Praise for Helen Whitaker

'Funny and frank'
Dawn O'Porter

'So well-observed, with a kind eye and an open heart'
Laura Jane Williams

'Emotionally smart and thought-provoking'
Clare Pooley

'A triumph!'
Mike Gayle

'Truly brilliant'
Emma Gannon

'Hilarious'
Woman

'Packed with wry humour'
Woman and Home

Helen Whitaker is a journalist and author living in London. Formerly the Entertainment Director of *Glamour UK*, her day job is currently Editor of *High Life* magazine. She writes books in her lunch hour, in the evenings and in any free time she has around parenting. Her writing has been published in *Grazia*, the *Telegraph*, *Fabulous*, *Stella*, *Red* and on BBC Three. Helen has written two previous novels, *The School Run* and *I Give It a Year*. *Single in the Snow* is her third novel.

Also by Helen Whitaker

The School Run
I Give It a Year

HELEN WHITAKER

Single in the Snow

First published in Great Britain in 2022 by Hodder & Stoughton
An Hachette UK company

This paperback edition published in 2022

1

A CIP catalogue record for this title is available from the British Library

Paperback ISBN 978 1 399 71301 6
eBook ISBN 978 1 399 71299 6

Typeset in Plantin Light by Hewer Text UK Ltd, Edinburgh
Printed and bound in Great Britain by Clays Ltd, Elcograf S.p.A.

Hodder & Stoughton policy is to use papers that are natural, renewable
and recyclable products and made from wood grown in sustainable
forests. The logging and manufacturing processes are expected to
conform to the environmental regulations of the country of origin.

Hodder & Stoughton Ltd
Carmelite House
50 Victoria Embankment
London EC4Y 0DZ

www.hodder.co.uk

For Al and Zee, my big air buddies

Chapter One

JEN

Jen pressed 'confirm Uber' with one hand while untangling her pants from her jeans with the other, a humiliated sob forming in her throat. Meanwhile Nathan, her ex-boyfriend of ten minutes, was already settling back down to sleep. As far as he was concerned their casual relationship had ended with no hurt feelings on either side, so what else was there to remain conscious for? Jen was madder at herself than with him. He'd just been who he was; it was her who'd spent ten months pretending to be fine with no commitment.

She checked her phone. The Uber was a minute away. She gave up on her jeans and pulled them on with her knickers still knotted in the leg, hitting Maxie's number as she edged her way out of the bedroom. Nathan might have grunted a goodbye as she closed the door, but then again he could just have been snoring.

One ring, two . . .

'If you're not dead, I'm pissed off,' her best friend's voice husked down the line, as Jen shivered outside Nathan's flat in the chilly mid-October morning.

'Max?' Her voice quavered and her cold breath clouded in front of her as she spoke. 'I know it's

6.30 a.m. Can you meet me for a coffee before work? I can come to you.'

Thirty minutes later they were in a café in Leyton that was marketing itself as a hipster hangout by virtue of charging £7.50 for a round of toast. 'What happened?' Maxie asked.

'I was lying in bed worrying about what would happen when we got to Vancouver, so I woke him up and asked him if we'd be moving in together when we got there.' Jen rubbed a rough recycled napkin over her tear-swollen cheeks. Her long blond hair was unbrushed and had been hastily pulled into a ponytail-cum-bun, while her blue-grey eyes were red-rimmed and underlined with dark circles.

'And?'

'And he looked like he was about to wet his pants.'

'Right.' Maxie seemed concerned and knackered, but she didn't seem surprised. Her three-year-old son Noah was across the room poking a cactus artwork with his Dr Who Sonic Screwdriver. Single mum Maxie had had to bring him with her on a diversion to preschool. 'But what did he actually say?'

'He said, "Sure, we could totally crash together at the start if you need a place."' A bitter snort-slash-weep emerged from Jen's throat.

'Fuck.' Maxie glanced over at Noah to check he hadn't heard.

'And then I told him he obviously didn't want to go out with me any more.' Jen forced a laugh, even though it wasn't funny. 'I broke up with *myself*, Maxie, BYOB dumped.'

'That's shit. I'm sorry.' Maxie fixed her brown eyes on Jen and smoothed down her usually curly, but now, after Jen had forced her out of the house too early to undertake her usual grooming regime, frizzy, dark hair. A second passed. 'Do you think though,' she said carefully, 'that it might actually be a good thing?'

Jen picked up her tiny flat white and chugged it in one. It was cold. She grimaced. 'I thought he could be The One,' she said miserably.

Jen could have sworn she caught an eyeroll. 'What?' she demanded.

Maxie's voice had a hard edge. 'You *thought* he was The One? You'd *know*. And did you ever *say* you wanted anything more than something low-key?' Her head tilted to one side as she scrutinised her best friend. 'He was nice enough, Jen, well, aside from the man bun, but he was just some bloke. Which, as we know, is kind of your thing.' Jen felt her face collapsing; she was under attack. Maxie swiftly moved on. 'I hate to see you sad, but think, will you actually miss *him* or just miss having a boyfriend?'

Jen started to protest and then absorbed what Maxie was saying. That this break-up could, really, have been any of her break-ups from the previous fifteen of her twenty-nine years. But she was too upset for self-analysis. What she needed right now was unbridled sympathy. 'Please don't tell me that this is an opportunity to grow, Max. I just want you to tell me he's a shit and that I will be happy again.'

'You *will* be happy again. But – don't freak out – *you* have to make you happy again.'

Jen ignored her, instead crumbling up the remains of her artisan croissant and inspecting the pieces.

'Don't pretend you can't hear me because we're getting to a tricky bit,' Maxie said, raising her voice. 'I've said this to you before, but maybe it's time to address why you're never on your own. I can't remember the last time you were sing—NOAH!' Her son's tiny hand was dangerously close to the succulent installation. The barista gave her a pointed look and she stared him down. 'He's not actually touching it,' she muttered. 'Keep your 'tache on.' She turned back to Jen, looking as though she wanted to say something else.

Jen rested her eyes on her warily. She'd lain awake for two hours before plucking up the courage to wake Nathan, and now her eyelids burned with tiredness and humiliation. 'What?'

'You stick at relationships that are rubbish, you turn flings into boyfriends, and you end up going out with people who should have been, at best, a one-night stand. You're such a boyfriend girl.' Maxie said the word 'boyfriend' the way other people might say 'The Taliban' or 'Mumford and Sons'. 'When you're with someone, you don't really ever seem to be anywhere near in love with them, but then you seem devastated when they're not invested in the relationship either. All these non-relationships are stopping you from finding someone you actually *are* into, or from being happy on your own.'

There were tiny stabs at the back of Jen's eyes that she wouldn't allow to surface as tears. Maxie was so together, even with the responsibility of being a solo parent to Noah.

But for Jen, having a boyfriend, even a rubbish one, made her feel safer. It proved that she knew how to make someone stay.

'By this age I thought—' she tried.

'What? That you'd have met your soulmate and started popping out babies?' Maxie's voice was scornful. 'Newsflash – sometimes you pop out a baby and the "soulmate" turns out to just be some dickhead. There's no guarantee.' Maxie's eyes flicked to Noah, who was munching on a pastry that she definitely hadn't paid for. 'I'm in no position to tell you how to choose a man, but at least take it from me that no man is better than the wrong man.'

'I know.' Jen pressed her lips together as Maxie reached for her hand. She sighed. 'It's just . . . why can't I find the "you complete me" sort of love you hear about?'

'No one needs someone to complete them,' Maxie retorted instantly. 'They need someone who recognises you're enough by yourself. But for that, you have to recognise it too.' She squeezed Jen's hand. 'This is one hundred per cent the best thing that could happen, I promise, and if you commit to being single for a bit, you'll see it too.'

Maxie was stronger than her. She had sworn off relationships when Leo – Noah's dad – had bailed, saying she was better off on her own. And with her it was true. She was so much herself, she didn't need anyone else. But seeing how sad her mum was after her dad left when Jen was thirteen made Jen feel like being single was the booby prize. Without a partner, her mum had withdrawn from the world, as though she should only be allowed to participate if she was part of a pair, and Jen had absorbed the message. Over the years, Jen had tucked her own personality away and become whatever her boyfriend at the time wanted her to be, prioritising boyfriends above everything else, even female friendships, aside from Maxie. She didn't know who she was on her own any more.

And despite her knack for metamorphosis, she still kept getting dumped. Each time, her self-confidence crumbled a little more, along what was left of her backbone. It had become a vicious circle.

'Is that your pep talk?' Jen said. 'No more boyfriends.'

Maxie rolled her eyes. 'It's seven in the morning and I have to get my kid to nursery before I go and work a ten-hour shift, so yes. My advice is to stay single for long enough to learn who *you* are and what you want.'

'How long does that take?'

Maxie widened her eyes in exasperation.

'No, seriously,' said Jen. 'What timeframe are we talking?'

'I don't know!' Maxie barked. She gave a disbelieving laugh. Jen still had her eyes trained on her, expecting a reply. She shook her head. 'OK, for you, I'd say take the biggest gap you've had between relationships and triple it. And then add another month. That's a bare minimum. But I can't remember the last time you were properly single to even be able to work it out.'

'Five months,' Jen replied, quickly doing the maths in her head.

'Is that all! It took me that long and several ill-judged online orders to truly accept that midi dresses don't suit me, so I'm not sure you can expect top-to-toe self-acceptance in the same timeframe. Round it up to six months and that's a start. Can I go to work now?'

Maxie was a paramedic, working long hours and never knowing what each day would bring. There was a chance she would save someone's life that day, leaving a patient dazed but eternally grateful. Or she could get abused by a staggering drunk. She treated both in the same caring but matter-of-fact way.

'Remind me again why I need to be single,' Jen said. Theoretically she knew why. But theories were as slippery as cheap tights. And just as likely to be binned.

'You're better than a dead-end relationship with someone who's not arsed about you, and your serial monogamy has so far been with people that aren't worth trying to cling on to,' Maxie affirmed. 'If you want love – *actual* love – then it's better that this relationship has ended because now you're free to find it. But what you need is time to work out what *you* want – and, yes, I'm going to say it – to love yourself first. No one needs to pick you, Jen. Pick *yourself*.'

'I'm getting you another coffee before you go.'

Jen got up as Maxie called after her. 'Something that's not served in a champagne glass or a jam jar or a bloody hanging basket, please.'

Jen returned with two more drinks; Maxie's was in a dainty china teacup. 'Sorry,' she said, putting it down in front of her.

'I'll let you off,' said Maxie, picking up the cup with both hands. '*If* you agree right now to stay single for a minimum of six months.' She held the cup out to induce Jen to 'cheers' her, and thereby pledge her commitment.

Jen's blotchy face crumpled in a pout. 'Fine,' she agreed, smashing her latte-filled mason jar against it. 'Six months of singledom. Who'd want to go out with me anyway?'

'Shush! That's *exactly* what I'm talking about. You're brilliant, you just don't know it. And with all this in mind, let's talk about Canada. You're still going, right? It's not like your visa is dependent on him.'

'Of course it's not.' Nathan had behaved like it was a happy coincidence that she had a year-long visa to work in Canada, and Jen had never corrected that misconception. Even though she'd always wanted to go, she would never have applied for one of the working visas issued to under-thirties if ten months ago she hadn't started dating a Canadian. 'But I can't follow my ex-boyfriend to Vancouver.'

'So go somewhere else in Canada, then!' Maxie almost shouted. 'You're always telling me you can't believe you're still stuck in the first job you got after graduation and that you want to travel more. This is your chance and you'll be too old next year.' Maxie was right. Jen's thirtieth was next June. 'I can't think of a better time or place to put a "staying single" vow into practice. Go to Canada and have some fun that doesn't involve having to crop out some placeholder boyfriend from the photos when you get back.' Her eyes searched again for Noah, who was now under a table playing with an upended bowl of sugar sachets. 'I'd bloody go,' she muttered.

The thought swooshed around Jen's head. Canada, but by herself.

Maxie was right. Because of that visa, the whole of Canada was up for grabs. Ten million square kilometres of possibility. The thought of it made her feel a bit sick. She'd had no particular hankering for Vancouver, but that was where Nathan was heading back to when his UK visa ran out, so she'd settled on the same. She still could. It was surely big enough that she wouldn't run into him if she went there?

Then another place crossed her mind. A chocolate-box impression of a ski resort two hours away from Vancouver that she'd stumbled across while Googling.

She'd fallen in love with the pictures of Whistler that showed it blanketed in snow, giving it a snowglobe-meets-Disney look. It had exactly the sort of small-town, festive feel she sought out in made-for-Netflix movies, and she'd daydreamed about heading up there for weekends from Vancouver, she and Nathan learning to ski before tumbling into a café for a hot chocolate.

Nathan might have evaporated but the resort was still there.

'Whistler,' she found herself saying to Maxie now. 'I want to go to Whistler.'

Maxie grinned back at her. 'I have literally no idea where that is, but it's the first autonomous decision you've made as a single woman and I'm proud of you. Whistler it is.' She held up her china cup again and Jen clinked her tumbler with it, echoing, 'Whistler it is.' A flutter rose up in her stomach.

She couldn't work out if it was panic or excitement.

Either way, she was going to Whistler, alone.

Chapter Two

ART

Art stifled a yawn and took a sip of the coffee he'd brought with him in his flask. At the front of the conference room, Graeme – or 'Gram' as all the Canadians pronounced it – the Head of Outdoor Operations, was pointing at a wall-sized projection of the mountain terrain. Orientation day. Again. Art knew this stuff like the back of his hand. His good hand. The one without a crooked knobbly bit where his hand met his wrist that still didn't look quite like it belonged to him, almost four years later.

He'd been in this conference room three times before, and the lecture didn't change from season to season. In the years before he'd been aware of Graeme and his homilies about piste boundaries, muster zones and radio channels, Art had been dedicated to the opposite of everything he was now being taught: exploring hidden runs, ducking under boundary ropes and building off-piste jumps well out of sight of the manicured slopes and safety patrols. He stared at the projection now, all that space, with dotted lines to separate the official pistes from the backcountry and the unknown danger. He couldn't keep his eyes from an area that was unmarked on

Graeme's map but in Art's mind would always have a big fat 'X' scrawled across it.

No.

He massaged his right wrist with his other hand. It was giving him jip today. It always did when the weather transitioned. It started as an ache and then spread as a series of twinges through his entire body. Phantom pains or muscle memory? Whichever it was, his body burned with it. The only way to combat it was to live inside each second, and *focus*, keeping control of every single thought and movement, right down to the expression on his face.

Art looked around. There were at least three hundred people in the room for this lecture, all ski and snowboard instructors, some freshly qualified and straight out of university, and some decades-long veterans with craggy faces and perma-goggle tans. They all wore the regulation red polo shirts and sweaters above their jeans, leggings or trousers, and some faces were familiar, but most not. He'd stopped paying attention after the first year, staying deliberately lukewarm with colleagues, and keeping to himself. The older ones already had their own cliques and paid him no special attention, but the younger ones were all so sociable, so mingly, so *nosy.* Here for gap years and to have an *experience*. Occasionally one of them approached him, either after a shy enquiring glance that registered he was on his own and wrongly assumed he wanted to make friends, or – and these were the worst ones – people who recognised him from before. From past TV coverage or the archive of some snowboard brand's Instagram feed that still existed even if you switched your personal account to private and deleted your old photos. Those people would accelerate from a polite hello to a meaningful 'where did you work before here?' in thirty seconds flat. He'd found that if snapping 'all over' didn't shut them down, walking away usually did. They'd scuttle back to their just-this-second-made seasonal mates, complaining he was an arsehole, but he didn't care. This course was a mandatory pre-requisite for anyone working on the mountain – as it should be – but his day-to-day was private clients, which brought him into very little contact with the general rabble. No shared changing rooms or required work 'mixers'. It was the way he liked it.

Graeme switched the slide and started his mountain safety refresher segment.

'You all studied first aid and avalanche awareness in your instructor courses, which for the new recruits among you were only weeks ago,' he was saying in his thin nasal voice. 'But you need to pay close attention to everything we cover here.'

Art sat up a little straighter and arranged his expression into one of hyper-alertness, in case anyone glanced over and studied him for a reaction. But inside his mind he zoned out. He trained his eyes straight ahead, repeating David Bowie lyrics in his head to provide a focus. After exactly thirty seconds he allowed himself a small frown of concentration. The room was airless. Stale. He couldn't tell if it had been like that all along or if the oxygen had suddenly been sucked from the room. His palms tingled with nervous sweat.

What was the first line of 'Rebel Rebel' again?

He only had to get through a total of two minutes, because he knew from experience that that was how long Graeme spent refreshing the instructors on what to do in the unlikely event of the mountain splitting and tonnes of powerful snow plunging towards their students. In just one more minute, they'd be listening to the protocol for dealing with complaints, and what was and wasn't acceptable to post on social media about their jobs.

His phone vibrated where it was resting on the notepad on his lap. He waited for Graeme to say 'TikTok' – a word that sounded absurd coming from his mouth – before he let himself safely have a look.

Dinner on Tuesday?

Yeti.
It must be that time of year again.
Such an innocent question and only three short words, but ones loaded with the weight of the previous three years. If he didn't reply, Yeti would show up at his house one day unannounced. Then his mum might start calling. His phone would light up with the 'might be useful' website links she hoarded, and she would collude with Yeti to come up with 'a plan'. He tapped out a reply.

Sure.

Two ticks appeared immediately, and the bubbles started dancing on the screen. Art raced to beat him to the next word.

How about The Powder Room?

No one local went to The Powder Room. That was exactly why Art had picked it. A location popular with tourists was far preferable to a bar full of locals where someone he knew – had known – might drop in for a post-work beer and sit down for a chat. The bubbles stopped. He imagined Yeti looking at the message, knowing what Art was doing and then deciding what tactic to try. Whether to cajole or to accept; he'd deployed both in the past to the same failed effect.

The bubbles appeared again, and Art found himself hoping Yeti would wheedle, even though he'd pushed away all his efforts to do so in the past. Art gave so little of himself that it was to Yeti's credit that he kept trying at all. Still, the response when it finally came gave Art a flicker of disappointment.

I'll book a table. 7pm.

Chapter Three

JEN

'How long are you going to be in Canada and what is your final destination?' A grim-faced immigration officer flipped through her passport to her visa.

Jen knew her paperwork was in order; she'd checked it twenty times on the way to the airport alone. She felt guilty all the same. 'Whistler,' she said in a hushed tone. 'For a few months. But my visa is for a year, so I can go somewhere else after. Or not. It depends if I get a job.' She was babbling and couldn't stop.

Her sole aim had been to get on the plane without bottling it, and now she had landed at Vancouver airport she was forced to focus on the fact that there was no turning back. Over the last six weeks, Jen had Polyfilla'd the holes in her rented London room and quit her Human Resources job; there was nothing to go back *to*. When she'd originally been hired at Proctors as a graduate in the HR department, and at the height of the recession, everyone had told her she was lucky. But she hated her job. Actually, that was a lie, she didn't. It was just something she *did*. She showed up, she got on with everyone and she worked hard. In seven years, she'd had two pay rises and the word 'junior' knocked off her job title. To most colleagues at the mid-sized engineering company, she was a faceless name on an email who clarified their holiday allowance or sat in on their exit interview when they left. When they gave their reasons for leaving – to a bigger company, for a dynamic step up the career ladder, or to change direction – she was envious and wished she had the impetus to do the same. Then she duly went back to her desk, typed up their exit notes and did nothing about her own situation.

That changed today. She'd applied for an HR job in Whistler that she'd seen online, and she had an interview tomorrow. If she got it, she'd also get free staff housing to live in. If not – well, she couldn't think about that now.

'If you hate it, just spend the money you've saved up on an amazing holiday,' Maxie had told her when they'd said goodbye. 'You learn to ski or snowboard and come back after six weeks as though that was the idea all along.'

Six weeks. She could think in terms of six weeks.

'But don't go there and end up going out with someone,' Maxie had reminded her. 'You've done over a month's cold turkey already. Totally single, making your own decisions and not even looking at the apps. I'm proud of you.'

Jen had avoided making eye contact with her. 'I thought I might reinstall some apps when I get there.'

Narrowed eyes. 'What?'

Jen had shifted awkwardly. 'Just to meet people,' she said. 'Not to find a boyfriend.'

'No, Jen! No Tinder, no Bumble and no Raya.'

'I've never even heard of Raya.'

'You're not famous enough anyway. Promise me you'll stay single for the whole six months, like we agreed. Until April. That's basically an entire ski season, right?'

Jen nodded. It was the end of November now. The first six weeks had been easy: even Jen would have been hard pushed to make time for dating amid the whirlwind of getting ready to leave the country. But with five more months stretching ahead of her, in a country where she didn't know a soul (except Nathan, and even Jen knew that staying in touch with him was a terrible idea), the temptation to download an app made her thumbs itch just thinking about it.

'So, until the spring, when the snow melts and the resort becomes whatever the hell a ski resort becomes when there's no snow,' Maxie pressed. 'Every decision should be *by* you and *about* you. The only love I want you to find is—'

'Oh God, please don't say self-love.'

'OK, I won't say it.' But she nodded sagely, before hugging her tight. 'Noah and I will be out to see you as soon as we can afford it.' The chance of Maxie being able to afford a holiday to Canada was slim to none. 'This is going to be the best adventure ever . . .'

'Ma'am, can you move along, please.' The poker-faced immigration officer didn't share Maxie's excitement or respond to any of her burbling about job dilemmas. He merely stamped Jen's passport and gestured for her to go.

Winding past Horseshoe Bay on the bus from the airport to Whistler, Jen peered out of the window. Mountains and hills spread as far as she could see in the distance. A ferry was starting to cruise over to Vancouver Island, which lay on the opposite side of the water, and on her other side a looming rock face spat out a waterfall as a bird of prey circled above. The first big snowfall of the season hadn't happened yet – it was due any time around now, in late November – so the road was wide and clear. She couldn't imagine it blanketed with so much snow that Whistler was cut off from the city, but she had read that it used to happen before the new highway was built.

Her phone beeped. Maxie.

Progress report.

On the coach to Whistler. Jetlagged and cacking it. Will text again when I have wi-fi.

Jen turned off her iPhone. Before she'd got on the bus, she'd bought a cheap flip-up Telus mobile, both to save money and because without a smartphone she'd be incapable of cyber-stalking Nathan or reinstalling those apps. She set it up now, sliding the SIM card into the back and trying not to dwell on the fact that she didn't have one person's phone number in this time zone to enter into it. She thought of her mum back home. After Jen's dad had left, her mother had never taken any risks, even small ones. She'd never put herself out there again – and had kept her world small, terrified of getting hurt. Jen was determined to be different, but while she made half-formed plans, she was always too wimpy to follow through on anything properly. Not on her own, anyway. Mum had just about accepted Jen going away when it was supposed to be with Nathan, even as she fretted about her daughter leaving her 'good job' and solid flatshare. When it turned out Jen was going alone, she'd tried to talk her out of it. It had been the same when Jen had left Leicester to go to university in London, which was the last time she'd ignored Mum's voice in her head and done anything remotely adventurous.

Ten years ago.

The bus turned off Highway 99 and into an alcove in the shadow of Creekside's Whistler Mountain. The panorama was familiar to Jen from the 2010 Olympic coverage she'd been briefly obsessed with back in sixth form. She recognised the wide green downhill ski run with fir trees lining its perimeter, and ropes of gondola cable that snaked up as far as Jen could see. The carriages were static now, with the wink of ice so high up Jen had to crane her neck to spot it. At the top the peak nudged cloud. At the bottom, neat apartment buildings and upmarket hotels were dotted around the lower edges of the mountain.

The bus's doors opened, and Jen jogged down the steps, the only passenger getting off the half-empty bus at this stop. A blast of cold, fresh air hit her, and a middle-aged woman walked past with a husky so large it made all British dogs seem pointless. Jen stopped to admire it for a second and a flash of something – homesickness, panic, fear, longing – whooshed through her head. She hauled her backpack out of the bus's cargo hold, straightened up, disguised the waver in her step and crossed over the road to the hostel she'd booked for the night.

* * *

'This is you.' The hostel manager Donna, a tight whip of a woman in sagging leggings, gestured at a small, utilitarian and very empty room. Four bunks lay undisturbed around her. The whole place smelled vaguely of damp.

'Do I have a specific bed, or is it first come, first served?' Jen asked, looking around. She took off the brand-new white Roxy snowboard coat she'd bought expressly for this trip. It was too hot in the poky room.

Donna unfolded a slow, languid smile. She had the voice of a heavy smoker. 'We got another couple of bookings later in the week, but for now you got the dorm to yourself.'

'Great,' said Jen. Relief. Talking to fellow hostel dwellers in the kitchen was one thing, but despite the independent traveller vibe she'd been channelling when she booked a shared dorm, she didn't *actually* want to share a bedroom with strangers.

Donna rattled through the house rules. 'Kitchen's communal, bathrooms are down the hall, phone's free for local calls, no unauthorised visitors, no smoking inside. If you need anything' – Donna mimed taking a drag on a joint – 'ask me at the desk.'

'OK.' Was this the stoner hostel? Jen guessed that if you needed to ask that, you didn't belong in the stoner hostel.

'Is there free wi-fi?'

'Yeah. Password's SWEETASS.' Donna handed her a key and shuffled through the door.

It was so quiet. No traffic noise, no voices, just hush. Back in London there was always something: teenagers shouting as they walked down the street or night buses whooshing down the main road. Jen went to unpack her pyjamas and a wave of anxiety broke over her. She was almost thirty. What was she doing in a stoner hostel in a town where she had no job and no friends? Her hands itched to call Maxie and say she was coming home, but instead she forced herself to pick up her coat again. Her jet lag exhaustion had mutated into a jangling anxiety. She needed to get out of this unwelcoming room.

Outside, her eyes followed a line of dense trees that stretched as far as she could see down the road, before snagging on a neon sign winking 'Bar'.

She pulled open the heavy wooden door.

Inside were dozens of mismatched tables and chairs, with a few people scattered around them. At 4 p.m. it was far too early for the deafening tones of Aerosmith booming out from the vintage jukebox that stood next to the doorway, but it helped to drown out the thought that she was a loser, sitting in a bar alone. The exposed wooden floorboards were scratched and there were overstuffed sofas dotted around the room, along with band posters, moose antlers and other knick-knacks nailed haphazardly to the walls. Again, there was a smell of damp.

A lanky guy in his mid-thirties was hunched on a stool behind the bar, fiddling with his phone. He was good-looking in a surfery sort of way, with scruffy dark hair and a deeply ingrained tan on his cheeks. The skin around his eyes was pale where he was obviously well used to wearing ski goggles.

'Welcome to Canucks. What can I get you?' the man hollered over the music, standing as Jen approached the counter. His voice had an Australian inflection.

Jen hesitated. She always had whatever anyone else was having; it was easier. Nathan's drink was rye and ginger, so she'd drunk a lot of that over the last ten months, but she hadn't actually liked it that much. White wine? That was her go-to, but it seemed safe and boring.

'What do you recommend?' she asked.

The barman laughed and pushed his hair out of his eyes. They were hazelly green, with long dark lashes the same colour as his hair. Maxie would have shouted at her for noticing.

'I could do you a beer and clam.'

Jen had no idea what that was. 'OK, yes, thanks.'

The barman stood up, revealing just how gangly he was at full height. At least 6'4", with limbs sticking out at all angles from a giant Guns N' Roses T-shirt and baggy jeans.

'Just arrived?'

Jen shrugged off her coat for the second time in twenty minutes. She nodded. 'I'm here for the season.'

'You don't seem like the gap-year type.'

Jen prickled. 'Because I'm about ten years too old?'

The barman grinned. The skin around his twinkly eyes crumpled a bit as he did. 'Pretty much.'

'I know. I'll see how the next few weeks go,' she said, trying to sound more peppy than she currently felt. 'I need to get a job, somewhere to live, and to make some friends. Currently I know no one and am wondering what I'm doing here.'

He set down a pink-tinged pint glass in front of her. 'Well, now you know me. I'm Rob,' he said. Was he flirting with her?

'I'm Jen,' she replied, imagining Maxie watching the exchange, and avoiding his eyes. She looked around the bar. 'Is it always this empty in here?'

'You wait. In two weeks it'll be rammed with people coming off the mountain and heading here for après.' Rob gestured at a small, raised stage at the far end of the bar. 'The band will be playing over there. You'll be lucky to get a seat.'

Jen couldn't imagine it, but she nodded politely and took a sip of her pint.

Fish. The drink tasted of fish. She gagged right there at the bar, eyes streaming and saliva dripping out of her mouth.

'What have you put in it?' she choked out.

Rob's laugh was even louder than the jukebox. 'Clamato juice. It's a mixture of tomato and clam juice. A Canadian speciality. You said you wanted one.'

'I didn't know what it was!' She pushed the pint to one side, still gagging. She clawed at her tongue to get the taste out, not caring what she must look like.

Rob was still laughing. 'Lucky for you, it's happy hour. Buy one, get one free. I'll get you another beer without the clam juice.'

The front door slammed and Rob looked up. 'SNOWY,' he called, his voice at once ten shades more Aussie. 'Pint radar in operation, mate? There's a spare one here.'

A short, squat man with tiny eyes and a shock of white-blond hair ambled over, contemplated Jen, and picked up the pint. Jen put him in his late twenties, like her.

'It's poisoned with fish,' Jen muttered darkly as he swigged half the pint down his throat in one swallow.

'This is Snowy,' said Rob. 'He works here too. He's the chef. Jen's just arrived for the season.' He put down Jen's new pint and then went over to clear glasses from some tables.

She took a tiny experimental taste before deeming it safe to drink.

'Where're you working?' Snowy asked, swigging down another enormous mouthful.

'Hopefully at The Redwood Resort. I've got an interview tomorrow.' She realised her carefully chosen interview outfit was still crumpled in the rucksack she hadn't yet unpacked.

'La-di-da.' Snowy whistled. 'Good luck.'

Rob reappeared with a tray of shot glasses filled with a nuclear green liquid. 'Let's get the season started properly, people,' he called, addressing the whole room. 'On the house.'

A middle-aged couple in hiking gear came over before Snowy picked one of the shots up. This was not the way Jen's afternoon should be going. If there was one thing working in HR had taught her, it was how to prepare for a job interview. This was not it.

Rob could sense her reluctance. 'Want to be less fun than them, Jen?' he said, nodding at the couple in waterproofs. He winked at her. A clear challenge. Jen snatched a glass from the tray. Another Aerosmith song started playing as Rob did a quick circuit of the room with the rest of the shots, and returned with the tray empty but for one. 'EVERYONE READY?' he boomed. 'GO.'

The crowd – such as it was – cheered and knocked them back. Jen followed suit, some sort of apple-flavoured liquor burning all the way down, but thankfully annihilating all residual trace of the clamato juice as it did.

Chapter Four

ART

Yeti's real name was Russ, but everyone called him Yeti because he looked like one. At sixty years old, his height and bulk were still solid with youthful muscle and he had shaggy grey hair that grew from every area of visible skin on his body. His beard was grey and bristly, and he had piercing blue eyes that peered out astutely from a thick fringe. Right now they were fixed on Art as he lowered himself into one of the velvet bucket chairs in The Powder Room.

'Hi Yeti,' he muttered. They were both glazed in the sickly neon-pink glow of the signs that picked out the bar's name across its mirrored walls.

'Jedi,' Yeti gruffed back, and Art paused, halfway between sitting and standing, before continuing to sit down. Yeti was the only person Art still saw who called him that. The joke had started years ago when he was Yeti's most promising protégé – the Luke Skywalker to his Obi-Wan Kenobi – and at one time everyone had known his nickname.

Before.

These days he actively hid the fact that at one time he was Art 'Jedi' Jenkins, Great Britain's most promising

Olympic snowboard slopestyle prospect. After a school trip to Castleford snowdome in secondary school had revealed a natural talent, he'd soon got hooked on the sport and started entering competitions. Winning them had got him hooked on success, and then he'd been scouted by Yeti, a born-and-bred Canadian who coached a small squad of up-and-coming Brits back in his hometown of Whistler, where there were the world-class snowpark facilities to train them in.

Once Art finished his A levels – which his mum had insisted he complete in the face of a sporting passion she didn't understand – he'd moved over, using Whistler as a base while travelling all over the world to compete. Under Yeti's tutelage, Art got to within a whisker of Team GB for Sochi. Three years later, he qualified for PyeongChang and was ready to go.

Right up until the Christmas before the Games.

Yeti leaned over the hot-pink table that separated the two chairs and looked down at Art's left leg, as though he could see through his black jeans to the ugly five-inch scar on his ankle. The table juddered as it bore his weight.

'How's that doing?' he asked, jutting his chin.

'Fine.' Something about these coerced meetings made Art revert to the sullen fourteen-year-old Yeti had first met in Leeds.

'And that?' His eyes flicked up to where Art had his left hand clamped unconsciously around his right wrist, rubbing the bone as he flexed his fingers in and out.

'It gets stiff when it's damp.' Art gave a practised shrug. 'But it's as fine as it will ever be.'

Yeti was nodding, his wiry hair dancing in the fuchsia glow. 'Are you still seeing the physio?'

Art suppressed a sigh. 'No. There was nothing else she could do for me. I have to stay mobile and follow the exercises at home, you know the drill.' They both knew his ankle wasn't the problem. Nor was his wrist. They had both healed, to a degree.

'And what about—'

'What can I get you?' A waiter appeared to take their drink order, cutting Yeti off. Maybe now he would stop prying.

'Beer, please,' Yeti replied. 'Art?'

'The same. Thanks.' Art knew he had to be careful about how much he drank around Yeti. One beer was fine, normal even, as were two, but any more than that and he'd get sloppy and it would be harder to keep a lid on everything. Yeti knew Art better than anyone; he'd spent months and years coaching him. He could interpret every squint and jaw clench, knowing what each meant about Art's state of mind.

That was why he'd learned to control every expression.

The waiter withdrew, and Art looked around the bar to avoid Yeti's eye. But Yeti didn't give up easily. It was why he was so good at coaxing people to a personal best or to get back up after their fiftieth wipeout of the day.

'You ever see our guy?' he said gruffly.

'Our guy' was code for the eye-wateringly expensive sports psychologist who Yeti had enlisted after Art's physical injuries had healed. Art had only gone along with it to keep Yeti quiet.

'His job is to help elite athletes overcome mental obstacles and get them back to optimal performance.' Art flicked a hand at his leg, the one he didn't even like to look at in the shower. 'I'm never going to be an elite athlete again.'

'OK,' Yeti conceded, nodding slightly. They both knew his injuries had been too severe for him to make a comeback on the international stage. 'I just thought he'd help with the other stuff.' Another euphemism that hung there. The 'other stuff' he wanted 'our guy' to help with was mental health.

'I couldn't afford him even if I wanted a shrink,' Art said bluntly. 'Besides, he's too in demand with people who actually stand a chance of winning a medal at the next Games.'

'Someone else, then,' Yeti said, as the waiter silently put their beers and a bowl of nuts down in front of them. 'Someone more suited to the everyday.'

'I'm fine,' Art said politely, taking a sip of his beer and trying not to shrivel under Yeti's stare. He looked around the room. The bar was almost empty aside from a few dressed-up couples. Early-season tourists, hopeful that their best snow days were ahead of them.

'If you need money, there's always a job for you with me,' Yeti started. 'You'd make a great assistant coach. I've caught sight of you tutoring on the mountain and how patient you are. Plus, you have insight into competing at an international level. That's a real asset.'

'I like teaching little kids,' Art replied. That, at least, was true. He did. The vicarious joy he felt when one of them nailed it and started whizzing down the nursery slope was as close as he got to the freeing buzz he'd once felt himself. Plus, he was completely in control with under-nine beginners. Most snowboarded no more than once or twice a year, and were happy to be taken down the easiest green and red runs, with a few rudimentary tricks thrown in for good measure. After that, they graduated to a tutor who could guide them down the black runs and half pipes, while Art patiently started again with a new set of tiddlers. To do what Yeti did, to coach people who stood a chance of making a national squad, you needed an element of the daredevil inside you. That was how you encouraged people to push their boundaries and how they progressed from being merely good to being excellent. Art did everything he could to avoid being a daredevil these days.

Yeti was staring at him over his drink and picking at the bowl of nuts. 'If you ever change your mind—'

'If I need money, I'm better off where I am,' Art chimed in before he could finish. 'My regulars book me in for their kids' next holiday before they've finished their current one. Didn't you once tell me that coaching pays less than minimum wage if you work out the actual hours involved?'

It was a low blow but Yeti took it with a sanguine grin. 'It's more than a job to me, you know that.' He took another sip of his beer, froth fizzing on his whiskers. 'Besides, one of these days I'll train someone that not only wins medals, but has the sort of face every advertiser wants on a billboard. Then I can forget the cold and buy a place in Hawaii.'

Even Art had to smile at that.

Yeti had practically come out of the womb on skis and would never leave the mountains, they both knew it. He'd had moderate success as an athlete, but after he retired, he found his true calling as a coach. He was nurturing but no-nonsense, his work ethic matched only by his enthusiasm for the mountains. Why else would he spend long hours of his life training teenagers in freezing conditions?

'Your mum called,' said Yeti, abruptly changing the subject. 'She asked me if you were going home for Christmas this year.'

'What?' Art's smile dimmed. 'Why did she ask *you*?'

'Because she said she'd messaged you a few times, and you hadn't got back to her.' Yeti lowered his glass. 'She's under the impression I see a lot more of you than I do.' That hung in the air too. Art managed to swerve most of Yeti's invitations, but the pre-Christmas meet-up was one he dutifully accepted in order to avoid this exact conversation.

'I'll give her a call.' Guilt pulsed through Art. It had been so long since he'd talked to her properly, he no longer knew what to say. It was easier to suppress any feelings that threatened to bubble up. If he allowed himself to miss her, a cascade of missing people could flood him.

'Do.' Yeti's eyes flashed, his unruffled façade dropping for a moment. 'She worries about you.' His voice lowered. 'We all do.'

'Well, there's no need,' Art snapped impatiently. 'I'm twenty-eight years old and holding down a well-paying job. What is there to worry about?'

Yeti's look said it all. *You know.* What he said was: 'You haven't spent Christmas in the UK for three years, nor will you let her come over here to you.'

'She knows that Christmas is my busiest time of year. Families want a perfect white Christmas on the slopes, which means the parents want me to take their children off their hands so they can ski in peace.'

'But you haven't been home at all since—'

'I'm just busy! An athlete's career is short, so stockpile the cash while you can. Who taught me that? *You*.'

Yeti made a gesture that said, 'OK, you win'. 'Well, if you can't get home for Christmas, come to us. You'll be done working at around three.' Art knew he couldn't argue with that. Yeti knew the rhythms of mountain life more intricately than anyone. Lessons stopped just before the light dropped and then families went back to their plush accommodations for a five-star, fully-catered Christmas dinner that the seasonal hospitality lackeys had spent the day preparing. That was the reality of a ski resort. For every holiday of a lifetime, there were dozens of underpaid people who were desperate to finish their shift so they could catch one run before the lifts shut for the day. It was the whole reason they'd moved to a resort to start off with.

'Maybe.' Art tried to shrug him off. 'Thanks.' He didn't want to go to dinner with Yeti and his lovely but inquisitive wife Lori. He planned to spend Christmas the way he'd spent it for the previous three years. Alone.

'You shouldn't be on your own,' said Yeti as though reading his mind.

'I won't be! I told you, I have back-to-back lessons and then after that I'll be exhausted. Have you ever taught a stream of children on Christmas Day when they're hopped up on chocolate?' That exhaustion was exactly why, aside from the money, Art agreed to work every year. The vigilance required to look after children on the mountain, combined with their endless pull for attention, meant that some years he'd fall asleep by 7 p.m. Then the day was done.

But Art could tell Yeti didn't believe him.

'Besides,' he said, changing tack. 'There's the Misfits meal every year, remember. I might go there.'

'Like you did last year.'

'Yep.' The lie slipped out easily. Last year, he'd told the Misfits that he'd gone to Yeti's. He'd tell them the same thing this Christmas.

'You don't need to decide now,' Yeti was saying. 'Just turn up if you want. There's a place for you, anytime, but especially at Christmas. I know it's a hard time of year . . .'

Art tuned him out, concentrating on the neon sign again until the light burned white spots onto his eyes.

A snowmobile had loosened the snow. That was what had set off the cascade. As they'd hiked up that morning, Art had seen the pair of snowmobilers and Shauna had tutted about the reckless turns they were making, but Art had just ignored them. He was too busy plotting his line before they set off. Shauna had soon forgotten and gone back to fiddling with the camera attached to her helmet. She always wanted to film everything to stick on the YouTube channel she had big ambitions for. It drove Art nuts. The sensation of soaring weightlessness couldn't be done justice on film, but he knew if the channel took off it would be a revenue stream, which would in turn stop them having to beg brands for kit because they'd have their pick of sponsors. Besides, the videos did look cool. A few of the bars in town had started playing her edited reels on their big screens during après hours.

Conditions that day were perfect – a two-foot dump of fresh powder with clear blue skies – and he was spending it snowboarding with the woman he was falling in love with. Christmas Day didn't get better than that, especially with the promise of the annual Misfits dinner once they'd had their fill of off-piste snowboarding for the day. The Misfits – their mish-mash of friends who were too far from home and too seasonally employed to have anywhere else to go – would be working their various shifts before meeting for the meal, usually catered with a combination of home-cooked dishes and leftovers swiped from any five-star places of employment. Art knew he was lucky that his day job *was* snowboarding so he didn't have to work in the town's tourist-driven service industry.

Art remembered visualising his route, the way Yeti had started encouraging him to do during practice runs. Some big-shot sports psychologist had convinced him of the power of manifesting and it had turned out to be less wacky than Art had initially assumed.

'Ready when you are!' Shauna had shouted, and off he'd gone, leading the way so she could film him from behind as he swooped down, creating fresh tracks in the snow. Days snowboarding for fun, and not to beat some personal best, were few and far between this close to the Games, and he was determined to make the most of it. He had raised his face up to the sun and grinned, playing it up a little for the sake of the camera.

Then came a noise like a diesel engine, and a juggernaut impact that flattened him. The shock was pierced by the thought that he'd been hit by one of the snowmobiles. Later they told him that he'd been buried under two metres of snow, but he didn't know that then. He just knew he was pinned face down, unable to move his legs, with his chest crushed. Then he remembered clawing uselessly as his breath ran out. Suffocating in white silence. The rest Yeti told him when he woke up in the hospital a month later. There'd been an avalanche. His ankle and wrist were shattered. Shauna was dead.

The snowmobilers had seen where the mass of snow had dragged and then buried him, and they'd pulled him out after four minutes. But they couldn't find Shauna. It turned out she'd managed to flip the signal on her transceiver, meaning Mountain Rescue arrived in under ten minutes. They located her, but it was too late. She'd been paddling for air in the wrong direction. Her helmet camera had recorded the whole thing.

Art still had dreams where he dove into the snow searching for Shauna. His desperation would build and build as he strained for breath. And then he'd find her. He'd reach his hand out just as he ran out of air. Then he'd wake up, drenched in sweat, panting.

Yeti was still talking about Christmas Day, but Art hadn't heard any of it. He looked down at his hands. They were shaking. He told himself that Christmas Day was just another day to get through. But it was also the day that time had frozen for him.

Almost four years later, he was still trying to thaw out.

Chapter Five

JEN

'Unfortunately, the position is no longer available.'

'What?' Jen was already rattling with nervous hungover energy when Eduardo, an ultra-tanned fifty-something with a solid grey block of North American news-anchor hair and eyebrows that looked like they'd never recovered from the nineties, informed her that the job – *her* job – as Human Resources Officer at The Redwood Hotel had evaporated, and along with it the staff housing she was relying on.

Whatever Eduardo was using on his face – was that contouring? – it was too bright for Jen's delicate hungover eyes. She winced. 'Why didn't anyone let me know before I came for the interview?'

Blurry scenes from last night in the bar with Rob, Snowy and a cast of other characters kept coming back to her in snippets (was one of them called Clyde? And was his girlfriend Kelly? The one with green hair was definitely Darren). At some point, the shots had stopped but instead of taking that as her cue to leave, when Rob had announced a lock-in Jen had insisted on trying another pint of beer and clam. The fishy taste repeated on her again as she tried to make sense of what she was doing in the anonymous, file-lined personnel office of the hotel if the job she had applied for no longer existed.

Eduardo held a printout of her CV in his hand. 'Your resumé,' he said, proffering it to her. Jen's head hurt too much to know whether it was a question or a statement, so she took it from him and looked at it, as though she didn't already know every line in there.

She'd woken up fully clothed on her hostel bed with her phone dead in her hand before realising she had less than an hour to make it to The Redwood Resort and Hotel for her interview. It had taken her longer to prise a barely working iron out of Donna at the hostel than she imagined it would to score a hefty block of weed, but half an hour later Jen was in a cab in a crisp white shirt, slim-fit navy-blue suit and block-heeled boots, having been very liberal with her perfume in an attempt to mask the booze that seemed to be seeping out of every pore. Her arrival was heralded by a sign at the bottom of a drive stating 'The Redwood Whistler' with five stars displayed beneath it. At the top, a faux castle stood in the shadow of a ski slope that started where the castle ended. White with dove-grey turrets, it seemed to gleam against the backdrop of the mountain's panorama, although once the snow dropped, it would be cleverly rendered almost invisible.

'Yes, it is,' Jen replied to Eduardo now, which seemed like the safest response. She took a shaky alcohol-infused breath and willed her years of experience from sitting in on job interviews back to the fore. 'Perhaps you could keep it on file in case a suitable position comes up—'

'That's just it,' Eduardo cut her off smoothly. 'As well as being the hotel's overall Talent Director, I'm the head of the Platinum floor here at The Redwood.'

Jen had no idea what that was but nodded along while trying not to laugh. She imagined suggesting that the fusty HR department at her old company rebrand as 'Talent Acquisition'. 'Platinum is the most exclusive floor for our ultra-VIP guests,' Eduardo explained, smoothing down a non-existent stray hair from his block. 'And I'm very well-versed in identifying the expertise we need.'

Jen raked her memory over her CV. Her last job in anything approaching 'hospitality' was ten years ago, serving strong beer to indiscriminate students in her university campus pub. It was hardly sourcing white lilies for J-Lo. What could possibly qualify her to look after VIP clients in a five-star hotel?

Eduardo pointed to her CV. 'It says here you went to Marlborough High School?'

'School?' Jen was momentarily thrown and then realised what Eduardo was getting at. It had been a running joke among her friends that the name of their Leicester comprehensive was similar to Marlborough College – one of the UK's top boarding schools, and somewhere more likely to attract a minor royal than the catchment area cast-offs found at her state school.

'Yes,' she replied. If Eduardo had a better impression of her because he incorrectly believed she'd spent her formative years hobnobbing with the upper class, then she wasn't going to rectify it.

'Wonderful.' He smiled. His teeth were even more dazzling than his skin. Jen's eyes throbbed with post-tequila energy. 'I'd like to offer you a seasonal job as one of our Assistant Luxury Concierges on the Platinum floor.'

'But don't I need extensive customer service skills for that?' asked Jen, bewildered. Dealing with members of the public all day – *loaded* members of the public – wasn't something you could just blag.

'It's more of an attitude than a ticklist,' Eduardo said airily, making less sense by the second.

'And what's the salary for one of your Platinum employees?' she asked.

Eduardo named an hourly rate so low Jen almost laughed. 'But of course, it also comes with the hotel's standard seasonal accommodation,' he added.

'I'll take it,' Jen agreed before she could stop herself. She was woefully underqualified for the job – she didn't even know what an Assistant Luxury Concierge was – but while she had money saved for the trip, it wasn't enough to live on until the spring. She was fast discovering that rental prices in a premium Canadian ski resort made London look budget. A foggy memory of Rob telling her that at thirty-five, he and the others could still only afford to live in a four-person houseshare, drifted back to her.

'I'll have the paperwork drawn up.' Eduardo sounded genuinely pleased. 'You're *exactly* the element we're looking for.'

'Great!' she said brightly, hoping he wouldn't start asking her what going to school with Princess Eugenie was like.

'I'd like you to start on Monday. While it's quiet enough to start the rigorous training.'

What happened to it being more of an attitude than a ticklist?

He stood up and Jen automatically held out her hand to shake. He ignored it and instead flicked his eyes over her, his gaze appraising. 'And, Jennifer, *FYI*, our words to live by are "immaculately groomed".'

The staff hamlet was only half a mile away from Whistler village, but Jen regretted walking there with her rucksack when she found herself winding up a steep road with no pavement on either side of the street. As she breathlessly rounded a corner hidden by trees, she contemplated turning back. Luckily, at that point it appeared ahead of her.

The word 'hamlet' implied quaintness, but the difference between the staff accommodation and Whistler Village itself couldn't have been more pronounced. If Whistler's aesthetic was 'chocolate-box charm', staff housing's was 'Russian gulag'. There were seven squat, concrete utilitarian apartment buildings labelled from A to G, with paths that ran between them in a matching shade of grey. She consulted the paperwork Eduardo had handed her back at the hotel, and headed to the site office.

When she opened the door to her apartment in Block C half an hour later, she silently rejoiced. Not because the flats seemed any cosier inside than out, but because she was only going to be sharing with one other person. This, the site manager had explained, was very unusual. Most of the apartment buildings consisted of fifteen five-person flats with two or three to a bedroom, but hers was a two-bedroom flat for two people. A bedroom each. In staff housing terms, she was in the penthouse. In reality, a circuit of the whole place took less than thirty seconds. The tiny living room consisted of an entry-level, two-seater IKEA sofa and coffee table, and the space bled into a kitchen area with a length of worktop running along one wall. At one end was a sink and at the other was a cooker and hob. A mini fridge sat below and the kitchen's one cupboard contained two sets of white crockery, two glasses and two sets of plain steel cutlery.

There was dark grey carpet throughout – the dense, hard-wearing kind that doesn't show muck – and the bedrooms were off a short corridor from the living room. The bathroom was at the end. Sink, toilet, shower. No bath.

There was no sign of the flatmate that the woman in the office had told her had already moved in, and no magazines, rogue shoes, or smoothies in the fridge to indicate what type of person she might be. Just a green toothbrush and a tube of Colgate toothpaste in the tiny bathroom, and one bedroom door that was locked, leaving Jen in no doubt that the open one – housing a smaller-than-average single bed, a rickety pine bedside table and a clothes rail – was hers.

It took her ten minutes to unpack, hang her clothes and arrange her toiletries in the bathroom, giving her plenty of time to sit on her bed and study the lengthy notes Eduardo had emailed to her ahead of her first shift. She started the day after tomorrow and began at 5 a.m. A smooth handover from the night shift staff was, according to the missive, 'paramount', so she needed to be at the top of her game. Tomorrow was Sunday and likely, Eduardo had warned, to be the last weekend where she wasn't working, although he had given no indication as to what her shift pattern actually was, or how much notice she would be given as to her working days. Still hungover, she decided these were all questions for her first day. Right now, she couldn't concentrate on anything else until she had some carbs. She went back through to the living room to investigate whether there were any flyers for a local Domino's concealed in one of the kitchen drawers.

'Hey.' A voice from near the living room window made her jump.

A very tanned, topless, box-shaped man had materialised cross-legged on the floor in front of the sofa. He had a Celtic band tattooed around one biceps, which carbon-dated him to between forty-five and fifty, and was wearing white, drop-crotched fisherman's yoga pants on his bottom half. Make that white-going-on-see-through. He beamed at Jen, looking right at home, from the lotus position.

'Mickey?' Jen asked cautiously. That had been the name of her allocated flatmate. She'd assumed it was a woman, and her name a North American thing. How did he move so silently? She hadn't heard him come in.

The box-man nodded back. 'Good to meet you. Just doing my practice. I do it as soon as I get in to reset.' Mickey took a giant gulp of breath and leaned forward, placing his hands on the floor in front of him, before lifting his legs off the ground. His torso muscles were one tightly woven sinew beneath all that hair, and he steadily contorted himself into what Jen recognised from Instagram as 'advanced yogic shit'.

'Are you a yoga teacher?' she asked, sitting down on their too-small couch.

'Sometimes,' replied Mickey. His accent was Canadian. 'Over the summer mainly. I'm usually too busy in the winter.'

Jen imagined it was something outdoors. He had that action-adventure Bear Grylls look about him. 'Doing what?'

'A bit of everything. Massage therapy for money, but as much snowboarding as I can when I'm not working.' Mickey moved into another pose. Jen could see *crotch outlines* through the thin, unforgiving fabric of his trousers. He wasn't wearing underwear. She perched uncomfortably on the arm of the couch, as far from Mickey's crotch as she could get.

'Are you good at snowboarding? I want to learn while I'm here.'

He flipped himself down from a headstand. 'Wait, you've never done it? I'll teach you. Are you free tomorrow?'

'Er, yes.' Jen gestured out of the rapidly darkening window. 'But, there's no snow.'

The noise Mickey made sounded like *Pffft*. 'They blow artificial snow out of the cannons on the lower slopes until there's a good dump. It'll be fine.' He walked over to where she was sitting, scrutinised her for a second and then pointed at her shoulders. 'You're holding a lot of tension in your upper back. It's toxic to leave it there.'

Jen bristled. 'It's been a stressful few days, moving to a new country, trying to get a job.'

'Hmmm. It looks more deeply ingrained than that to me. You need a massage. I'm the best massage therapist I know, but I also know that's exactly what a creep would say, so I'll recommend you some people. In the meantime . . .' Mickey bustled into his room and returned – thankfully – with a hoodie thrown over his bare torso but also clutching the biggest bag of weed Jen had ever seen. He settled back on the floor cross-legged and expertly rolled a spliff.

'Smoke?' he asked, firing it up.

A pulse of anxiety surged through her. 'No, thanks,' she said as casually as she could, as though she were offered drugs all the time. 'I was going to order a pizza though if you're hungry.'

'Sure.' He beamed. 'I brought back some beers if you want one. Grab them from the fridge.'

This was safer ground, even if the lingering memory of how much she drank last night gave her a moment of internal protest. She quickly pulled the drawers open and, finding nothing useful on the takeaway front, fetched her ancient laptop to check what the Deliveroo situation was in Whistler.

'Nice to meet you, roomie,' said Mickey, clinking his bottle against hers. 'Let's get to know each other.'

Jen laughed, sitting back down on the couch, but properly this time. There was something very childlike about

Mickey and already she was warming to this slightly odd middle-aged man. 'OK, you go first.'

Mickey took a toke on his spliff, chased down by a swig of his drink, and a thoughtful look crossed his face. 'First of all, I should tell you about the time I took acid in Disneyland.'

Chapter Six

ART

'What if a baddy came down here and shooted the snow cannons at us?'

Art squinted at Buddy, one of his two five-year-old charges for the afternoon, and arranged his expression into one of serious contemplation.

'We'd put a call out for Iron Man and then he'd come and rescue us.'

Satisfied, Buddy, with one foot strapped into his tiny snowboard, turned away and scooted over to the magic-carpet travelator that would carry him back up to the top of the nursery slope. Art called out some instructions, while keeping an eye on Juno, Buddy's twin sister, who was waiting at the top for her next go.

'Lift your back leg up and put it on the board. Then balance there until you get to the top. There you go, superstar, you did it.'

Buddy beamed. 'Will I go a hundred miles an hour on the way down?' he shouted excitedly.

This was why Art liked teaching children. They asked constant questions, but they were interested in everything but Art himself. Aside from fielding the occasional query about his 'funny' British accent, Art found that his students couldn't care less about who he was, his background, and why his social interactions were limited to an annual forced drink with a sixty-year-old man. They wanted to know who would be faster at skiing, Hawkeye or the Hulk (Hulk; he's heavier), what would happen if it snowed every single day forever (everyone would have to snowboard everywhere all the time) and – when one of his students was feeling particularly tantrummy – *why* they couldn't do it (they just need to practise). His mind was constantly occupied by their conversational non-sequiturs, and when he wasn't answering their questions, he was assessing the area for potential peril. God forbid he lose track of a five-year-old on an 8,000-acre mountain range.

There was a chill in the air that Art knew meant the first big snowfall was imminent. Fat, low-hanging clouds drifted past and wind snapped at his cheeks, whipping up puffs of fine snow from where the cannons were pumping it onto the slope so that lessons could commence for the season. The two he was teaching today, the children of a Silicon Valley executive, were very cute and very enthusiastic. They had been in awe – as all his beginners were – when he demonstrated a little jump at the start of their lesson and told them that in a couple of days, he'd have them doing it too. They couldn't wait to get started.

At the top of the slope, Juno and Buddy were heavily wrapped up against the cold, their bulky layers making them almost as wide as they were tall, with mirrored bug eyes from goggles that were too big for their faces.

'Try your falling leaf again, Juno,' he called to her.

Juno shakily swayed from side to side, zig zagging in the 'falling leaf' technique that Art had been teaching them as the way to steer their boards. There was no fear in her face at all, purely exhilaration. Her pink cheeks shone around a little mouth that was puckered in concentration.

She made it to the bottom and Buddy set off, tentatively at first and then with more confidence as he got the hang of it.

'Yes!' Art shouted, walking over to where they stopped at the bottom and holding his hand aloft for high fives. 'Are you *sure* you're not experts? Are you supposed to be *my* teacher?' The children giggled and slapped his palm as hard as they could. 'We've never done it before,' Juno said.

'I can't believe it,' Art replied. 'Right, shall we go back up and I'll show you how to do falling leaf with your *bums* facing down the slope.'

Talk of bums and butts never failed to induce hilarity and the children sped towards the lift again, laughing. He walked up beside them as they rode the travelator, helping them clip their back legs back into their snowboard bindings when they struggled, and getting them into position.

With his hands clasped on Buddy's, he said, 'OK, Buddy, put your weight onto this foot' – he pointed to his left – 'and you're going to turn. I'll keep hold of you, so you don't speed off.' Buddy did as he asked, a big grin appearing on his face as he realised he was making a turn. Art loved seeing kids register the fun and freedom of snowboarding: as pure as speeding down a hill on your bike. He let go of Buddy to help Juno with the same move. As he did, Buddy snagged the front edge of his snowboard and fell, landing face first on the snow. Art rushed over, picked him up and brushed the snow from where it had encrusted on the front of his coat. Buddy's expression faltered, his lip trembling as he decided whether or not to cry.

'OK, so *now* you're a real snowboarder,' Art said. Buddy blinked back at him, confused. 'Didn't I explain? Hey Juno, come here.' She obediently scooted over. 'You can only class yourself as a real snowboarder when you've had a proper wipeout. And that' – he gestured at Buddy – 'was a totally rad wipeout, dude.' Buddy looked unsure. 'I'm telling you,' Art continued, 'it's part of learning. Do you know how many times *a day* I fall over?' He threw himself onto the floor theatrically. 'I just did it then!'

Buddy barked out a laugh, forgetting he was upset. Juno looked utterly delighted and threw herself on the ground. 'I've wiped out too!'

Art got up and pretended to slip again, causing more hysterics, before getting the two of them to pull him up by his arms. 'OK, so we're definitely all going to fall over,' he told them. 'Sometimes it might even hurt. If that happens, we just need to take a break until we feel better. But sometimes we'll fall and it won't hurt, but we'll be upset that we can't do it. Those times, try to remember that *everyone* falls over sometimes. Even me. Even the best snowboarder in the whole world.'

'Are you the best snowboarder in the whole world?' Juno asked seriously.

'Maybe like, top twenty,' he quipped back. 'But when I fall over, I stop, check my body feels OK, and if it does,

I pop right back up and try again. That's how we get better.' He nudged them back onto the travelator. 'How do we get better?'

'By trying again,' they chorused back, sailing back up the hill.

'OK, let's go,' said Art. 'This time, I'm not going to hold on to you.'

He watched them go up and then cautiously start coming down, calling words of encouragement as one and then the other veered off a little fast but then brought themselves under control.

'Juno, that is brilliant! Now shift your weight again and you'll go the other way. Yes! If you're going too fast, press your heels into the snow to slow down before going for the next turn. Buddy! You're doing it. Bend your knees a little more. Amazing.' They made their way down and Art marvelled at the way the twins automatically made space for each other and kept out of each other's way in wobbly symmetry.

Until a figure in white, screaming 'SHIIIIIIIT', tore through the gap between them. Completely out of control, the person narrowly missed Juno as she shakily went to make another turn. The noise and shock startled her into forgetting Art's tuition, and she leaned back, just as the nose of her board was pointing down the slope. It took off at speed, and fear spread across her face as she realised she didn't know how to stop. Art sprinted up to her, helping her come to a controlled stop before checking Buddy had made it to the bottom unharmed. Meanwhile, the figure carried on swearing right until they hit the netting at the end of the nursery slope. There was a bank of ploughed snow behind it and the figure crumpled into it with a noisy 'OOF'.

His heart thudding and fury rising, Art guided both kids back to the bottom of the lift, checked they were unshaken and instructed them to wait there, before hustling over to where the figure was lying on their – her, as he realised it was a woman – side. She had the nose of her snowboard stuck in the snowbank with netting wrapped around her.

'What the *hell* was that?' Art shouted, adrenaline surging. His mind was replaying alternative versions of what had just happened, all of which ended with her skittling one or both of the kids to the ground. 'This section is clearly marked for children, and there's a speed limit for a reason. You could have hit her.'

Another person – also snowboarding stupidly fast – skidded to a halt beside him. 'I'm sorry, man,' he said in a broad Canadian accent. He was wearing the most worn-out kit Art had ever seen. His mismatching jacket and trousers were held together with bits of duct tape, and when he flipped up his scratched goggles, it revealed red-rimmed eyes in a craggy, suntanned face. 'I was giving her a lesson further up and she picked up speed before I could stop her.'

The woman attempted to undo her bindings and pull her board off her feet, which helped to extricate her from the snowbank, but she was still doing battle with the netting.

'I picked up speed because your only instruction was to say "follow me" without actually telling me how to do it,' she called to the man with irritation. She had a British accent. Northern or maybe Midlands. She pulled off a glove with her teeth and pushed her weight into the snow to try to lever herself up. 'Can someone help me?'

Art ignored her, his attention on the man. 'I haven't seen you at the mountain safety courses. What's your name?'

'Mickey,' the man replied, lazily holding out a gloved hand for him to shake.

Art ignored it. The faint aroma of weed drifted up to his nostrils from Mickey's vicinity.

'I haven't done any of those courses,' Mickey added, as though it wasn't obvious.

'So you're up here,' Art dropped his voice to a hissed whisper so the kids wouldn't hear, '*stoned*, while teaching a beginner and you haven't got any teaching *or* safety qualifications?'

Mickey rolled his eyes. 'Dude, chill out. Those classes aren't mandatory unless you're employed by the mountain as an instructor. I'm just giving a friend a few pointers on how to get started.'

Art looked from the woman back to him. 'And how's that going?' he deadpanned.

The woman, who had now lost her hat, her goggles and the other glove while attempting to haul herself upright, stomped over. She was about the same height as this Mickey, around five seven, with long blond hair stuck up at all angles, a face that was rosy with exertion and a dusting of melting snow on her cheeks. She looked simultaneously dewy and indignant. She was pretty, Art registered. He hated himself for noticing.

'Stop having a go at Mickey,' she said as she stopped in front of Art. He set his jaw and deliberately kept his goggles down so she couldn't make eye contact with him. She opened her mouth to say something else but then stopped, wincing. She tentatively pressed her fingers along the length of her neck. Art knew that hitting a snowbank at speed was a recipe for whiplash, especially when your body was as tense as most adult beginners were when they first started learning. The woman blinked through what Art assumed was a bolt of pain and started again. 'It was me that almost bashed into the children, not him.'

'He shouldn't be up here teaching without proper training,' Art ploughed on. 'It's basic health and safety.' This place was full of people who didn't think the rules applied to them, who ignored signs and safety information. It was one thing if they broke their own bones but quite another to put other people in danger. He felt a rising sense of panic and closed his own eyes for one second, two, before locking the sensation out. He glared at Mickey, who looked at him like a schoolboy who'd been caught smoking at the back of the playing field. He had a suitably chastened look on his face, but it was undercut by a rebelliousness that Art knew wouldn't stop him from doing it again.

'Sorry,' Mickey muttered, not sounding sorry at all. Art shook his head dismissively before turning his attention back to the woman. 'And you,' he said, crooking a finger at her, 'should have arranged some real lessons before going anywhere near a snowboard.' He knew he was ranting but he couldn't stop himself. He took *every* precaution to keep his students safe but something like this reminded him that there was no way to prevent other people's reckless behaviour.

'I had every intention of doing that, I promise,' the woman said. The flakes of snow on her cheeks started to melt as her face flushed with embarrassment. 'But I've just arrived and my new job starts tomorrow and I don't know when I'm going to get any more days off, so when Mickey offered to teach me I jumped at the chance . . .' As she burbled out excuses, Art was thinking about what *could* have happened again. It made his insides itch.

'The impact of hitting a five-year-old at high speed on a snowboard is the same as hitting them in a car.'

The woman stopped talking abruptly. The rosiness drained away. 'I'm so sorry. I am. I'm so sorry,' she called out again, directing it at the children themselves. 'I didn't know how to stop and when I tried, I just went faster. Then I fell over.'

'That's OK,' Juno called back to her. 'You get better by trying again, don't you, Art?' She smiled at him adorably, visibly proud of herself for remembering what he'd told them.

'That's right,' he said cheerfully, before turning his head away so they couldn't hear him mutter, 'When you're five. You two should know better.'

'Yes. And I told you I'm sorry,' the woman repeated.

'Get yourself some lessons,' he replied. Her mouth tightened into a straight line. He could tell she thought he was going on. She nodded and then gave him a pointed look, as though to subtly say, 'Finished?' With him silenced, she made her way carefully back to the snowbank to retrieve her hat and goggles. Art could tell from where she was distributing her weight that she was masking a pain somewhere, probably in her knee, which had borne the brunt of her crash.

'Are you hurt?' he said brusquely.

'I'm fine,' she said politely. The way someone would speak to a guy who'd been giving them unwanted attention in a pub as a hint to stop talking and go away.

He was happy to oblige. Once he had completed his mountainly duty. 'Just one more thing,' he said, and she lifted her eyes to his face warily. 'You can get thrown off the mountain for swearing, so next time you do a kamikaze run, watch your language.'

This time there was nothing subtle about it. Her sarcastic double thumbs up was a clear 'fuck off'.

Chapter Seven

JEN

'Here at The Redwood we have a policy that dictates if we're going to do something, we do it right, you know? It's something countless failed Platinum employees have been unable to recognise.'

Jen nodded, although the frequency of Eduardo's 'you knows' didn't always seem to warrant an answer. It was 5.45 a.m. and so far, her on-the-job training had consisted of Eduardo cataloguing every previous staff member's ills and having Jen agree how deplorable they were.

'We do not do excuses at The Redwood. We accept, and then we fix. You know?' Jen stared at his hair, distracted. What *did* he use on it to make it into one solid block?

'You know?' Eduardo said again, more firmly this time. This one was obviously not rhetorical.

'Oh right, yes, of course.' Her voice felt unfamiliar in her mouth. Since Eduardo had assumed she went to private school, she'd started imitating Princess Diana on *The Crown*.

'Good. I also ought to remind you that we don't think of our time here as a shift. The set hours are more of a guideline – we stay here until the job is done and the clients are happy.'

Jen tried not to roll her eyes. From looking at the rota in the staff room that morning, she knew she was going to be spending more time here than at her apartment anyway, but she didn't say that to Eduardo, who was sermonising about impeccable service, client expectations, and how he hadn't received any complaints at all last season due to his terrific gift for 'anticipating needs'. Jen had no doubt that the job was hard – the long list of tasks in his email was testament to that – but it was already clear that Eduardo wasn't the kind of boss who would show solidarity and whisper about the guests' outrageous demands behind their backs. He actually believed it was important, meaningful work. Only with a pitiful salary.

She'd already been reprimanded for arriving at the hotel via the guest entrance because she hadn't known she wasn't supposed to. But at least she'd managed one look at the main lobby before she was relegated to the discreet rear entrance used by the help. Inside, there were low, rectangular, white velvet sofas, and a gigantic open fire. Polished timber columns reached from floor to ceiling, and there was exposed stone brickwork in muted earthy tones. Plates of complimentary cookies rested on sturdy wooden coffee tables, and they in turn nestled on thick rugs. It was the first building Jen had been into so far that didn't smell of damp; instead the deep woody smell of the fire mingled with a delicious, but discreet, foresty smell, that, Eduardo had informed her, was a very expensive signature scent created by a renowned 'nose'. The ninth floor – where Platinum was located – was even more impressive. Thick cream carpeting ran along the fifteen-suite floor, offset by pale blue walls that Jen noted must need touching up every time a suitcase so much as thought about brushing against them. Then there was the panorama of the mountain seen through the giant windows, and framed by heavy, platinum-coloured velvet curtains. It looked even better from the hot tubs on the balconies, which every suite had. Through the window they were passing now, she saw flakes of snow drifting down outside, and wondered if this was the big snowfall everyone was waiting for.

On the other side of the corridor, there were no windows and the rooms were part of an inner sanctum that housed the discreet staff-serviced rooms – kitchens, linen, the staff changing room Jen had used to change into her all-black uniform, and the passage they used to reach the rest of the hotel so they didn't thud past the suites unnecessarily. Not that anyone would thud without being instantly dismissed. Eduardo had already told her that. Three times.

So that Jen could learn the layout, Eduardo had given them special dispensation to pad – quietly – past some of the suite doors and down to the concierge desk. Jen followed him slowly due to the pain in her left leg from that stupid crash on the mountain yesterday. Every time she took a step, she bit her lip to stop herself wincing with pain from the enormous black and purple bruise that stretched from knee to thigh under her trousers. She concentrated on the doors, which were platinum in colour too. It was all so incredibly *elegant*; the sort of understatement that cost a fortune. On this floor, prices began at $1,000 a night.

Eduardo led her to the sleek, wooden concierge desk that stood near the lifts, where an iPad was fixed onto a stand. He pulled up a screen showing the list of current guests – sorry, *clients* – and Jen was relieved to note that only three suites were currently occupied. That would change this weekend when the flow of visitors to Whistler, and with it moneyed Redwood-bound clients, started to increase, Eduardo was explaining. He flipped between the current guest list and one for just before Christmas, when they were fully booked, to show the difference. It was a spreadsheet with icons next to each name. Some of the names were of Disney characters or long-dead film stars, which she quickly deduced meant a paranoid celebrity checking in under a pseudonym.

'Who's Elmer Fudd?' Jen interrupted.

Eduardo pursed his lips, clearly weighing up whether she could be trusted. His hair was now gleaming under the flattering lighting. *A wig?* she wondered idly.

'I think it's better for us to deal with that nearer the time.'

He pointed at a weighty ring-binder. 'Right now, I need you to familiarise yourself with the icons and what special requirements they relate to. It's all in here.' He followed it up with a closer scrutinising look at Jen. She was wearing the black cigarette-style trousers and a long-sleeved black shirt she'd been given as a uniform when she arrived that morning, along with strict instructions that she was only to change into it when on site. As though she would otherwise choose to wear the flimsy material to wait at the bus stop in freezing temperatures each day. The fit, however, was surprisingly good, and for a work uniform it was actually quite chic. Jen was wearing her black French Sole ballet pumps with it, and thought the overall effect was quite Audrey Hepburn. If Audrey Hepburn had ever dyed her hair blond and curled it into boho waves.

'Long hair should be neatly tied back,' Eduardo said, gesturing at her head, 'and if you can't look after your own nails properly' – Jen looked at her hands; her nails were short, neat and unvarnished; what could possibly be wrong with them? – 'then I suggest you visit the village salon who give a discount to Redwood employees.' He leaned in and looked at her intensely. 'Immaculately groomed, remember.' Before she had a chance to react, he swept a hand in front of him to indicate they should swap places in front of the iPad. She dutifully did, and a spear of pain ran from her knee to her thigh, which forced her to take the weight off her left leg. Her hip flew up in response, leaving her lopsided. It hurt more when she had to stand still than when she was moving.

'Why are you standing like that?' Eduardo hissed. 'Your posture is appalling.' Jen froze and then tentatively distributed the weight evenly again between both her legs. She tried to absorb the pain, but it was a slow-burning agony.

'I had a little accident learning to snowboard yesterday,' she gasped, 'but I'll be fine in no time.' She desperately hoped that it was true. After the bollocking that sanctimonious snowboarding teacher had given her, she'd been far too proud to admit how much pain the crash had left her in, and she definitely wasn't going to tell Eduardo about it now.

'Just don't let any of the clients see you hunched like a crack addict in an HBO drama.' Eduardo scowled. 'And I suggest you stay away from the slopes from now on.'

'But that's why I've come here—' Jen started to say, as the lift doors dinged and Eduardo shushed her, fixing a phony customer service smile on his face.

'Welcome to Platinum,' he said as the doors opened, his smile fading as he registered there was no VIP alighting.

'There he is,' he said instead, in a tone that wasn't exactly friendly but was still about a thousand degrees warmer than the one he'd been using with Jen. A handsome, vaguely familiar-looking man who looked to be in his late twenties walked up to the desk. He was broad-shouldered, around six feet tall, wearing outdoorsy gear, and had scruffy, disobedient dark brown hair and a few days' stubble covering his chin. That described approximately fifty per cent of the local male population, so didn't help Jen place him. The sense of recognition niggled at her even as she tried to surreptitiously check him out.

'Jennifer, this is Art, our children's snowboarding tutor,' Eduardo said in a bored voice to her. 'He'll be here doing daily pick-ups and drop-offs for lessons, so you'll be spending a lot of time liaising with him. And Art, this is Jennifer, Platinum's newest recruit.' It was only when Art's deep brown eyes widened in recognition and his mouth morphed into a glower that Jen realised where she knew him from. Half of his face had been hidden behind goggles yesterday but now she had a perfect view of the bad-tempered expression that sat above the snowboarding instructor's sanctimonious mouth.

Chapter Eight

ART

It was her. Looking about a thousand times less bedraggled in the all-black Platinum uniform, a full face of make-up and the sort of blond artful curls Art understood took a lot longer to create than they appeared to. Her eyes were grey-blue and flinty.

'We've met,' she told Eduardo, her voice as flat as her expression.

'Fabulous,' Eduardo replied, oblivious to the tense atmosphere. Then again, Eduardo wasn't that interested in his employees other than whether they went to the right school or if they measured up to his impossible standards. The staff turnover on Platinum was constant. Chances were she wouldn't be working there long.

'You probably already know, then,' Eduardo was explaining, 'that Art doesn't work for the hotel itself, he's freelance. But he's requested by so many of Platinum's guests that he's an honorary member of the team.'

Art's eyebrows shot up. Eduardo had never seemed like the team-spirit type to him. That was one of the reasons he continued to work for the Platinum floor.

'How wonderful,' Jen said evenly. Her voice was a lot posher than when she'd spoken to him yesterday. 'I'm sure the guests – I mean clients – feel very safe in his hands.' Her face was expressionless, her eyes stony. Art noticed a spray of freckles across the bridge of her nose.

'He teaches under-nines, so their parents naturally need to be assured that safety is paramount,' Eduardo said, distracted. He was frowning at something on the screen. 'Art, who are you picking up today? I don't have any lessons scheduled until tomorrow.'

'It's a new client. Newton Oates is the child's name,' Art said quietly. He was used to projecting his voice during lessons to make sure the children both heard and understood him clearly, but amid the hushed elegance of Platinum it automatically dropped. It wasn't the sort of place you shouted. 'They asked me to meet her before the lessons start and' – Art looked at his watch – '6 a.m. was the only time they could do.' In a different life he'd have railed against having to be somewhere, well presented and on his best behaviour, at this time – but today, like so many others, he'd been lying awake for a couple of hours by the time he got up. He liked having somewhere to be. It put a limit on alone time with his thoughts.

'Sure. Just let me call the suite,' Eduardo said. 'Take a seat.'

Eduardo picked up the receiver. 'Mrs Oates, good morning, Eduardo from the desk. I have Art Jenkins here to meet you ahead of the snowboard lessons you've booked for Newton.'

Eduardo nodded, the slightly creepy smile that was permanently on his face during customer interactions in place. He murmured, 'Of course,' before hanging up.

'She said she'll be out soon,' he said to Art.

'Soon' in rich-people speak could mean any time between now and lunch. Art had learned that his clients broadly fitted in to one of two categories: firstly, those who were so busy that they gave you 0.5 seconds of their time and attention before hiring you, but also wanted 'measurable results' in their child's snowboarding ability and a detailed breakdown thereof emailed to them each day. This usually went hand-in-hand with a 'mop-up session' over the phone on how to improve productivity during the next lesson. Then, there were those who operated on a 'centre of the world' schedule – 'creatives' fit heavily into this category. They claimed to be ultra-laid-back but actually wanted their staff to be constantly available, even when they themselves were hours late.

Art slotted his tall frame into one of the Eames chairs in the all-white seating area near the lifts and prepared to find out which category Mrs Oates fell into as Eduardo continued to talk quietly to that girl at the desk. Art lowered his gaze a little but watched them out of the corner of his eye.

'Jennifer, while I remember, can I get your passport to scan for HR?' Eduardo said, his attention still on the screen.

Art noticed a stricken expression cross Jennifer's face. 'Um, I don't have it on me,' she said, the posh accent slipping slightly.

Eduardo's head shot up and he glared at her, silent annoyance radiating from him.

'Sorry,' Jennifer said, chewing her lip slightly and blushing. 'I forgot to bring it.'

There was a tense pause. 'You're going to need to be more organised than that,' he said neutrally. Art could tell even from where he was sitting that there was nothing neutral about it, but at that moment the phone chirruped. Eduardo snatched it up and whispered a few urgent words into it, before declaring: 'I need to deal with this.' A brief expression of anxiety passed over his face. 'Cara should arrive on shift any moment but, Jennifer, I'm going to need you to man the desk until I get back.' He stalked off, managing to keep his exit almost completely silent despite the clip he moved at. If Platinum taught you one thing, it was how to be stealthy. Eduardo was the master of it, much to the horror of any employee who'd dared to slag him off without realising he was standing right behind them.

'It's Jen, not Jennifer,' Art heard her mutter, even though she'd waited until Eduardo had disappeared from view before she risked saying anything at all. Her blond hair fell over her face as she scrutinised a giant binder on the desk in front of her. Her forehead wrinkled a little as she concentrated.

Art pulled out his phone to kill some time. He had a client enquiry from friends of Buddy and Juno's parents. They would be 'wintering' in the resort and asked if he was free to teach their kids. It took him only a couple of minutes to tap out his polite reply, offering his availability and rates, but he felt self-conscious in Jen/Jennifer's presence. He had an awareness of her just *being there* building under his lashes, which made him uncomfortable, but he couldn't quite pinpoint why. Probably because he'd bawled out plenty of idiots on the mountain, but he rarely had to face them again afterwards. There was the odd burly bloke whose embarrassment at being reprimanded made him aggressive and fighty, but Jennifer (or Jen) wasn't like that. She wasn't speaking to him at all.

Art stared at the weather app on his phone and tried to sneak a glance at her to see if she was looking his way. She wasn't. Good. They could just sit here in silence until Mrs Oates came out.

'How's the whiplash?' he found himself blurting.

'I don't have whiplash,' she replied snippily. But then she went to turn the page of the folder and shifted her standing weight. He caught her flinch as she did it, even though she pressed her lips together to try to suppress it. 'My leg's quite sore today though,' she admitted.

'That's because you barrelled into a solid block of snow at about twenty miles an hour,' he said, about to follow up with some advice about how to relieve the pain.

'Yes, I get it,' she said, cutting him off. 'I was stupid.'

The phone chirruped again, and she jumped. 'Hello. Platinum floor, Jen speaking,' she said as she picked it up, her posh voice back in residence. The receiver continued to ring in her hand and she started stabbing her fingers at the display. 'Hello? Platinum floor, Jen speaking.' It rang again and her voice took on a panicked tone. 'Shit, how do you actually pick this thing up?' She peered at the display.

'What does the number seven mean?' Her voice was getting shriller by the second and Art tried not to roll his eyes. She didn't even know how to answer a phone. Further evidence that she was some posh, if older than average, gap-year type who'd probably never had a proper job before. He sighed.

'It's coming from Suite Seven,' he told her.

'What?' she snapped. Her face had flushed and the phone was still ringing.

'The number on the display tells you what suite it's coming from,' he explained. 'But you need to press the green "accept" button to pick up. You know, like a normal phone.'

Art had thought she'd at least be grateful. Instead, she muttered, 'Unbelievable,' before doing as he said, and then answering the phone in a velvety-sounding tone.

'Platinum floor, Jen speaking, how may I assist you today?' The fixed smile on her face dropped as she murmured, 'Aha, sure, of course, so that's . . . oh.'

She pulled the receiver away from her ear and looked at it in her hand. Her eyes had widened, feathery lashes framing them in surprise, and the veneer of indifference had dropped. 'They hung up,' she said incredulously. 'They asked me for something that I was about to repeat back to them as a way of confirming, and now they've hung up so I don't know if I got it right.'

'Well,' Art said, slightly impatiently. 'What did they ask for?' Jen was never going to last in a five-star hotel if she expected to be hand-held through every task. 'Just fetch them whatever it was or find someone who can.'

'All she said was "caffeine". Which I assume means they want coffee, right? But what sort? And how many? And where do I get it from?'

'Grande bone-dry triple-shot ristretto,' said Eduardo, reappearing behind her like a bright orange spectre. 'Go and find Cara in the kitchen and she'll tell you where to get it.' He caught Art's eye and threw his own skyward as though they were united in noticing Jen's incompetence. Art looked away. He wasn't on Eduardo's side. He wasn't on anyone's side.

'Well *go on*, then,' he hissed, shooing her away.

'Right,' he heard Jen reply, her voice trembling a little. She set off for the kitchen, visibly limping, as Eduardo shout-whispered after her. 'And sort out your gait.'

Chapter Nine

JEN

'Stupid fucking patronising dickhead,' Jen muttered as she pushed open the 'staff only' door. 'Why is he everywhere I go?'

'Eduardo? Yeah. You get used to that.'

Jen jumped as she entered what looked like a well-appointed show home kitchen, where another black-clad twenty-something woman, with giant, amused brown eyes, and hair so short it had to have been cut with clippers, was pottering around within. That look, combined with the black uniform, made her look incredibly cool.

'Not him.' Jen realised she had no idea who Art's allies were. For all she knew, this woman was his girlfriend, and she couldn't afford to make any more enemies on her first day. 'Someone else,' she finished. 'Anyway, I'm Jen, and I'm very new.'

'Yes, I guessed.' The woman's accent was Canadian. She held out her hand. 'Cara.'

'I love your hair,' Jen said.

'If I had to listen to Eduardo tell me one more time that my ponytail wasn't neat enough, I was going to scream. So I thought: if long hair has to be tied back, instead I'll wear it short.' She smiled. '*Really* short. The buzzcut drives him nuts but he can't say *anything*.'

'So it's not just my appearance that's up for discussion, then?'

Cara shook her head with an expression that said 'oh so much to learn'.

'I have to get a really complicated-sounding coffee for the people in Suite Seven,' said Jen.

'Got it,' said Cara, beckoning her over. 'Come and see the breakfasts.'

Cara stood in front of a bell lift holding another iPad. She had the current guest list pulled up and a list of food items next to each of their names, along with the time for each meal to be delivered. There were a lot of meals for just three rooms. 'Most people on our floor order room service for breakfast rather than going to the hotel's restaurants. Each day the main hotel kitchen makes up the guests' food, which has been tailored to the guests' individual requirements. Then it gets sent up in the lift. If they're new clients, the dietaries are usually sent to us by their PAs in advance of their trip and if they're return customers, we already have it on file but cross-reference it before their arrival to make sure it's up to date,' Cara explained. 'It could be anything from gluten-free to vegan to macrobiotic to whatever Gwyneth's pushing right now.' She raised a perfectly arched eyebrow. 'And often it changes from trip to trip.'

'Does anyone just order from the standard hotel menu?'

Cara pulled a face. 'I wish. Up here, there *is* no menu. They order whatever they want.' She gestured at the list. 'And sometimes more than one meal option. Luckily there are incredible chefs to prepare the food, but half the time they don't even want it by the time it's delivered.'

'What do you mean?'

'I mean that sometimes the *clients*' – there was none of the reverence Eduardo had infused into that word – 'receive their Paleo baked eggs, and they decide that what they *actually* want is a mason jar of organic coconut yoghurt and chia seeds, so we have to send down to the kitchen to have that made up and then re-deliver it.'

'Can't they just change their original order?'

The look on Cara's face said it all. 'Don't get too hung up on the waste, the expense, or the total freaking pointlessness of what goes on up here. When a guest on any other floor orders room service, they pick up the phone, place an order and wait for it to arrive. Up here, we order it for them, and then it's our responsibility to make sure it's done right. If there's a mistake, it's *our* fault. Even if they forgot to actually *tell* us they meant freshly squeezed organic apple juice when they said orange. The guests always say to us it must be great to work on Platinum, as if we spend our time just buzzing off rich people's auras. Um, no. It's great to *stay* on Platinum.'

The unconcealed resentment was enough to make Jen grimace. 'So what are you still doing here?'

'Occasionally you get a tip so good that it makes up for the people who've spent their whole trip being shitty to you. Like, rent-paying good.' Jen had forgotten about the gratuity-based customer service industry in North America. If she could summon up a veneer of charm, maybe her salary wouldn't be quite so terrible after all.

'Also,' Cara continued, 'I get four days off a week to ski.'

'Four days?' Jen choked out. She hadn't had one scheduled day off on the rota in the staff room. 'How did you wangle that?'

'You try working here for three years, honey, and you'll need that much time off too. If you work your tips, you can cut your hours. It's the only thing that makes it worth it. And once you and Sasha – that's the other new starter – get up and running I might actually be able to drop all the overtime Eduardo keeps making me work.'

A buzzer sounded behind them, and Cara opened the lift to reveal some brown sludge in a glass and some seeds on a plate. She sighed. 'Here we go.'

Jen didn't stop for the next eight hours, and neither did the falling snow. But as she helped Cara tick off the breakfast orders, she didn't get to admire the whitening landscape through the floor-to-ceiling windows – because Cara wasn't wrong about the guests changing their minds. Those three rooms kept her busy re-ordering a constant flow of new breakfasts, two of which she had to Google before she was confident enough of their existence to ring down to the kitchen without worrying she was being hazed on her first day. Even then she could hear herself stutter as she explained to the incredibly friendly kitchen staff that their baked eggs had been rejected in favour of a single tablespoon of raw coconut oil to arrive in a shot glass so it could be swilled around in a guest's mouth. The kitchen weren't the least bit offended that their food had been rejected, and only chuckled wearily upon hearing the next round of requests. One of them signed off the call with 'Watch out for that gluten, eh?' after Suite Twelve announced they were coeliac after apparently days of not being.

It was menial, finicky work, but at least while shadowing Cara in the kitchen there was no chance of running into Art again. Plus she got to avoid facing any customers, the thought of which terrified her.

By the time Jen left at three o'clock, with her feet throbbing and her brain addled with half-remembered instructions, the ground was ankle deep in creaking snow and the sky swollen with more. She'd worn trainers on the journey to work – it had been bitterly cold but dry when she left – but on the walk home she kept slipping. The steep walk back to staff housing was slow progress, punctuated with little skids as she slithered around. She eventually made it to her building, where the snow around the porch area had been foot-thawed into slush, and had to jump over a freezing puddle. 'Shit!' she shouted when she didn't quite make it.

Feet sodden, she trudged up the stairs to her apartment. The hallways smelled of other people's cooking and her eyes homed in on the dirty black streaks on the white walls, relics of years of skis and suitcases being scraped along them. One day on Platinum had thrown her basic accommodation into sharp relief. It was only as she reached her door that she realised she hadn't got any food in the apartment. All she wanted to do was take off her damp clothes and collapse onto the tiny sofa but now she had to go out again.

She opened the apartment door where the smell of freshly smoked weed hung in the air but there was no sign of Mickey. If only she could call up to Platinum and have what she needed delivered. Instead she pulled off her wet shoes, swapped them for some Doc Martens and left for the village supermarket, avoiding the puddle this time around. It was still snowing, and Jen pulled her coat up around her face, marvelling at white as far as she could see. Even staff housing looked almost like a cosy alpine retreat when it was blanketed in snow. Almost.

She made her way back to the road and down the hill, the day quickly darkening, along with her mood. Soon she was walking on a pavement-less road with no lamp posts, barely able to see the ground in front of her until a car drove past and illuminated it briefly with its headlights. She was glad when she neared the village. A brightly lit town square Christmas tree was already up presiding over everything, and casting the snow-dusted shops and restaurants in a festive glow.

There was an ambient muzak version of Wizzard's 'I Wish It Could Be Christmas Everyday' playing as she walked through the supermarket door, and that, combined with the Christmassy scene outside, helped to dissolve her bad mood. Christmas was only four weeks away and she'd be spending it in a Christmas-card scene come to life.

As she picked up a basket, she spotted Snowy from Canucks standing in the fresh produce aisle. He was in baggy jeans, torn at the bottom, and a T-shirt with an obscure band name on it. No jacket, despite the weather, and his white hair was sticking out at all angles. His clothes contained all the right hipster elements, yet the overall effect was endearing rather than cool. His basket was full of exotic-looking vegetables, the sort Jen always bypassed because she didn't know how to cook them, and a multipack of toilet roll. For some reason, seeing someone buy toilet roll always made her uncomfortable. As she stared at it, wondering whether to say hello, Rob came barrelling around the corner of the aisle and put a six-pack of beer in Snowy's basket.

'J-Dog,' he said, clocking Jen standing there. Snowy looked up, saw her and chorused the same.

'You coming to the bar later?' Rob called, bowling over. He looked just as gangly – and just as cheekily good-looking – as he had the other night.

'I wish,' said Jen, pulling a face. 'But I'm back at work at 5 a.m. tomorrow and I daren't turn up hungover. I need to be efficient and capable.'

'You got the job,' said Snowy. 'Congrats!'

'I got *a* job,' Jen replied. 'I'm working on the Platinum floor.'

Rob whistled. 'Give it a week and you'll be begging for a drink after work.'

Jen laughed. 'I probably will.'

'Oh and put New Year's Eve at Canucks in your diary now,' Snowy added. 'There's a big party every year and everyone will be there. It's the best night of the season. You should come.'

Jen smiled. 'I will, thanks.' At least her social diary had one plan in it, albeit for five weeks in the future.

She peered into Snowy and Rob's basket again as the three of them awkwardly made their way down the snack aisle together. The supermarket was busy and it was tricky to walk along without bumping into someone. 'What are you buying? I need some dinner inspiration.'

'I'm knackered, so something easy,' Snowy said. 'Probably soy-poached chicken and lemongrass brown rice.'

'Sure, easy,' Jen said, laughing. 'I forgot you were a chef.'

'Come over to ours sometime and I'll cook,' Snowy said. 'In fact, what are you doing for Christmas dinner?'

Jen hadn't even thought about it. None of her situationships had ever got as far as negotiating where they were spending the day and with whose family, so she'd always been back in Leicester with her mum, older sister Alison, Alison's husband and two kids. Her sister had married at twenty-six, and had two kids by her early thirties. While she and Jen had never fallen out, they had never been that close either, so their relationship was all surface civility and regularly spaced meet-ups. Alison put all her energy into her husband and kids rather than her extended family, which Jen's mum approved of. Every year she asked Jen if she'd be bringing someone along, making her feel as though she'd be much more welcome if she had her own partner and kids to contribute. Jen had felt both guilty and relieved that her trip gave her the perfect excuse to opt out this year.

But what *was* she going to do? She had a feeling Mickey would have the same feelings about Christmas as he had about steady jobs, structured snowboard lessons and societal expectations, which was that they were a claustrophobic construct to be avoided at all costs.

'I'll probably be working,' she said, thinking about the Platinum rota. At least she'd found one plus of never having a day off: if she had to work, she didn't have to worry about being alone.

'We usually all are at some point,' said Rob. 'But we do a drop-in dinner every year that goes on for the whole day. We tell everyone to come along before or after their shift. Or both.'

Rob grabbed some crisps from the top shelf behind her head. With his height it wasn't even a stretch. 'Everyone's welcome. There's nothing more depressing than spending the whole of Christmas Day making sure other people have a magical time and then when you finish work, the restaurants are all full and you can't afford to eat in any of them anyway.'

'OK.' Jen smiled. 'Thanks.' She picked up a bag of pasta and a jar of sauce. 'What should I bring?'

'Whatever you like. Snow does most of the cooking but all booze is welcome. Some people bring a dish they always have at home if they have time to make it.'

Jen thought about the tiny, underequipped kitchen in her staff housing apartment. She didn't think it was up to her mum's cauliflower cheese.

'Failing that, just swipe some leftovers from the Platinum floor,' Snowy said with a grin. 'From what I've heard they chuck Michelin-star-quality stuff away all the time.'

Jen nodded, intending to tell them about the breakfasts. 'You've got that right—'

'Oh wait, sorry, I just want to catch the butcher to ask if he ordered the meat I asked for.' Snowy ducked off with an apologetic look, heading towards a guy with a rockabilly quiff who was wearing a butcher's apron. Rob raced after him. 'Don't spend as much on a turkey as you did last year, Snow,' he shouted. 'We'll see you soon J-Dog,' he called back over his shoulder with a full-beamed smile. Was it her or was his look lingering slightly?

It's irrelevant, she told herself sternly.

She waved, now feeling slightly less friendless in this unfamiliar town, and meandered around the shop. She picked up some bread and milk and then decided to buy a bottle of wine. A night at Canucks was a bad idea ahead of another early shift but a glass of wine would be fine, and she was sure Mickey would join her. She lobbed a few other bits in her basket and joined the queue, which was stretching all the way back down one of the aisles. Standing still again, her feet throbbed, but she prepared to wait. There was only one cashier serving.

'ID please,' she said when Jen eventually reached the front. She automatically reached inside her pocket, but her passport wasn't there, she remembered. It was back in her apartment, where it had been when Eduardo asked for it earlier too.

'Sorry, I don't have it. But look, I'm clearly over eighteen. Or is it nineteen here? Either way.' She gave an exaggerated smile, pointed to her face and then laughed, thinking the cashier would join in.

The cashier, a middle-aged woman wearing a take-no-shit expression, didn't blink. 'No ID, no wine,' she said.

Jen's laugh shrivelled. 'I'm almost thirty,' she said. 'I guess I should thank my moisturiser.' Maybe Rob and

Snowy could buy it along with their groceries. 'My friends are in the shop somewhere. Can they get it for me?'

'Buying alcohol for a minor is a criminal offence,' the cashier said.

'But I'm not a minor!' Jen burst out. She wasn't even bothered about the wine, really, but this was ridiculous.

'You're holding everyone up,' a voice called out from somewhere behind her.

Jen turned around, noticing just how big the queue had become. 'Oh God, sorry,' she said, going red and getting flustered. 'It's fine, I'll forget about the wine,' she went on, shooting apologetic smiles to each of the people waiting in turn, and hoping they didn't think she really was some sort of underage chancer. She was buying prosciutto, for God's sake. Who buried their illegal teen booze in a basket that contained overpriced artisan meat? She worked her way back, mouthing 'sorry', and as she reached person number three, her insides lurched. It was that snowboarding instructor Art, with his brows furrowed, looking at her in the same unimpressed way he had when she was struggling to get to grips with the Platinum phone system. Why did he always turn up in the midst of chaos? And how dare he look so handsome and brooding, even when he was being bad-tempered and glowering?

The cashier plucked the bottle of wine from the conveyor belt and put it to one side with a heavy sigh before ringing up the rest of her groceries.

Jen could sense Art's disapproving eyes on her back the whole time.

'Thirty twenty-five,' said the cashier. Jen thrust her card at her and the cashier stuck it into the machine, which took an interminable amount of time to register. Jen prayed her UK bank wouldn't decide now that they needed to do an authorisation check.

The machine was handed back. 'PIN number.'

She typed it in and, after a thousand years, her card went through. She loaded the groceries into her rucksack at random, not caring if the tins of soup were squashing the bread beneath, and made for the door.

Just as she reached it, Snowy's voice rang out from somewhere near the back of the line. 'Hey J-Dog! Was that you causing the hold-up?' She sought out his face and saw him laugh and jokingly roll his eyes. She grinned back.

'Sorry!' she called back. 'Forgot my ID and caused a red-wine-related kerfuffle.'

'Serves you right for looking sixteen. Hey, if we don't see you before, remember Christmas. Find me on social and I'll send you the address.' He and Rob both threw up their hands in farewell and she found herself mirroring them. Their enthusiasm was contagious.

'Will do,' she called back. As she turned back to the door, she chanced another glance at Art, expecting him to still be shooting daggers of disdain at her.

But he was looking behind him, back at the queue, with what seemed to Jen like a haunted look on his face. He wasn't looking her way at all.

Chapter Ten

ART

Art never went to the grocery store in the village, precisely because it was the only decent one in Whistler and therefore was always full of people who might know him. Instead, when he wasn't organised enough to get his groceries delivered, he drove thirty kilometres to the one in Pemberton.

But today he needed essentials – milk, bread, eggs, toilet roll – and was too tired after a fractious night's sleep, his pre-lesson meeting with Mrs Oates, and a tricky lesson this afternoon with a child who decided immediately that he hated the snow. He'd figured he'd be in and out of the shop in less than five minutes. But then he found himself confronted – again – by the Platinum Princess, as well as Rob and Snowy.

They were exactly why he drove to a supermarket thirty minutes away. The characters from his previous life carrying on in normal situations, as though on a track parallel to the one the railway points had switched him to. Remembering there was an alternative world that he could exist in caused the tourniquet around his mind to loosen. The sense of loneliness and loss started to haemorrhage out.

Art didn't hang around. He ditched his basket in the queue and left, his boots heavy as he traversed the car park where snow was falling as it had been all day. The car park had been gritted and, mixed with wheel-churned snow, it had transformed the ground into dirty slush. He stalked across it and was behind the wheel of his battered blue truck before he could even fully register what he'd done. As he leaned back in the seat and steadied his breath, he saw Rob had raced out of the supermarket door. His eyes snagged on Art's truck, before he looked straight through the windscreen at him. Art hit the ignition and reversed out of the parking space, steering so aggressively that the turn quickly cut off the look of bewilderment on Rob's face. The wheels threw up slush as he sped to the exit but he didn't slow down.

He just wanted to get away.

Had to.

He drove out beyond the town limits, half heading towards Pemberton and the other supermarket, but he didn't want to go to another brightly lit room where there was a chance – however small – of seeing someone he knew. His only thought was to stop the cascade of anxiety, anger, grief and loneliness. He just wanted to be numb.

A couple of kilometres down the road he saw the sign for a rough dive of a locals' bar, one he'd never been to because it only welcomed true locals and, even after ten years living in Whistler, he knew he was still a newbie in their eyes. On impulse, he steered into the car park at the back, taking the corner too fast and feeling the rear end of his truck slide on ice as it overshot. He'd sit inside a while, until he got himself together enough to go home.

But then he walked in, and felt self-conscious in the quiet, dimly lit room. One drink to settle his nerves, he decided, ordering a Jack Daniel's before sequestering himself in the dark corner of a booth under a speaker that was playing eighties music too loud. That reminded him of Rob; his musical taste was stuck in that era. Art took a pull on the drink, ice cubes banging against his nose as he tipped it too hard. There were only a few people in the bar, mainly men in their sixties who looked like they'd been there since the eighties. No one was looking at him, but he felt like everyone was, and that they could see into his damaged, churned-up mind. He took another swig.

His phone vibrated in his pocket and he pulled it out, registering a message from Rob. His old friend had sent a single question mark.

?

It lay there accusingly. Art's limbs felt heavy, and even the music couldn't drown out the roaring in his head. Keeping a tight grip on every aspect of his day was supposed to stop him feeling like this. It was supposed to stop him feeling anything at all. He'd thought cutting his friends off would be another way to stop thinking about life before, but they had a habit of popping into his brain. Their unexpected appearances made their absence from his physical life hurt even more.

The question mark was Rob being upset rather than angry, and that was worse. At least if he'd called him a dick for ignoring him it would be normal. Plus, if Rob had a go at him, he'd have a genuine reason to cut him out of his life. Instead he avoided him and Snowy and the others because he was so full of rage that they were alive. How can you say to someone, 'I'm furious that you exist when Shauna doesn't, and that you can live your life without feeling like I do about the world'?

Art's glass was empty. He ordered another drink, a double this time. The Jack Daniel's had warmed him up and he was thirsty for another. He stared again at the question mark. Twice he started to answer and then stopped to order another drink.

After that, time sped up.

He ordered another Jack Daniel's, his fifth in under an hour. By now, he could tell the waitress didn't want to serve him, but, as he wasn't being obnoxious or sleazy, she had no reason to refuse. She gave him a worried look as she placed it down in front of him.

The question mark started to double in his eyes, and then it blurred completely.

Some more time passed and he was on the floor. Yeti appeared next to the booth. How? He hadn't called him, had he? Did the old guys in the bar know him? He tried to ask but couldn't make his mouth form the question. Wordlessly, Yeti held out his sizable arm as a gesture for him to get up. He clamped the other one around Art when he stood, only for his legs to buckle.

The waitress hovered above them. 'Thanks for calling me, Elaine,' he said. 'I've got him from here.'

So she was the grass, Art noted as the bar gave way to the parking lot. Even there, he couldn't be totally anonymous. Poor pitiful Art, his life all but ended by an avalanche.

Outside the bar Art took in a lungful of frigid air. It misted his breath as he exhaled. It had stopped snowing and was quieter out here, but he still couldn't understand what Yeti was saying. His brain just wouldn't process his words. A few seconds later he felt him rifling through his coat pocket before pulling out his car keys, half hauling him into the truck and turning on the ignition.

'How will you get your own car home?' Art managed to slur from the passenger seat.

And then everything went black.

Art gasped awake the next morning, fully clothed on top of his bed but with his coat neatly folded on the chair in his bedroom and his boots arranged next to the door. He could feel his pulse in his head, and his temple throbbing as the memory of Yeti in his truck came back to him. He sat up.

Mistake.

Nausea rushed through him. He took a gulp of air but his mouth flooded with saliva, so he closed his eyes again to steady himself. The memory gap between getting from his truck to bed physically stabbed at his brain. It forced him up, his body vibrating with self-loathing as he padded into the living room to see if Yeti was still there, perhaps snoring on the couch as he'd been known to do from time to time, long ago. He looked at the green velvet sofa. There was no physical sign of disturbance.

He flicked his eyes over the room. From the outside, his four-room wooden chalet in the neighbourhood at the opposite end of town to Rob and Snowy's looked exactly the same as the other seventies residences on the quiet street, but unlike most of the older people who lived around here, who'd moved in decades ago, Art had given the inside of his place a full renovation. It was decked out with high-spec tech and sturdy, minimalist wooden furniture. The sort of decor people throw a lot of money at to look like a really expensive version of a shack. Most people his age in Whistler were still renting, and their furniture was a combination of the cheapest Ikea and second-hand stuff they'd picked up from thrift stores. Art owned his place and didn't even have a flatmate, never mind the four or five people seasonal workers often packed into their two-bedroom places to keep down the astronomical costs in a town where tourism had stretched the rental market to its limit.

Financially he was lucky, but his home and all the trimmings had been paid for with compensation from the snowmobile company. The company had emphasised that while no one would be able to *prove* the avalanche had been the fault of their riders, they didn't want the negative publicity of a lawsuit. Not with one semi-professional snowboarder dead and an Olympian capable of giving interviews about how the tragedy had snatched away both his career and his girlfriend.

Art walked over to the fancy bronze kitchen mixer tap and ran it, cupping his hands under the water to drink from them and glancing at his watch. He was supposed to be at The Redwood to collect Newton Oates at eight thirty and it was 8 a.m. now. For once he'd slept past 4 a.m., but only due to – he shuddered as he remembered – at least half a bottle of Jack Daniel's. Last night he'd thought it was the answer, but it had just made everything worse. With no time for a shower, he quickly changed into his outdoor gear, automatically turning his head away from his scar-criss-crossed left leg as he pulled his trousers on. Then he grabbed his keys from the counter next to the door, where Yeti must have dropped them last night.

In his truck, Art momentarily hesitated, wondering if he was fit to drive, before winding down the windows as far as they would go and turning the ignition anyway. The snow had stopped for now, but there was the promise of more and the light was grey and flat.

On the way, he passed low buildings, hotels and condos, all enveloped by the snow's white mouth. The supermarket flashed past, and he kept his eyes trained on the road, not wanting to see or even think about it.

Ten minutes later he was at The Redwood, stomach twisting with nausea and anxiety. He'd be fine once he and Newton were outside on the slope. He'd have to be.

It was too hot in the lift, and the cloying smell of the diffusers that were all over the hotel seemed to snag on the hairs inside his nose. He resisted the urge to slump against the padded, silver quilting of the lift wall as it rose through the building, and he could feel himself swaying on the spot. It had been so long since he'd got drunk that the hangover felt like it was crushing him inside and out, and the fact that his body was taking a moment to keep up with his intentions made him think he wasn't entirely sober yet.

He shouldn't have come.

He shook his head to push out the thought.

The lift doors donged and he came face to face with – of course – Jen, who was standing in position at the concierge desk. She was everywhere. Her customer service smile faded as she registered him standing there and she quickly looked down at the iPad.

'Morning,' he said to her quietly. His voice sounded strange, forced. She didn't return his greeting, just continued studying the screen in front of her. What was her problem? Today, her hair was tied up in a high bun, emphasising the sweep of her cheekbones and a jaw that was set.

'I'm here for Newton Oates,' he added.

'I know,' she said without taking her eyes from the iPad. 'But you're fifteen minutes early, so I'm not going to call them yet.'

'Right.' He wobbled into one of the reception chairs without taking his rucksack off. It forced him to lean forward, applying a pressure to his stomach that made him think he might be sick. Despite being climate-controlled, this room felt too hot too, and his face was tight with sweat. What he really wanted to do was put his head between his knees, but he settled for resting his elbow on his knee and his forehead lightly on his hand.

'Thanks for soaking me last night,' Jen said in his direction. 'Really appreciate it.'

His head jerked up. What was she talking about? If a guest were to come out of their room, they'd see a well-put-together employee chatting pleasantly to the snowboarding tutor. In two days, she'd already managed to pick up the reassuring lilt of a long-time Platinum employee. But somehow the gentleness of the delivery made the comment hit all the harder.

'What?' Suddenly what Art was feeling wasn't just prickle-palmed hangover paranoia, it was a rising sense of guilt. Had something happened at the bar? Why would Jen be in that bar?

'When you drove out of the supermarket car park – like a maniac – you drove through a massive puddle and drenched me.'

He didn't remember that. But then again, he hadn't been paying attention. Jen's voice was level but the accusation was clear: she thought he'd done it on purpose. Whatever.

'*If* I did it, it was an accident,' he said levelly. She resumed looking at the screen.

'Yet you neither stopped nor said sorry. *And* you were driving too fast.' The tone of non-threatening friendliness didn't change.

'I'm saying sorry now,' Art said defensively. 'And I was driving fast because I had somewhere to be. I swear I didn't see any puddle before I went past.'

She looked up and gave him an inscrutable look before dropping her gaze again, her light eyes dipping below her dark lashes as she tapped something onto the screen. 'Interesting,' was all she said.

He shouldn't engage but he couldn't help himself. 'What's interesting?' he said wearily.

This time Jen stopped what she was doing and stared hard at his face. 'That when you do something "accidentally"' – she drew bunny ears in the air as she said the word – 'I'm supposed to accept it and move on, but when *I* made a mistake on the mountain, you wouldn't stop going on about it. Tell me, is the double standard because I'm a woman and you're a man or because you're a dick and I'm not?'

Her words were too clever and too quick for the state he was in. She may even have had a point, but he couldn't cut through it to be sure.

'I'd argue that you're not *not* being a dick about it, so I guess we're even,' Art retorted but not as fast as he'd have liked. He was having trouble forming the words properly.

'Right. *I'm* being a dick,' said Jen. The pleasant tone was gone and her voice was getting louder.

Art suddenly felt caged in, and sitting down wasn't helping. He stood up, but it was too fast and spots appeared in front of his eyes. A wave of dizziness pulsed through him and he wobbled, all the blood draining from his face. He was going to faint, he realised, before grabbing onto a portion of the hand-painted wallpaper with a sweaty hand.

Whatever Jen had been about to say next, she stopped. 'Are you OK?' she asked instead, her eyes widening in concern. She came out from behind the desk and offered him a hand. 'You don't look well, let me help you.'

'I'm fine,' he muttered, gesturing for her not to. He attempted to pull himself together with a deep breath out. By then Jen was right next to him and she wrinkled her nose. 'Hang on, are you *drunk*? You smell like you've been on an all-nighter,' she hissed, revulsion all over her face.

'I'm not drunk,' he fired back immediately, even though truthfully, he didn't know.

Jen shook her head at him. 'How could you turn up here like this?'

'I'm fine,' he said again tightly, even though he was feeling worse by the second. It was one of those hangovers that got progressively worse and then bedded in. If she'd just stop talking, he could try to regroup.

He made to step away from her but wobbled again. Jen glanced in the direction of the 'staff only' door to the back corridors.

'You're clearly not fine,' she said, frowning. 'Go home and sleep whatever *this* is' – she flapped a hand at him – 'off.'

'I've got a lesson,' Art said emphatically, articulating each word. 'I'm not going anywhere.' He turned to take his rucksack off his shoulder but couldn't quite grab it. He ended up following it around like a puppy chasing its tail.

'Look at you!' she yelped, before lowering her voice back to the Platinum-approved hush. 'If you stay here, you're getting fired. And even if you don't, you're not sober enough to look after a seven-year-old.'

The sentence struck, as it was supposed to. What was he thinking, taking a risk when it came to a child's welfare? 'I can't just leave,' he said quietly. 'I'm supposed to be starting the lesson in ten minutes.'

Jen pursed her lips as she thought. 'I'll say you called in sick. I used to work in HR, so I know the right things to say to avoid any questions. Luckily for you, half the hotel staff has food poisoning today from a leftover shrimp tower that was put out in the staff room. No one ever wants details about food poisoning.' Jen grimaced, and Art's stomach roiled at the thought of warm, sweating shrimp.

'I never go in the staff room,' he said.

Jen rolled her eyes impatiently. 'Assuming you're not BFFs with Eduardo, how would he know that? Now go, before he materialises. If he sees – or smells – you he'll know straight away we're lying.'

He nodded and then paused, feeling a pulse of paranoia. Jen didn't like him. What if this was a trap? 'Why are you helping me?'

She shrugged like it was no big deal. 'Because my working life will be harder if you're fired and I'm tasked with finding a new private snowboarding tutor. Besides,' – she flashed him a brief, kind smile that only served to make him feel worse – 'maybe I'm just not as much of a dick as you.' She looked worried and glanced at the door again. 'Eduardo will be back any second. He only disappeared to bollock the barista for reheating a guest's coffee in the microwave rather than preparing a fresh one.' She strode ahead of him and pressed the 'call lift' button before he could say anything else. 'So, go, *now*.'

The lift instantly pinged and Art got back in, now defeated. But as the doors started to close, another question threatened to burst out of him. He lunged at the closing doors and held them open.

'I saw Snowy and Rob talking to you in the supermarket. Did they tell you?'

Jen's face wrinkled in confusion. 'Did they tell me what?' Her eyes were narrowed and she was looking at him as though he was mad. 'Wait, are you guys *friends*?' She looked like she couldn't believe it.

'Not really. Not any more. Why?'

She shook her head, now looking like she was stifling a laugh. 'They're so chilled out and funny and you're, well . . .' Her raised eyebrow finished the sentence and he let go of the door, allowing himself to slump against the padded interior this time.

He left the hotel with his head down and his hood up, although he supposed if questioned, he could argue that he was leaving in a hurry because of his stomach. He wondered again if he could trust Jen, or if she'd renege on what she'd said, instead taking great pleasure in watching him get sacked.

Not that he didn't deserve it.

She'd done the right thing in stopping him. He shouldn't have even thought about looking after a child in this state.

He left his truck in the staff car park and instead started walking home. A long trudge in the snow was small penance to pay for his reckless decision to drive earlier, while likely still over the limit. Slogging along stretches of knee-deep snow kept his concentration in the moment and not on how the last twelve hours had unravelled coping mechanisms he'd been knotting together for years.

You're not coping, a voice said in his head.

He upped his pace. It took him forty minutes to get home, by which time his heart was pumping and he was blowing out plumes of visible breath.

Art let himself in, bracing for the claustrophobia he often felt when he returned home. It was only 9 a.m. and without a lesson, the day stretched out ahead of him. He couldn't let himself sit down and dwell, he had to keep busy. He'd make breakfast, something elaborate that required him to follow a recipe and have someone else's instructions inside his head. Eggs Benedict with a homemade Hollandaise sauce, something that required concentration. Not that he could face eating, but that wasn't the point.

He made it as far as his fancy coffee machine in the kitchen when he remembered he still didn't have the groceries he'd originally gone out for last night. He paused, wondering what he could make instead, and, as he scanned the mason jars of food on shelves around the kitchen, his eye snagged on a folded piece of paper propped up next to the cooker. He'd been in such a rush to leave earlier, he hadn't seen it.

The ragged piece of paper had been ripped out from a notebook and folded in two. 'Art' was written in Yeti's barely legible scrawl on the front.

Yeti's job as a coach meant he was seasoned in giving pull-no-punches feedback and as Art unfolded the paper, he readied himself for a litany of judgement. But there were only four words written there.

Stop hiding. Get help.

Chapter Eleven

JEN

How's the job going?

Jen was halfway through replying to Maxie's message when Art reappeared the next morning. Even though she'd been expecting him any time from 8 a.m., his arrival, signalled by the dong of the lift, startled her enough to press 'send' prematurely.

I'm a 29-year-old dogsbody was all Maxie received, which in fairness was not wrong.

'Morning,' Art said, as he pulled off his woolly hat and approached the concierge desk looking worn out, but still ten times healthier than he had the previous day. He was in the same navy baggy snowboarding trousers as yesterday and a green Burton-branded jacket. His hair, wet and freshly showered, curled onto the tops of his ears as it dried in the warm hotel, and his nose was red-tipped from the cold. His brown eyes looked focused and they rested now on Jen, who stuffed her phone into the concierge desk drawer, despite angry vibrations suggesting that Maxie was replying, no doubt pressing her for more information.

Jen waited, assuming some sort of apology or explanation for his behaviour the day before was imminent. But instead he furrowed his dark brows and said, 'What happened to your face?'

Jen raised a self-conscious hand to the swollen red lump on her cheek that she'd tried unsuccessfully to cover up with make-up that morning.

'It's from snow tubing,' she said. 'I had a crash. With the ground, not a person,' she added quickly.

Art looked confused and opened his mouth to say something else. But he wasn't getting in the next word, not today.

'Don't even,' she chided. 'It's entirely your fault that I was snow tubing at all.'

His usual combative look was back. 'How do you figure that?'

'Because Newton Oates didn't have a snowboarding instructor yesterday, so her parents were looking for an activity to keep her occupied. I – helpfully – suggested the tubing park, but as her parents are here to work, she didn't have anyone to take her – again, because she was *supposed* to be in snowboarding lessons all week. So her mum asked me to go with her.'

Art's eyebrows darted up in surprise. 'They let you out of work for that?'

Jen snorted. 'Eduardo was furious, but he also couldn't say no because we couldn't find a stand-in teacher for you and Newton's parents were desperate.' Jen had watched Eduardo getting frantic as they rang around, knowing that no one was going to be available in the first week of December at short notice. If they were, it was doubtful Eduardo would think they had the credentials to teach a Platinum guest's child. 'I was dispatched on the proviso that I'd make up the "break" time at the end of my shift.' She couldn't keep the bitter edge from her voice. 'Because obviously, babysitting a seven-year-old was a small holiday for me. Anyway, she loved it, while my face loved it less. However, Eduardo is so enraged by the state of my face and the fact that I "skived work" yesterday that he's making life even more hellish for me than usual.'

'Oh,' was all Art said. He looked suspiciously like he was trying not to laugh, which only served to piss her off more.

'Wait, what was that?' Jen pricked up her ears theatrically, causing Art to do the same.

'What?' he said, looking around for Eduardo.

'I thought I heard someone say "thank you, Jen" but I must have been mistaken.'

Art took another step towards the desk and Jen inhaled, checking to see if he still smelled of stale whiskey and clothes that had been slept in. He didn't. Instead, she got a lungful of the citrus-scented shower gel he must have been using.

'I was about to but I haven't been able to get a word in edgeways. But I *am* grateful for you covering for me yesterday, so thank you.'

'Oh.' Jen reddened, not knowing what to do with the unexpected sincerity. 'Well, you were out of order. Massively.' Her voice came out as sullen and teenage.

'I was.' Art nodded. 'And you were right. I shouldn't have been teaching.'

Why did Jen always feel like she was on the back foot with him? Sheepish shame-faced Art was more perplexing than bad-tempered Art or even argumentative half-cut Art. Were they being *nice* to each other now? He was infuriating.

She was about to tell him it was OK, but then reconsidered. He didn't get to be prickly and then just change the script to suit him. He wasn't one of her ex-boyfriends. Or her dad. Her father was someone she'd ended up seeing so rarely that she was always on her best behaviour when she did, in the hope he'd make his visits more frequent. She always tried to be accommodating so that people would like her enough to hang around. It had been the same pattern since Matt, her first boyfriend at fourteen, had asked her out, and she'd said yes without really analysing if she wanted to. She quickly discovered that having a boyfriend gave her instant validation. After he broke up with her three years later, along came Chris at university, then Ollie – a couple of years with each and serial dating in between. Nathan was the latest in a long line of guys who trundled along and she trundled alongside, never pushing them for anything more than they were offering. They certainly never saw the less obliging sides of her personality. But Maxie had told her to stop that. And right now some guy who wasn't even a friend, never mind her boyfriend, was expecting her to mould her personality around him to keep the peace. Not this time. She wanted an explanation.

'So, what was it all about?' she asked.

Surprise rippled across his face.

'Yesterday,' she persisted. 'Why were you in that state? And what did you mean about Rob and Snowy telling me? I don't know you very well, but public drunkenness seems out of character.'

Whatever warmth had been briefly there had gone; the stony look in Art's eyes was back and the shutters were down. 'You're right, you don't know me very well.' His voice was clipped.

'Jennifer!' Eduardo's whisper was somehow louder and more resonant than if he'd shouted. He emerged from the staff door and his eyes lasered in on her cheek, though she could tell it was through irritation rather than concern. The one good thing about Art's annoying presence was that it provided a welcome distraction from Eduardo's criticisms.

'Feeling better?' Eduardo said to him, his voice almost friendly.

'Much, thanks,' replied Art awkwardly, glancing at the floor. Dead giveaway that you're lying, Jen noted. She'd seen it all the time with people fiddling their annual leave back at Proctors.

'I would *never* eat anything left out in the staff room,' Eduardo said with a sniff, as though the mere idea of a broke employee taking advantage of a free meal in a five-star hotel after a long shift was hideously déclassé. Jen had never willed someone to eat a dodgy prawn more. 'Anyway, I'm glad you're back. Yesterday was *impossible*, what with Jennifer gallivanting all over the place with Newton Oates.'

The look he threw Jen indicated that he blamed Jen entirely for the 'gallivanting'.

'I'm sure she did a great job of looking after her,' Art said, catching Jen's eye and giving her a small smile. She ignored him. 'But I'm here now.'

Eduardo simply looked at Jen's cheek again and raised his eyes skyward in horror. 'Ah, here she is,' he said in the warm voice Jen now recognised would never be used towards any of the Platinum employees. Newton Oates's mother, trailed by Newton, was walking down the corridor.

'Good morning,' they all chorused dutifully.

It was only when Mrs Oates arrived in front of the desk that Jen clocked her exasperated look – and Newton's downturned mouth and red-rimmed eyes. She'd either already been crying or was about to start.

'Hi Newton!' Jen said in her most jovial, cajoling voice. 'Your teacher Art is back today. His tummy is all better, so he can start your classes. Are you excited?'

'NO!' Newton was small for a seven-year-old, and with her forehead furrowed and her ponytail wobbling in anger, she looked like she was on the verge of a full, toddler-style meltdown.

Mrs Oates's eyes found Jen's. Her hair was wet and she was in the sort of non-descript leisurewear that two short days on Platinum had taught Jen was stealthily expensive. Her mouth was a tight straight line, but she gave a small, forced laugh.

'Newton has got it into her head that snowboarding is going to be scary and so she doesn't want to go, but I have a *big* meeting this morning that I have to get ready for, so she will be *much* happier having fun on the slopes.' She angled her body so that Jen and Eduardo could see her face, but Newton couldn't.

'Help me,' she mouthed.

'Scary?' exclaimed Jen, ignoring the pain her cheek that the enthusiasm caused, as well as the one in her knee, which was still twinging whenever she transferred her weight. 'No way will it be scary. It's going to be so much fun. Isn't it, Art?' She threw him a warning look, unnecessarily as it turned out, because he'd already come over and dropped himself down to Newton's level so that they were looking at each other eye to eye. He gave Newton a big genuine smile, the type Jen had never seen him crack around her. He was disarmingly good-looking when he wasn't scowling or drunk. Or both. 'Tell me what's scary and let's see if I can work it out with you.'

Newton frowned and stood there, deep in thought for a moment. 'I don't want to get lost on the mountain,' she said eventually.

Art nodded as though he was giving the idea serious consideration. 'That's a clever thing to think about,' he replied. 'Sometimes it does happen to adults who don't pay attention to the rules.' Newton's eyes widened in fear. 'But I promise you that it won't happen with me,' Art carried on. 'Do you know why?'

She shook her head.

'Because I have taught at least three hundred children to snowboard. And do you know how many I've lost?'

More head shaking.

'None. Zero. Nada. I'll tell you why – one, I have eagle eyes.' He swivelled his head from side to side to demonstrate, and Newton followed it with hers. 'And two, I'll be right beside you the whole time. Does that make you feel better?'

Newton nodded, looking less tearful than before.

Jen was reluctantly impressed, noting the way he had contemplated what she said without seeming patronising. The opposite of how he was with her.

'So that's one thing we don't have to worry about. What else?' said Art to Newton. He popped up briefly, standing on his right leg and flexing his left foot out before crouching back down again.

'I'm scared of falling over and hurting myself.'

Art was nodding again. 'You probably will fall over but that's because *everyone* falls over. Even me, even your mum.' He pointed to Eduardo and gave a mischievous grin. 'Even this guy.' Eduardo stood a little straighter and forced a pained smile. Jen tried not to laugh. 'It only seems scary because you've never done it before, but you hadn't tried tubing before yesterday and that was fun.'

'That was because Jen was there.'

'Art will be there today and he's fun too,' Jen cut in, just about managing to keep the sarcastic edge from her voice. He had a good manner with children, she'd give him that. But fun? She couldn't imagine it.

'Can you come?' Newton said to Jen in a small voice. Her lip wobbled a little.

'I have to work here.' Jen could feel Eduardo looking at her, radiating disapproval.

'But you came yesterday,' Newton persisted. 'Why can't you come today?'

Jen dropped down so she was level with Art and Newton. 'I came yesterday because I got special permission. But that was because Art was poorly, and he's better now. Besides,' she added, 'I don't know how to snowboard.'

Newton's face crumpled in confusion. 'Neither do I. Why can't he teach us both?'

The idea of Art getting to boss her around in an official capacity made her want to curl up into a ball, but she couldn't tell Newton that. 'He's a children's teacher,' she said instead, hoping to shut the whole thing down. 'And I have to work today.' Art stood back up and stood a little removed from the scene. *Any time you want to jump in*, she thought. Eduardo looked on, wearing a neutral expression.

Newton's mum broke the silence after a worried glance at her Apple Watch. 'Jen, you did such a great job yesterday that Newton hasn't stopped talking about you. If there's *any* way you could be spared for a couple of hours' – she directed this part at Eduardo – 'I – *we* – would *really* appreciate it.'

Jen found herself caught between Eduardo's stern and Mrs Oates's imploring looks, her eyes tracking across them both to see who would win out. She leaned back a little so instead they were facing off against each other. The last thing she wanted was to be in close proximity to Arsehole Art for two hours. Not that working on Platinum under Eduardo's perennially disapproving gaze was much better.

'Of course, *I* don't mind, if that's what Newton needs to help her confidence.' Eduardo smiled. A dead-eyed shark smile. 'But as Art is a *private*, paid instructor, another student would have to pay too.'

Jen's heart plummeted. She had no idea what Art's fee was but judging by everything else in this hotel, there was no way she could afford it. Nice that Eduardo was forcing her to be the bad guy though, by saying that she wouldn't – or couldn't – pay.

'I would obviously cover the cost of Jen's lesson,' Mrs Oates said briskly. 'Just add it to our bill and send me an invoice.'

Eduardo's shark smile dimmed as it sank in that he'd lost. Mrs Oates wasn't around to see it as she had already started back down the corridor, trailing farewells to Newton and satisfied that the whole situation had been resolved. The three other adults stood there, exchanging looks that showed that none of them were happy about how this had turned out.

'But,' Jen started, grasping for a reason why she couldn't spend *more* time with Art. 'I don't have any of the right clothes with me to have a snowboarding lesson,' she finally landed on triumphantly. But Newton's mum was gone, the door to their suite shutting softly.

'For God's sake,' hissed Eduardo, any semblance of professionalism evaporating along with Mrs Oates's presence. 'Go to lost property and get kitted out.'

As their group of three made their way from the hotel to the gondola, the snow-dipped peaks that had been concealed by early-morning mist in the village sharpened into focus, backed by deep sunshine. It made the thick blanket of snow that had been falling gleam beneath it.

Jen walked slowly to the gondola, partly through reluctance, but mainly because the unclaimed lost property at The Redwood had turned up a bright pink Gucci ski suit so tight that it corseted her ribcage. Any joy triggered by wearing her first designer outfit had been squeezed out via the serious camel toe she was sporting. Luckily, the padded silver Moncler ski jacket – so shiny you could see it from space – was four sizes too big for her and hung down far enough to camouflage her entombed crotch, even if it further hindered her movement by dangling close to her knees.

'Leg still sore?' Art asked. Though there was no sign of inclement weather or wind, his goggles were pulled over his eyes, so she could only see the stubbly bottom half of his emotionless face. It was like talking to Robocop.

She nodded in agreement. It was simpler to lean on that as an excuse than to explain that yes, while that was true, she was hobbling mainly because her vulva was being severely constricted.

Newton was quiet on the journey and held on tightly to Jen's hand, which was sweet, but it made it difficult to carry the snowboard she'd borrowed from the hotel's equipment rental centre. The snowboarders she saw around the village held them so naturally that they looked like extensions of their arms, as did Art, who was carrying his own board as well as Newton's. But any position Jen tried felt cumbersome and artificial.

'Why are we going up the gondola and not to the nursery slope down here?' Jen asked uneasily. After Mickey's horrendous attempt at teaching her, the only thing providing comfort was the idea that her professional tutor would be guiding her to the gentle, enclosed incline she'd crashed into a few days ago – even if said professional was Art. But as they'd left the hotel, Art had announced they would be going further 'up the hill'.

'Like I told you the other day, that area is for children's lessons,' he replied. 'We need to go to another section if I'm teaching you too.'

Jen analysed his voice for sign of annoyance but there was nothing she could pinpoint. She'd expected him to rail against Mrs Oates's fait accompli, but he'd passively accepted the decision, pointed Jen in the direction of lost property and said he'd take Newton on ahead to sort out snowboards for both of them. As they'd waited for the lift, he'd asked Jen her shoe size and when she'd responded, 'Six,' he'd given her a small push, not hard enough to tip her over but enough to make her cry out in surprise. In turn it had made Newton giggle.

'Goofy,' he'd said impassively when she looked at him, wondering where this weird display of overfamiliarity had come from.

He'd pointed to her feet, where she'd put her right foot out to steady herself when he'd knocked her off balance. 'If you have your right foot at the front of the snowboard, it means you ride goofy. That trick is an easy way to tell which leg a beginner favours.'

'I think I tried it left foot forward the other day. I was

using one of Mickey's spare boards and that's how it was set up.'

'That explains a lot.' Had there been the ghost of a smile on his face? His attention had quickly returned to Newton, who was saying, 'Push me over now, push me.'

They reached the queue for the gondola, which was so long it almost stretched back to the car park, but Art side-stepped it into a separate lane marked 'Ski School'. He guided Newton in front of him and gestured for Jen to follow, corralling them onto the cable car.

He stashed his and Newton's boards in the holsters on the outside of the gondola doors and then reached for Jen's and did the same. It was a tiny chivalrous act that made her wonder who had body-snatched bad-tempered Art and replaced him with this friendly professional. They had the cabin to themselves and, as the cable car rose up from the village's surface, it hugged the side of the mountain. The snow below reflected the low-hanging early December sun. Newton sat down next to where Jen lowered herself carefully, her groin feeling bisected by the ski suit. Art made for the far side of the cabin and sat looking out the window.

'I hope you're going to wait for me,' Jen said, helping Newton pull her goggles over her eyes. Her cheeks were pink and rosy beneath them. 'I have a feeling you are going to be *so* much better at this than me. I bet I spend most of my time on my bum.'

Newton giggled as Jen had hoped she would. 'I'm still scared I won't be able to do it,' she said, leaning close to her and shooting a quick glance at Art.

'Me too. How about we look after each other up there?' Jen asked, a conspiratorial look on her face.

'Deal,' Newton replied, holding her mittened hand out to shake on it.

'It's my job to look after my pupils, so neither of you has to worry,' Art chimed in, looking over. His Robocop exterior cracked to reveal a warm, genuine smile. His second that morning, Jen noted. 'I promise, it's going to be fun,' he said.

Satisfied, Newton started humming while looking out of the window, occasionally pointing out skiers and snowboarders below as they swooped down the piste.

As they approached the mountain's mid-station, Art stood up, gesturing for them to do the same.

They spilled out onto a flat, open area, with signposts pointing the skiers and boarders to pistes in all directions. There was more of a wind up here and it whipped up and amplified people's voices around them. It was disorientating but thrilling.

Art led them to a roped-off section, where several red-clad instructors – the official uniform for instructors employed by the company that owned the mountain resort – were presiding over their groups: some adults, some children and some mixed family groups who were taking lessons together. It made Jen feel marginally better that she wasn't the only person over eighteen who needed tuition.

At the flat top of the small area's incline Art announced, 'Boards on,' while strapping his left leg into his front snowboard binding. Jen bent down to copy him, letting go of her board, which instantly slid away. Art, with cat-like reflexes, lunged, stopping it with his unstrapped foot. Newton shrieked with laughter and Art lifted his goggles and pulled a face to make her laugh more. He was a completely different person around children.

'Jen has demonstrated an important early lesson here,' he said, his voice taking on a more serious tone. 'Hold on to your board when it's not attached to your feet.' Still strapped onto his own board by one leg, he hopped over to where Jen was standing and passed her board back to her. Then he hopped over to Newton and held her board steady as he strapped her feet in, before grasping her hands and swaying her gently from side to side on the board so she could feel the motion but without the risk of falling.

Jen hoped he wasn't going to do the same to her, even though from the way Newton was cackling, it was a lot of fun. But Art left Jen to sort herself out, so she knelt down before shakily holding her board with one hand and stepping in an awkward crouch into the binding, and then leaning back to secure it. She immediately fell on her bum, landing with a soft thump. She stayed there, figuring it was easier to strap in like that anyway.

'We're going to do some side-slipping,' Art explained, strapping his back foot onto his board while still holding on to Newton and somehow being able to move around in all directions elegantly. He wasn't even looking where he was going, seeming to have an instinctive sense of balance.

'Boards parallel to the top of the mountain, faces looking down the slope,' he said, addressing Jen, as he physically guided Newton into the right position. Jen laboured to haul herself up but kept slipping back down. 'Then,' Art continued, giving an exaggerated squat to illustrate he was sticking his bum right out, 'dig the heel-side edge of your board into the snow to stay where you are.'

Newton copied him. Jen was still on the ground.

'Take the pressure off to start moving and then lower down again to slow down or stop.' He squatted and stood up several times to demonstrate. He made it look as simple as getting up from a chair. He slowly tugged Newton along with him.

This time, Jen got halfway up before she fell down. She was boiling inside her giant coat and condensation was forming on the inside of her goggles from where she'd been breathing hard. Her ski suit felt even tighter as the panic sweat caused it to stick.

Art casually unstrapped his board and took it off while he was still moving. He walked down the incline close to where Newton was successfully side-slipping, offering her words of encouragement.

'Bend your legs a little more and you'll find it easier. Good, keep going. No, you don't need to hold on to me,' he said, leaning away from her outstretched hands.

Neither of them was taking any notice of Jen, which gave her the confidence to try getting up again. It worked, but once upright, her poker-straight legs wouldn't bend into the squat Art had shown them. She couldn't blame the ski suit this time; they just wouldn't comply. Instead she panicked and slammed onto her backside again.

'That lesson with your friend has done more harm than good,' Art called up to her without looking. He and Newton reached the bottom together and Art unstrapped her from the board so she could walk back to the top to try it again. 'It's wrecked your confidence and now you're expecting to fall over.'

Jen bristled but his tone was matter of fact rather than critical. She also realised he hadn't been lying to Newton about having eagle eyes. He was paying attention even when she couldn't see him watching her.

'Just keep digging in your heel-side,' he shouted as she stacked it for the fifth or sixth time, he and Newton sailing past. 'Squat. Low. Bend your knees.'

'I am,' Jen replied through gritted teeth. The mountain wind was doing nothing to combat the sweat moustache forming above her lip, and she imagined her face was as pink as her ski suit. But slowly, and with her thighs burning, she reached the bottom for the first time.

'Back to the top,' shouted Art, and she dutifully unstrapped and trudged back up, scowling. She couldn't work out if he was more annoying when he was being encouraging or when he was being grumpy.

An hour later Jen was convinced there wasn't a part of the slope her bum hadn't connected with. By then, Art had progressed them from back side-slipping to front side-slipping, with about a ten per cent success rate for Jen versus a ninety per cent success rate for Newton. She was having a hard time not resenting a seven-year-old for being better than her. Then again, Newton had Art to grab whenever she wobbled. Not that Jen wanted to hold on to

Art, that would be weird. But he was solid and capable. Like a post. A baggy-trousered, floppy-haired post.

With his board back on, he was somehow controlling himself as well as an unsteady Newton purely by moving his weight around. At one point he managed to snowboard *uphill.*

'Slowly move your weight into your heels,' he called, for once resting his gaze briefly on Jen. He and Newton were right next to her. 'Now lean your weight forward again to regain control.'

Slowly, Jen did as he said. She promptly fell on her face, air bursting from her lungs as she thwacked onto the snow.

'Try again. A little slower. A little less weight.'

Jen repeated the same move, then found herself trapped face down. Her core muscles weren't used to the effort and she couldn't summon the strength to flip herself over. Her armpits prickled with stress sweat, and she squirmed, trying to lift her legs and turn but she couldn't. A lump of ice that had worked its way over the hood of her coat burned as it melted down the back of her neck.

'Give it a second and then try again,' she heard Art say above her.

'There's no point. I'm never going to get it,' Jen fired back. She had to twist her neck uncomfortably to look at him.

She thought she could see his mouth twist in amusement, but he didn't laugh at her. 'You will get it. But not while you're lying on the slope.'

He reached her under her armpits and pulled her up, spinning her around so he could grab onto her hands the way he'd done with Newton. Jen's instinct was to snatch them away, but she knew if she did, she'd be on the cold slope again in seconds. Whatever she thought about him personally, she had to begrudgingly admit he was a good teacher. His tone was soothing and his demeanour was unflappable. He came across as quietly capable. Nothing like the petty-seeming man she'd encountered a few days ago. She felt a flash of heat work its way across her body that was nothing to do with her screaming glutes.

'Bend your knees,' he said, still holding on to her. There were layers and layers of padded clothes between them but the position felt weirdly intimate. 'Tuck your pelvis under and get your weight right onto your heels, so the back edge of the board is parallel to your bum. OK good.' He started to pull her gently and they stuttered their way down the slope. He was looking at her, nodding slightly in concentration, the whole way, his defined jaw set. 'See?' he said as they reached the flat of the bottom. 'Could you feel that's where you needed to be?'

Jen could. A tiny but vital difference in her stance that felt right the second she found it. 'Yes!' she exclaimed. 'It's like finding the biting point in a car.'

'Exactly,' he agreed, still watching her. He nodded again, this time in approval, leaving her to it as he made his way back to Newton.

Her confidence bolstered, she raced back to the top, strapping on for another go so she and Newton could set off at the same time. Art started walking backwards down the slope and said it was time for them to give it a go without him. Without a trace of her earlier fear, Newton got going.

Jen set off, mentally running through the steps Art had told her. As she did, something clicked. She couldn't stop smiling as she made it the whole way down without falling over. She'd done it, she was snowboarding. Doing something totally new, for herself, miles away from home. Maxie would be cheering her on, while her mum would be sick with worry, focusing on the ways it could go wrong. She concentrated on Maxie's hypothetical reaction instead.

Art was holding his palm aloft for a high five with Newton as she reached where he was standing. As Jen wobbled towards him, he kept it there. Not caring if it was cheesy, she smacked his gloved palm with hers, grinning like a loon. He shot a delighted smile back and her legs trembled a little as she came to a stop. From the exertion. Obviously.

Chapter Twelve

ART

'You need to make sure you stretch.'

Art saw Jen freeze. The morning's lesson was over and the three of them were in the cable car descending the mountain when Art demonstrated a few moves to help alleviate the inevitable aches the following day would bring.

Jen stood motionless in one spot. Newton did the opposite. She immediately pulled her ankle up behind her thigh to stretch out her quads and started hopping around on one leg. The cable car carriage wasn't busy, but she still caused a few passengers to move out of the way as she sprang about as though made of elastic. Jen, if anything, appeared to melt further into the background – not easy for someone wearing a coat so shiny she gleamed like the FA Cup. She had a frown on her face that made it seem as though she didn't approve of him telling her what to do.

Art's heart sank. He hadn't been thrilled when Mrs Oates volunteered him for an extra student but he had considered the lesson – undoing the damage that Mickey the idiot had done with his 'tutoring' – as a way to thank Jen for covering for him yesterday, and she'd made good progress. She'd thrown herself into it, and hadn't complained about being cold or hurting herself, even when she'd fallen down hard. He'd decided that maybe she wasn't such a princess after all. Plus, he could see from her face during the lesson that not only was she learning, but she was enjoying herself too. Something had flickered inside him as he registered the look on her face as she managed to make a turn: the swooping and swooshing that made your stomach dip during the transfer of energy. There was no feeling like learning to snowboard. Actually, there was.

It was a little like falling in love.

He bent over in a hamstring stretch and shook his head to remove the thought.

On the slope she had accepted the teacher/student dynamic without question, but now the lesson was over she was acting as though he was patronising her. Newton was completely unaware, standing with one of her legs propped up on the cable car grab rail.

'Come on, Jen. Art says we need to stretch,' she said.

Jen backed even further into her corner. 'I'll do it later,' she muttered. She and Newton had been a little team so far. Jen had been setting a good example when it came to following Art's instructions, so it made him feel marginally less singled out that she was fobbing her off too. There was an element of making a fool of yourself involved in learning anything new; a self-consciousness that small children didn't seem to have, and that adults had to get over if they wanted to improve. Maybe she just didn't want to stretch in a small cable car in close proximity with strangers. Fair enough.

'It doesn't have to be right now, Newt,' he said. 'We can wait until we get out at the bottom.'

'It's OK. I'll do it when I get back to work,' Jen said quickly.

Art squinted at her. 'Sure. But you do need to make sure you do it. Your muscles will be agony tomorrow if you don't. Snowboarding for the first time uses muscles you don't know you have, as well as ones you don't use that often in everyday life.'

'I will stretch, I promise!' Her voice came out as a squawk. She seemed to realise she'd overreacted and then dropped it. 'I just can't do it now,' she said cryptically. Art looked at her in confusion.

'Why not? It's easy.' Newton dropped into a totally unnecessary downward-facing dog.

Jen muttered something but it was too quiet to hear. Art instinctively moved closer and leaned in. Teaching children meant he'd learned the hard way that when you can't quite catch what they're saying, it's usually them announcing they're desperate for the toilet. 'What?'

She pulled an 'I don't want to tell you' face and then said quickly, 'I might rip my trousers.' She glanced down at the hot-pink ski suit she'd got from the hotel's lost and found. It was form-fitting and so bright it practically vibrated.

Art couldn't help it. He burst out laughing.

'It's not funny! You have no idea how *tight* they are!' she huffed. 'You say my muscles will be in agony from the snowboarding tomorrow – try learning to do it when your whole outfit is a resistance band!' She was mock infuriated, but she was laughing too now. 'If I try to do a lunge, there may be irreparable *chafing* or a rip that will get me arrested on a public obscenity charge, do you understand?'

'Is it like that episode of *Friends* with Ross and the leather trousers?' Art burst into a fresh round of laughter, which set Jen off properly. Her face wrinkled up in mirth, the freckles dancing across her cheeks as she belly-laughed.

'Oh God, don't. My stomach muscles already hurt. In fact . . .' She undid her coat and then unzipped the front of the ski suit, audibly sighing with relief as she was released from the luminous pink encasement around her middle. She then caught Art's eye, which set them off again. Every time Art tried to stop laughing, they looked at each other and erupted again until he actually felt weak. He couldn't remember the last time he'd creased up about something so completely ridiculous.

Newton, still showing off her stretches, looked back and forth at them. 'What?' she kept asking, giggling because they were both so utterly helpless with hysterics, but not understanding why.

'I can't do the stretches,' Jen gasped, 'because' – she had to stop because she was still shaking so much – 'my ski suit is too tight.' They'd caused enough of a commotion that the rest of the people in the cable car were looking at them with expressions of amusement on their faces. 'I don't know why I'm laughing so much. It's not even that funny,' Jen said, before wiping a tear away from her eye and transferring a smear of mascara to the back of her glove. 'Oh

God, what are the chances of me adhering to Eduardo's "immaculately groomed" directive now?' She started laughing again and shrugged. 'Oh well.'

Their laughing tailed off into silence, with Art and Jen catching each other's eyes now and again and sharing an amused, if now a little embarrassed, smile. Now it was over, the whole thing felt exposing.

The cable car glided into the terminal and Art ushered them out, grabbing all three boards from the holsters on its exterior.

He led them back through Blackcomb village, past the little restaurants and cafés, ready to deposit Newton back at the hotel for lunch. It was almost noon and the sunny day meant the cafés all had people spilling out of them, sitting outside eating toasties or drinking coffee while wrapped up against the elements, but with their sunglasses on. It was the perfect weather for a holiday skier: cold but bright and with fresh soft snow on the mountain.

'Can we get a hot chocolate from there?' Newton asked, pulling on his coat sleeve and pointing in the direction of a particularly twee coffee shop. It was called The Chocolate Box, and its wooden cabin design was adorned with a series of life-sized renditions of mountain animals – bears, cougars, marmots, squirrels – decked out with ski equipment, outdoor-wear and jaunty woollen hats. The owners had clearly had a tween audience in mind when they submitted their business plan because Newton's eyes were wide and shining with excitement. 'Please. My mom gave me some money.' She rooted around in the pocket of her coat and pulled out two crumpled ten-dollar bills.

'I ought to get back to work,' said Jen, although she was looking at the café with a curiosity not entirely dissimilar to Newton's.

In ten years of living in Whistler, Art had never entered this kitsch nightmare of an establishment, but he knew it was a big attraction for the children he taught.

'Sure,' he said. Newton started dancing on the spot with joy. 'I have another lesson in an hour though, so I need to get you back to the hotel soonish.' He looked at Jen, who so far today had surprised him with her attitude: she'd been less fixated on having the last word and more of a good sport than he'd expected, particularly in keeping her sense of humour in what he now knew were the world's tightest and brightest trousers. He suppressed a chuckle as he glanced at them again. 'If you want to come, we won't tell Eduardo that we've been drinking hot chocolate instead of snowboarding, will we, Newton?'

Newton shook her head. 'Come with us, Jen!'

She looked doubtful, shooting a worried look in the direction of the hotel, the turrets of which were visible over the low buildings in front of them.

'You must be allowed a lunchbreak,' Art continued. He could tell she wanted to come, and in that moment he didn't want to break the spell between their gang of three. 'Do you really want to miss this?'

Jen's eyes flicked to the café again. Fairy lights flickered in the window and as a customer left, the sound of Christmas songs wafted through the open door. 'OK, but then I really have to get back. I have to make the time up at the end of my shift so won't be finished until 7 p.m. instead of 4 p.m. now.' She groaned. 'I don't know how I'm supposed to see any of the mountains when I'll be spending most of my time behind that desk.'

Newton had skipped ahead to the café door. 'Come on, you guys! There's a table right next to the bear inside.'

'Grab it!' Jen called, following.

'How can you say you're not seeing any of the sights when you're now going to Canada's cheesiest café?' Art stashed their snowboards in a stand outside and held open the door.

Jen gave a wry smile. 'That's true. Besides, I can't really complain, seeing as I've just spent the morning having a private snowboarding lesson with Platinum's go-to guy. I was planning on signing up for group lessons, so thank you for giving me such a good start. Oh, good Lord . . .'

Jen's eyes widened as they stepped inside The Chocolate Box. Twinkling lights dangled from the ceiling, candy canes adorned every available space, and the air was filled with the sickly-sweet aroma of melted chocolate and marshmallows. The piping music was played at slightly higher speed, giving the Christmas songs a Chipmunks quality. Newton had already ensconced herself at the circular table she'd spotted and was cuddled up to a gigantic faux-fur grizzly bear. Art and Jen took off their coats and hats, Jen now seeming unbothered by the gaping front of her undone salopettes. They slipped into the seats at either side of Newton. None of them could stop gazing around; in every nook and cranny, there was a fresh 'treasure' to behold and Art and Jen kept pointing to things, their noses wrinkled and mouths wide in amusement. The warmth of the café after the cold outside meant that soon their damp coats were steaming on the backs of their chairs and Newton's face was shining and rosy. She was holding the menu, which had pictures of each of the offerings, and pointing to a concoction that looked like a root canal waiting to happen: hot chocolate topped with whipped cream, marshmallows, chocolate shavings, sprinkles, edible glitter, miniature animal biscuits and the *pièce de résistance* – a candy cane sticking out of the whole thing.

'This,' she proclaimed. 'It's fifteen dollars, so I have enough.'

Fifteen dollars for a hot chocolate! Art tried not to react.

'You're sure?' he started saying, but Jen swiftly chipped in.

'Do your parents let you have sweeties?' she asked. She raised an eyebrow at Art. 'The Oateses' breakfast orders definitely run to the sugar-free side of things,' she said, with a slight eye roll. 'Art, you have her mum's number, right?'

He nodded.

'We're just going to call her quickly, OK?' Newton started to protest, but Jen said firmly, 'We have to check. We could get in trouble if we don't.' Jen held her hand out for his phone, and he handed it over. A flash of discomfort pulsed through him as he thought how long it had been since someone else had held his phone, even to look at a video or text message.

His old phone had been smashed in the accident and several iterations of an iPhone later he'd yet to set a screensaver. His apps all stared out from the default background, revealing nothing personal about him at all. Jen didn't notice, or if she did, she didn't say anything, instead just saying, 'Can you unlock it and get her number up?' and politely looking away while he did. Her cheeks and nose were as pink as Newton's. It made him think about what he must look like, all sweaty and dishevelled, which was something that never usually crossed his mind during lessons. He ran a hand self-consciously through his hair where it had flattened from his hat.

When he passed the phone back, she pressed 'call' and cleared her throat, her posture straightening. He felt as though he was seeing her get into her Platinum character after a morning where she'd shrugged off her work persona. She stood up and moved slightly away from the table as she made the call, before returning to Newton's hopeful and expectant look. After three hours of full-on exertion on the mountain, the kids always crashed, going from exhilarated to exhausted in moments and their tempers resting on a hair trigger. Art sensed that the overall mood could plummet depending on what her mother had decreed.

'OK. Your mum – mom – says you can have the hot chocolate.' Newton's face lit up again. 'However,' Jen added, 'she says it's a special treat and you'll be having lunch when you get back to the hotel, so you have to eat that too.'

Newton nodded eagerly. 'I will. I promise I'll eat all of my wagyu beef later.'

Jen looked like she was trying to stifle another laugh. 'Sure.'

'I wouldn't want to eat again after one of these,' Art said to Jen out of the side of his mouth.

'Me neither,' she replied. 'But her mum can deal with that. As long as we have her permission for the drink, that's not our battle to fight.' She clapped her hands together. 'Let's order. It's unlikely Eduardo would drop by here, but I wouldn't put it past him. I think I'll have' – her grey-blue eyes danced up and down the list – 'this one.' She pointed it out to Newton, who gasped 'yes' in agreement. Jen shrugged and flipped the menu around so Art could see. 'When in Rome, or rather, when in a stuffed-animal fever dream,' she said. She was pointing at a red velvet hot chocolate with a cherry on top and a Santa-shaped cookie attached to the rim of the mug.

'Can I just have a coffee?' Art tried.

They both shook their heads at him.

'Not unless it's a mocha topped with whipped cream and covered in snowflake dazzles,' Jen informed him.

'What are snowflake dazzles?'

Jen pointed at another drink on the menu where some iced gems floated on top of one of the drinks. 'No coffee is complete without snowflake dazzles,' she said seriously. Art couldn't help but snort with laughter. Being away from the hotel and Eduardo's watchful eye agreed with her.

Newton nodded in agreement, and Art helplessly held out his hands.

'OK, you win. I'll get something with snowflake dazzles.' He stood up to go to the counter and Newton held out her pocket money. 'That's OK,' he said, gently pushing it back in refusal. 'I'll get us the drinks.' He got in the rapidly growing queue to order, registering that as every drink on the menu involved several elements, he might be there for some time. He started running over his schedule for the next few days. The weather this week was supposed to stay fine, so he and Newton would be out every day, getting her ready for some easy green runs. If Jen were able to get some days off and some group lessons booked, she'd be able to build on today's basics and soon be on her feet too. At this stage, snowboarding was all about building confidence and making it fun.

He looked over at the table, where Jen and Newton were daring each other to touch the claws of the bear that loomed over them. A high-pitched version of 'Santa Claus Is Comin' to Town' started playing and he found himself humming along. Yeti aside, he couldn't remember the last time he'd been for a drink with anyone. Maybe it was because there was absolutely no pressure – this was less 'a drink' and more a liquidised sugar high – or maybe it was because The Chocolate Box was totally neutral territory with a kid and a woman who knew nothing about his past, but he felt almost comfortable. The situation wasn't making him want to get away as quickly as possible anyway, which was unusual when he was around other adults. He begrudgingly acknowledged that Jen's presence had added humour and ease to the morning. He actually wanted to buy her a drink.

An unfamiliar sensation swooshed through him, fleeting but definitely there. It had been so long that it took him a second to register the emotion at all.

Happiness. Right now he was happy.

* * *

'Newt!' Mrs Oates called from across the square. She was approaching the café when they emerged forty-five minutes later.

'Mommy!' Newton called, rushing towards her. She had dabs of chocolate at each corner of her mouth.

'My meeting finished ahead of time, so I thought I'd come and surprise you. I can take over from here,' she said to Art, as Newton grabbed her hand and implored her to come inside and see the animals. 'OK, but no more chocolate today,' she chided, smiling.

'You did great, Newton. I'll see you tomorrow,' Art said. He got no response. Newton was too busy pulling her mother to the door.

'See you tomorrow. And thanks again, Jen,' Mrs Oates called before they disappeared into the tinny music.

Art turned to Jen as the door closed behind them. 'That goes for me too,' he said. 'You really helped me out today. Again.' It was the second time Jen had come to his rescue in as many days, and he wanted her to know he was grateful.

'Are you actually *thanking* me?' Jen replied, eyes squinting into his own against the glare from the sun hitting the snow-covered ground all around them. 'Does that mean I did something right?'

Art's hackles instinctively rose. Sarcastic Jen wasn't gone, she was just behaving in front of the guests. But just as quickly he realised there was no edge to her voice and there was a smile on her face. She was teasing. He rolled his eyes back at her.

'Yes, I'm thanking you. I like to think that despite my occasional swerves into judgemental territory—'

'Occasional?' Jen questioned. She pursed her lips and raised an eyebrow.

'I like to think,' he repeated, ignoring her, 'that I can admit when I have been hasty, so yes, thank you for today. And yesterday.'

Jen smiled back at him. Her cheeks were flushed from the cold and her face was glowing in the reflection of her silver jacket. Her gaze lingered on him for a second, as though she was trying to get a read on him, so he cleared his throat and looked away. 'Are you heading back to the hotel?' He pulled his and Newton's boards from the ski rack outside the café. 'I'll come and drop these off at the rental shop.'

'Yes, I better get back.' She gave an exaggerated sigh. 'Who'd have thought the prospect of going to a five-star hotel could feel oppressive.' Art could sympathise with that. He'd hate to be cooped up inside all day, knowing the mountains were out here but that he wasn't on them. They started walking back to The Redwood, snow crunching below their snowboarding boots. The al fresco areas of the cafés and restaurants were getting rowdier now. Pitchers of beer and bottles of wine jostled for space on tables with carb-heavy lunches of bowls of nachos and plates of fries.

'Will Eduardo give you hell for leaving today?'

'Probably.' Jen groaned. 'Giving me hell seems to be one of his major interests, but I don't care what he thinks. This has been the most fun I've had since I arrived, even if I now have to work until late this evening to make up the time.'

'That's a long day,' Art agreed sympathetically. He felt a little buzz in his stomach. It was the most fun he'd had in a long time too.

'It's the early starts that are killing me, to be honest,' she replied. 'I have to be there for five in the morning and haven't got used to getting up in the middle of the night yet.' She shrugged, the snowboard under her arm wobbling as she did. 'Although compared to the packed tube in London, I love my commute. When it's dark but so clear and the moon is bright, I really like walking to work. That little wooded bit between staff housing and here feels like you're seeing a part of the world that no one else knows about.'

'You take that shortcut to work in the pitch black at five o'clock in the morning?' Art's voice was sharp. Jen flinched, not expecting the key change.

'The buses don't run that early,' she fired back defensively, 'so I have to walk. I was worried at first but there's usually a couple of other people from staff housing heading to or from work at that time. And everyone keeps telling me there's no crime here at all. Maybe the odd ski theft, but definitely no murderers.'

'It's not murderers you need to worry about,' Art said in the same terse tone. What was she thinking? 'It's bears.'

'Bears!' Jen exclaimed with a scoffing laugh. 'Apart from anything else, they'll all be hibernating now.' She was silent for a second and then looked at him sideways. 'Won't they?'

'Which is why one will be even more pissed off if you sneak up on it. You have to go around those woods. Promise me.'

'It adds an extra fifteen minutes to the journey,' Jen grumbled. 'It's hard enough to be on time as it is.' The look she gave Art reminded him of the one from the beginners' slope a few days previously. As though he was being a deliberate killjoy. He changed tack.

'Think of it this way,' he said, trying to lighten the mood. 'If you came face to face with an angry bear, Eduardo would only berate you for turning up late *and* covered in blood.'

Jen's pout gave way to a reluctant smile. The freckles across her nose crinkled prettily as she did. Art liked being the one responsible. 'True.'

'If you don't have time to go around,' he added softly, 'you should sing. Really loud.'

Now Jen burst out laughing. 'What?'

'I'm serious! You need to make a consistent amount of noise, so any animals know you're there and don't get spooked. Singing is the easiest way.'

Jen pulled in front of him and stopped dead so she could scrutinise his face. The fullness of her attention was unnerving. 'I can't tell if you're trying to trick me, and in a few days there will be a slew of complaints from the hotel about a mysterious off-key melody they can hear coming from the forest.'

Art widened his eyes at her as innocently as he could. 'I promise I'm not. Besides, would you rather be a bit self-conscious, or end up in your own version of that Leonardo DiCaprio film?'

'Good point,' Jen replied. 'I'm not sure matted fur is a good look for me. If I have to go through the forest, I will sing my heart out. Let me know any requests but I'm notoriously bad at knowing the words, so most of them will just be "la-la-la something something".' She danced on the spot as she sang tunelessly, looking cute and unguarded. Then, seeming to realise what she was doing, she blushed. She quickly turned back around, almost bashing him on the leg with the snowboard she was carrying under her arm, and continued to walk, picking up the pace as the hotel came into view. Art had to accelerate to catch up with her.

'I can return your board for you too, if you like,' he said, holding out the arm that was already carrying Newton's. She stopped again and smiled, passing it to him.

'Is that OK?' He nodded and pulled it into the crook of his bicep, arranging it next to Newton's. 'Thank you. It saves me a bit of time, and Eduardo will already be waiting to attack.'

'Worse than any bear,' Art deadpanned. 'Can't have that.'

Jen turned to go, and then turned back, wincing slightly, before sniggering.

'Even undone, this ski suit cuts in,' she said in explanation.

Art chuckled softly.

'Thank you to you too,' she said, looking a little shy. 'For the lesson this morning. Free private tuition from The Redwood's elite snowboarding instructor was not something I thought was going to happen today, so thank you for letting me tag along – and also for being patient with me. It was embarrassing how bad I was, especially compared to a little kid.'

Now it was Art's turn to go red. He jiggled the three snowboards he was carrying nervously. He wasn't sure he could handle Jen being sincere.

'Kids have a lower centre of gravity. It's easier for them,' he muttered.

'You could just say you're welcome,' she said. Was she being rude or trying for banter? She was smiling, so he decided to take it as a joke.

Art smiled back. 'You're right. *You're welcome*,' he said as earnestly as he could.

'Ha ha,' Jen said as she turned for the second time. 'See you tomorrow.' She trudged off, heading for the hotel's lobby before seeming to remember herself and swerving for the staff entrance.

'And watch out for bears,' Art called to her retreating back.

'La-la-la something something,' she shouted without looking back.

Art smiled again to himself and watched until she went inside.

Chapter Thirteen

JEN

Eduardo raised his eyes skyward in disbelief. 'Don't tell me you're injured *again*?'

Jen froze in the stance Eduardo had caught her in, with her hands clasped together and her arms stretched high above her head. She was attempting to stave off the rapidly stiffening muscles that Art had warned her about.

Half the pains weren't even in muscles she recognised. Her thighs and her bum, sure, but who knew that taking a snowboard on and off all morning could strain the fleshy bit between your thumb and your forefinger? She also felt a bit sick from the hot chocolate and marshmallows. She stood to attention at the concierge stand. 'No,' she replied. 'I'm just doing my deportment exercises. You know, ones we were taught at school.' She emphasised the word school, knowing that Eduardo was impressed by any allusion to her fictional alma mater. 'Books on the head and whatnot.' She turned to the guest list in front of her, picking up on a client request.

'A dog wedding,' she said slowly. 'Does that sound right?'

When her question met silence, she looked up again, but Eduardo's attention was now elsewhere. He was scrutinising the curtains, a look of intense concentration on his face.

'Eduardo?' she prompted.

'Hmm?' he replied without turning around. He was pinching bits of the curtain fabric. 'Call Al at Posh Paws.' He closed the curtains and then opened them again, inspecting the hang. 'He's our regular dog minister.' He stepped back. 'Do these curtains look off to you? The folds just aren't working for me now they're back from the cleaners.'

Jen looked. The curtains were made of silver silk velvet and had cost hundreds of dollars to clean, so she couldn't bear to think about how much they cost to make. To her, they looked exactly the same as they had before they'd been sent for cleaning. Pristine and expensive.

'I don't think so,' she said carefully.

'They're off,' he said, making her wonder why he'd bothered asking her to begin with.

'OK, they're off,' she agreed, then immediately regretted it. The dry cleaners would be made to suffer for it. She changed the subject. 'About the dog wedding.'

'What about it?' Eduardo said with irritation. 'Mrs Higham always travels with her prize-winning pug and is about to breed her. I assume she wants her to be married first. Ask her if she has a theme in mind and then call Al to firm up the details and officiate.'

'Right,' Jen said, feeling a bit like she was going mad, but Googling Posh Paws anyway. She picked up the phone to call the mysterious dog minister Al.

'Not *now,*' Eduardo hissed. 'Go and sort out your face first.'

Jen held up a hand to her cheek. 'W-what's wrong with my face?' she stammered. Art had dropped her at the hotel entrance, saying he'd return all their equipment to the rental shop, and, aware of the time, Jen had thrown everything in her make-up bag at her face to counteract the windburn and the fading snow-tubing bruise that annoyed Eduardo so much.

'Too much make-up is classless, Jennifer.' He flapped a hand in her direction. 'Sort it out.'

Jen repressed a frustrated scream and fled to the staff room, where Cara was in her civilian clothes and unlacing her hiking boots to get changed into her uniform. She had bleached her cropped hair white. 'Ooh, excellent hair,' Jen murmured, wondering if she could get away with it. Not the skinhead – no way was she cool enough for that – but a dramatic change of colour.

'Thanks! Whoa,' she added, catching sight of Jen's face.

'A bit too Kardashian?' Jen asked with a groan. 'Don't answer that, I already know. Eduardo just told me I look common.' She pulled her make-up bag out of her employee locker and started attacking her face with an eco-wipe.

'How come you're still here anyway?' asked Cara, pulling her thermal vest over her head. Jen caught a flash of an intricate tattoo that covered her entire torso as she shrugged on her black shirt. 'Shouldn't you have finished at three? Incidentally, I noticed my shifts have all been changed from earlies to afternoons, which I assumed Eduardo did on purpose because we get on.'

'Would he really do that?'

'Divide and conquer.' Cara shrugged. 'That's totally his management style. My boyfriend and I both worked on Platinum one season and despite repeated requests for us to have the same days off, he put us on opposite shifts, so not only did we never see each other at work, we never got a day off together either.'

Cara zipped up her cigarette trousers, ran a hand over her white crop and gave herself a cursory glance in the mirror.

'Do you need to borrow some make-up?' Jen asked.

Cara grinned. 'I told him I'm allergic to a compound found in all make-up brands so I can't wear it any more. Told him it's either no make-up at all or weeping sores on my face. Makes life easier.'

'Your skin is flawless as it is,' Jen grumbled, applying some colour corrector to her cheeks. She couldn't work out if they were red from the mountain elements or because she'd irritated her skin from using way more product than she was used to. 'Anyway, I'm here until seven, so at least our working day will overlap a little.'

'Overtime?' Cara asked. 'Or, don't tell me, someone's left?'

'Neither. I'm making up the time because I got to "slack off" this morning and go snowboarding with the Oateses' little girl. Her frazzled mum roped me into her lesson so she could go to work.' Jen dabbed a little powder on her forehead. 'Eduardo didn't consider it work and said I have to make up the hours.' She moved on to mascara and, in the mirror, caught Cara's reflection giving her a curious look. She stopped, her mouth hanging open mid-application. 'What?'

'You went to a lesson with Art?' she asked. Her voice was edged with an interested tone that Jen couldn't identify.

'Yes.'

Cara dropped onto one of the benches in the centre of the staff room and slipped her feet into some loafers. 'Wow,' she said, looking surprised.

Jen stopped what she was doing and turned from the mirror to better see Cara. 'I just got asked to organise a dog wedding, but *this* is weird?'

'Call Al at Posh Paws,' Cara said automatically.

'Yes, I know,' Jen replied impatiently. 'Enough about that. Why is having a snowboarding lesson with a snowboarding instructor so odd? Aside from the fact that I'm not one of his usual ultra-rich clients.'

Cara gave a stiff but inscrutable smile. 'I'm just surprised he went for it. He's kind of an enigma. Nice enough, not to mention *very* cute, but he keeps to himself. Although I'm not surprised after everything—'

'CARA! Your shift started four minutes ago, get OUT here.' Eduardo's trademark whispery shout came through the door, making them both jump. Cara jumped back up and pulled it open. He was lurking outside, wearing his benign customer service face while managing to convey his disgust through a laser glare. As the door started to close, he caught sight of Jen and stuck his foot in the door. 'Mrs Oates has just asked for you to attend morning lessons for the rest of the week with Newton, so come prepared tomorrow.' He let the door go, but managed to get in one last barb before it shut. 'I assume you haven't finished reapplying yet.'

The next morning, Newton and Jen were waiting for Art when he arrived at the Platinum floor.

'No pink today?' he said, looking at Jen's muted black snowboarding trousers, which she was wearing with her white Roxy coat. There was a crackle of humour behind his eyes.

'I thought I'd wear kit that I can move in today,' she replied with a smile. Eduardo followed the whole exchange with his lips drawn into a straight, disapproving line.

'Try to be back before the lunchtime rush, Jennifer,' he said. His voice was undercut with as much threat as he could get away with in front of Newton.

Jen waited until they were safely in the lift before huffing, 'What lunchtime rush? Everyone's here to ski, so they're all on the mountains at lunchtime. My shift ends as everyone comes off the slopes – *that's* when it gets crazy.'

'I'm sorry you have to work late to be able to come to the lessons,' Art said, looking genuinely apologetic. 'It's not like it's an easy job without adding three or four more hours onto your day.'

Jen's eyes flicked to an oblivious Newton, hoping Art would take the hint that they shouldn't talk about it in front of her. 'It's fine. Besides, for this week I get to spend the best part of the day on the mountain when usually I'm cooped up inside. Not many people in hospitality can say that.' Cara had been vocally envious of the set-up, before

Eduardo had spent the rest of yesterday's shift putting her everywhere that Jen wasn't. Which also meant that Jen had had no opportunity to follow up on what she'd started to tell her about Art.

She surveyed him now as they rode the elevator down to the ground floor. He looked different but she couldn't put her finger on why. All the usual elements were there: dark hair sticking out from a khaki-green beanie hat with goggles clamped around them, plus his usual instructor's outfit. She scrutinised his face and felt her stomach tug a little. The perma-frown was gone, that was it. He caught her looking at him and the ghost of a glower clouded his face.

'What?' he said.

Jen quickly looked away. Newton's attentive eyes were fixed on her.

'Do you have a boyfriend, Jen?' she asked, her nosy little face scrunched up.

Heat immediately rose to Jen's face. She glanced at Art and then quickly away again before she'd even registered that she'd done it. 'No, I don't,' she said in as clipped a way as she could get away with. That should shut the line of questioning down.

'A girlfriend, then?'

Jen remembered that children have no tact. 'No, not a girlfriend either. I like boys. Men, I mean.' She could sense Art's presence out of the corner of her eye. He was leaning against the lift wall, with his body angled away from them. But she knew he could hear the conversation. He couldn't not. Newton was very much using an outside voice.

'So why don't you have a boyfriend?' Even coming from a seven-year-old, rather than her well-meaning mum during the brief times Jen had been single in the past, the question seemed judgemental and loaded.

'Er.' She guessed that saying 'because I promised my best mate I'd steer clear of boyfriends to encourage me to grow a backbone' would only prolong what was becoming a very awkward conversation, and she didn't want to annoy Newton by being short with her. 'I only arrived in Canada a week ago,' she settled for saying lightly. 'Give me a chance!' She should say something about being single and empowered, something Maxie would approve of. Maybe she would have if Art hadn't been standing *right there*. His presence made the whole thing even more excruciating, but she was still able to register a flicker of failure that she didn't have a partner – followed by a flicker of irritation that she'd felt a flicker of failure.

'Maybe you could go out with Art?' Jen watched the floor numbers descending oh-so-slowly with increasing mortification as Newton turned her laser focus to Art. He'd been silent throughout Jen and Newton's exchange, staring at a fixed point on the lift wall as though he wasn't even taking any notice. Jen absorbed the sight of his profile – the moody jawline speckled with stubble, his intense brown eyes that she'd seen glitter when something amused him flat and empty. He was as impassive as a statue. But he *had* been listening, because as Newton opened her mouth to speak, he got in there first.

'Are you ready to get back out on the mountain today? The snow is *going off*!' He said the last part with a frat boy flourish, making Newton giggle. 'We're going to get some sick powder today, bruh.'

Jen wished she had the ability to take control of a moment like he did. To say what she wanted without caring about the other person's reaction. It worked. Probing questions forgotten, Newton nodded. 'Plus, guess what?' she said with a gleeful look on her face.

'What?'

'My mom says we can have hot chocolate again today.' She rummaged around in her coat and pulled out three crumpled twenties. 'She even gave me enough money to treat you two this time.'

Another hot chocolate expedition added an extra hour onto Jen's overtime, but as Art smiled at Newton, she realised she was more than happy to do it again. The prospect of having to stay at work with Eduardo didn't seem so bad if she got to hang out with these two first.

Chapter Fourteen

ART

Shauna was trapped in the snow. He knew exactly where she was, he just had to find her. Get down deep enough, make it in time.

He dove and dove. His desperation rose as he ran out of air. But – yes – he could see her. She was there, an arm's length, now only a hand's length, now only a fingertip away. He could reach her, but he needed to take a breath now so desperately. Just a little further, a little longer . . .

Art woke up, drenched in sweat. The recurring dream always left him feeling as though someone had just released their hands from around his neck, but this morning, after another cheerful day of lessons with Newton and Jen yesterday, it hit him harder than ever. It felt like a punishment. His panting breath sounded deafening in the dark, silent room.

He looked at his phone. 5 a.m. There was no chance of going back to sleep. There never was after he had the dream. He should probably be grateful it wasn't earlier, he thought bitterly.

He swung his legs out of bed, unable to lie there a minute longer, and massaged his left ankle with his hand through his pyjama bottoms. Then he stood up, pacing around his bedroom and the living room a few times.

He'd put some music on, that's what he'd do, and work through his physio routine: stretches and reps that forced him out of his head and into his immediate bodily needs. He started doing his standing heel raises, designed to strengthen his mangled ankle, wincing as he pushed through the first-thing-in-the-morning stiffness. Despite what he'd told Yeti, he'd been neglecting his exercises. Even when he was in top physical shape, there was a maximum range of motion he'd be able to reach, so he'd been told. Instead, the physio was about maintenance and giving himself the best chance to remain mobile as he got older. As a former athlete it was a reality that was hard to accept. How do you stay motivated when there's a tight cap on your potential for improvement? When you know you'll never have a shot at beating a personal best? Of being a winner?

To give yourself the best chance of enjoying life, Jedi, Yeti's voice whispered earnestly in his head.

He lay down on the floor and lifted his left leg up. He started tracing the alphabet with his big toe.

A-B-C-D-E

Keeping track of the letters gave his mind something to focus on but his attention kept slipping, back to the dream. Back to the day the dream was based on.

F-G-H

He blew out a ragged breath as his ankle spasmed. His leg cramped in pain and he tried to think of something to hold in his mind, a memory of feeling secure and normal, to push out the nightmare of how she must have felt as she died.

An image of Shauna dancing in the chairlift queue on the mountain, jiggling around on a particularly cold day to try to keep warm, slid into his brain.

No, not anything to do with Shauna. His brain clamped shut around the recollection.

Something else. Anything else. It wasn't easy to summon something that made him feel warm from the past four years when most of the time he was alone.

Come on, Art.

Teaching. That worked. He felt as close to normal as he ever got when he was teaching his classes. The kids' enthusiasm, the outdoors, the satisfaction of helping his students achieve something and witnessing them catch the snowboarding bug. He felt like himself again. His leg relaxed slightly and he ungritted his teeth. What letter was he on?

I

He followed the thought through. Yesterday. He felt normal yesterday. Newton had been tired and fractious after the first tiring day of lessons but he and Jen had coaxed her back into a good mood, and the three of them had felt like a team. He was even joyful at times, when the snap of the air combined with the glisten of the snow and their silly banter flew across the slope. There had been an ease to the day. He deliberately only offered lessons for children – adults asked too many questions – so it had been so long since he'd been snowboarding with anyone his own age, he'd forgotten what it could be like. Messing about on the mountains with friends who were on the same wavelength, seeing it all as a laugh rather than a competitive sport, and happy just to hang out.

Friend. Is that what Jen was?

His leg spasmed again.

Technically she was being paid to be there, and her entire job was to be pleasant and amenable. But it didn't feel fake, not like Eduardo's phony perkiness around the guests. Jen's openness seemed genuine, in direct contrast to his own closed-off emotions, and during the lessons watching her being wholly herself had made him lift the shutters, just a tiny bit.

Being near her seemed to still the constant thrum of anxiety he felt most of the time.

He had felt more like his old self, someone more carefree, someone that Shauna lov—

No.

It's been so long since you had any friends, you're making too much of it, he told himself. Jen could have been anyone he got on well with, of any gender, who didn't know his history. It was pure chance that she'd been assigned to the lessons. But she'd turned out to be someone he could have a laugh with. A friend who was disconnected from his past and didn't load every conversation with implications about what he'd lost; a friendly but formal relationship, where they could enjoy each other's company but with built-in boundaries that prevented them from getting too close.

It was 6.05 a.m. Art had almost two hours to try to rid himself of the agitation the dream always left him with, something he failed at every time. It hindered his ability to stay focused on the mountain with his pupils and he hated that.

His thoughts wandered back to Jen. She'd told him that Eduardo always put her on the early shift, so she'd be awake and working right now, just at the point where it felt as though the lonely night would never end for him. Even if he could bring himself to text them, all his old friends worked and slept late. Their schedules were completely at odds with the hours he kept and the times when he felt most isolated from his old life.

The lessons gave him an excuse to drop by the Platinum floor whenever he wanted. His students' parents always fed back that they loved his teaching approach: the way he insisted on meeting them and their children before lessons began in order to make sure everyone was happy and the set-up was a good fit. They didn't know that he'd originally instigated this policy because it gave him something to do, and a place to be. A place with its own rules where the focus was very much not on him.

Now with Jen there, it occurred to him that it felt more than just convenient; it felt welcoming.

It was a little earlier than usual and OK, he wasn't due to meet any parents today, but the structure and rhythm of the hotel was a place he could fit into. And with Jen's friendly face there, all the better. She'd have enough chat to calm him down and no knowledge of what had wound him up to begin with. Just shooting the breeze, staying away from difficult topics. Enough to kill the two hours he needed it to while he shook off the clinging memory of the dream? It was worth a try.

Alphabet forgotten, he started to pull on his snowboarding gear and grabbed his keys.

Chapter Fifteen

JEN

Jen rushed through the staff door and arranged her face into one of calm efficiency in case she ran into any guests or, worse, Eduardo. Sasha, the other new starter, had called in sick and they were short-staffed, so searching for and then retrieving the wool comfort pillow that Suite Four had demanded from the pillow menu at 5.45 a.m. had meant leaving the Platinum desk unattended. An enormous but unavoidable violation of one of Eduardo's eight billion rules. She sprinted all the way back from the store cupboard.

Luckily he wasn't lying in wait when she made it back to the concierge desk, so she quickly checked the iPad for any calls or messages that had come through during her short absence. It wasn't until a voice called out, 'Hey,' that she realised she wasn't alone.

Her head jerked up.

Art was sitting across from her in one of the lobby chairs.

'What are you doing here so early?' she said, still slightly out of breath. The lights in the public areas were on, but were kept at a flattering 'low glow' until 7 a.m. She had to strain to see him properly. He looked distracted.

'Is everything OK?' she asked.

She could see him under the dim lights, nodding.

'I just need to run through a few things about the lessons,' he said eventually.

'Now?' It was 6.20 a.m.

'I didn't think Eduardo would want you talking on the phone, but the guests are used to seeing me here, so I thought I could just talk to you between jobs. If that's OK.'

'Sure.' It was kind of a long way to go about it, but working in this hotel had exposed Jen to more eccentricity in just over a week than she'd ever seen before. 'Do you need to ask me two hours' worth of questions?' she worried. 'Am I being reprimanded?' The lesson yesterday had gone well, she'd thought. They'd practised the same exercises as the first day, with Newton making steady progress and Jen less so. Then they'd egged each other on to try different drinks from the hot chocolate menu afterwards. The scene hadn't been entirely unlike Jen's original cutesy daydream about what life in Whistler would be like. Aside from the addition of a small child and a man who was being paid to hang out with her. Perhaps Jen being so much worse than Newton was proving to be a problem, and meant Art wasn't giving enough attention to the person whose parents were paying the bill.

'Nothing like that,' he said quietly. 'I just figured it would be quieter to catch up before you started serving breakfasts.'

'Oh God,' Jen continued to fret. He must have made a special visit here to get things straight while Newton wasn't around. 'I really try and keep away from

Newton on the slope but I'm just not good enough to stop myself from sliding in the wrong direction sometimes. I'm so sorry.'

A strange look passed over Art's face, as though she'd somehow given the wrong answer. 'I'd hate to knock her over, or put anyone else in danger. What should I do? Maybe I'm just a lost cause. You can totally tell her mum and ditch me. Eduardo thinks it's interfering with my work as it is.'

'No, no, nothing like that,' Art insisted. 'You're learning and you haven't put Newton in danger. No one expects you to pick it up straight away.'

A reminder flashed up on the iPad in front of her. 'Just a sec,' she said, picking up the phone. Over the last couple of days, the suites had started filling up and the difference in workload was noticeable. 'I have to call down for Kopi Luwak coffee for the new client in Suite Nine so it's ready at precisely 6.30 a.m. as requested.'

Art's face crinkled in confusion. 'What's Kopi Luwak coffee?'

'It's made from weasel shit and costs more than I'll earn this week.' She pulled out the premium CBD oil Suite Nine's personal assistant had couriered to the hotel to add to the cup, as she cradled the phone between her ear and chin. The oil cost about ten dollars a drop, but so far didn't seem to be helping its owner chill out, most likely because any effects it might have were counteracted by the twelve jitter-inducing espressos he drank each day. She said a few words to the barista and hung up. 'Continue,' she said to Art.

'Huh?' he said, squinting at her.

'The stuff you need to run through.' Jen glanced over to the mineral water dispenser. 'Crap, that's empty. I'll be back in a second.' She went through the staff door to the store room and struggled back with a nineteen-litre refill. The hotel used glass ones for both aesthetic and environmental reasons, which may have been admirable, but meant they were *really* heavy and likely to explode into a thousand pieces if someone dropped one. Which she had. Twice. Seeing her waddling along, Art jumped up to help, removing the old one and grabbing the other side of the container to help her heave the new one to the top. Their hands touched briefly as they manoeuvred it into place, his on top of hers. She'd almost got used to the sensation of him correcting her stance gently on the slopes, but that was through layers of gloves and clothes. The touch of his bare hands now, though warm, was a shock. He must have felt the same as he pulled them quickly away.

'Thank you,' she said, rubbing her hands together slightly to dissipate the awkwardness. 'Eduardo refuses to help us with them because he says women doing manual labour is a matter of workplace equality, even though the picture on the side shows it's a two-person job. Then if we drop one he has a heart attack because it sounds like a cannon going off.'

'Mass heart attacks across the whole floor,' Art agreed with a wonky smile.

'The last person I'd want to give CPR to is Eduardo,' Jen said, wrinkling her nose at the thought of it. 'Although my friend Maxie says you can't discriminate between arseholes and non-arseholes when it comes to resuscitation.'

Instead of sitting back down again, Art was standing next to the water dispenser, flexing his right wrist in and out. 'Is Maxie a doctor?'

'A paramedic,' Jen replied. 'She was the person who told me I should train as a first aider in the workplace because everyone should be able to do CPR. She gets so many heart attack call-outs and hardly anyone knows what to do while they're waiting for an ambulance, so I made sure my last workplace signed up to all the first aid courses it could and got the MD to sign off on providing a workplace defibrillator.' She'd been quite proud of that actually. She'd had to campaign for it, but had eventually managed to convince Proctors to stump up the expense after explaining the odds of survival when one was provided on site. As someone who usually kept her head down and went along with the status quo, it was probably her most assertive act to date.

Art looked at her for a second, an inscrutable look on his face, and then looked away.

'What?' she asked. 'I'm not saying I'm a replacement for the emergency services or anything. Although,' she added, feeling that she needed to be self-deprecating in case Art thought she was showing off somehow, 'I was also a fire marshal. And as you've seen me in neon, you'll know that the gilet I had to wear during fire drills really suited me.'

She chuckled at her own joke, expecting him to bring up her pink ski suit and join in, but he didn't. 'I like to make myself useful,' she said instead, realising just how true it was. Maybe it wasn't assertive, maybe she'd actually done it to remind everyone of her value and convince them that she was worth having around.

The memory of an uncomfortable conversation with Maxie rose up, not from Jen's break-up with Nathan but from the one with Ollie, after he'd been offered a job in Dubai and accepted it without so much as a conversation with her beforehand about what it meant for them. 'It wasn't your fault that your mum was unhappy after your dad left, but her being unhappy on her own is the reason you've buried your own needs in every relationship since then. If you're no trouble and bring enough skills to the table, then you'll be enough. Guess what, that's impossible and you're enough on your own.' Jen blinked the recollection away. She hated that her neuroses were so basic. The room felt very quiet, as though it had muffled and absorbed the jokes Jen had made. Art hadn't laughed or joined in with the banter like he might have yesterday. He hadn't said anything.

'Well, I know who to come to if I need a clear exit down a smoke-filled stairwell,' Art finally said. He looked like he had something on his mind. Weary somehow, as though he hadn't slept. He raked a hand over the bristly stubble around his chin. Maybe he thought she wasn't taking his health and safety chat seriously, and she felt a pulse of disappointment that she had somehow let him down. She pushed the reflex away with a stern word to herself. He *came here to see* me. *I can talk about what I like. It is not my job to keep him conversationally happy.*

Still, this whole situation was discombobulating her. Art had said he wanted to talk, but it was as though it wasn't going the way he expected. Why didn't he just say what he wanted? Just then, a bellboy arrived with the coffee Jen had ordered. She deposited the CBD drop into the cup.

'I have to take this to the room and then you can fire away,' she said to Art.

He motioned to her that it was fine, and she left him standing in the same spot. But when she came back from delivering the CBD coffee, he was gone. When he came back to pick up her and Newton two hours later, he didn't mention their previous conversation at all.

Chapter Sixteen

JEN

After three mornings of lessons, something clicked, and it wasn't just her almost-thirty-year-old knees as she heaved herself up from her wipeouts. Her turns were still wobbly, but she could link three of them in a row without falling, and she started to instinctively look in the direction she wanted to go rather than at her feet. Occasionally she even managed to do the two things at the same time. On their final day, Art announced he was going to take them from their familiar learners' slope to a series of 'easy greens'.

The temperature was crisp, and it was cloudy, with occasional flurries of snow. Still the sun kept peeking out, and visibility wasn't too bad, so, after reaching their usual gondola mid-station, they made their way to another cable car, one that took them up to a higher elevation. It was a lot busier, and their little group was bisected by other people. Hemmed in by a big family group, Art and Newton retreated to one corner, while Jen ended up on the other side. A part of her was relieved. Since his disappearing act yesterday morning, things between her and Art had been awkward. And the harder she tried with him – which she had despite her telling herself she shouldn't – the worse it seemed to get. It was as though he was a boyfriend she was trying to please. A sick feeling bubbled up from her stomach.

Shit.

She watched the people on the piste below the cable car skiing down the mountain. The combination of them descending and the cable car ascending made them quickly diminish in size. Meanwhile, the carriage was so full it was getting very hot inside. Craning over people's heads, Jen saw Newton do a little wave from her spot next to Art. He was trying to shift over to carve out a bit of space for Newton but the people around them kept moving into it before Newton had a chance. Jen was glad again she was on the other side. The thought of being pressed up against Art in a clammy cable car made her nervous. Someone opened a tiny window, and she felt the relief of a jolt of cold air as it spread through the cabin. She let the breeze waft over her face, closing her eyes and lifting her chin up to meet it. When she opened them again, she sought out Newton to see if she was OK, but instead locked eyes with Art. Her skin started to burn despite the cold air and the thought arrived fully formed.

She had a crush on Art.

A week into her trip and she'd developed a crush on the most unavailable, and possibly the most unsuitable man in town – Eduardo notwithstanding.

Fancying someone who blew hot and cold, with whom she didn't quite know where she stood, was *so* her.

Art had made it quite clear he barely even liked her, so it wasn't as though she was at any risk of breaking her vow to Maxie, but she still wanted to kick herself. In the few weeks since making the promise, and definitely in the week since her arrival, staying single had started to make more and more sense. She was beholden to no one and – Eduardo's impossible standards aside – wasn't seeking anyone's approval. She had a seasonal job, a slightly bizarre flatmate and the rest of the season to figure out whether she – Jen – was OK with both of those things, or wanted to change them. Now she fancied Art, and previous experience had taught her that she'd soon start to mould herself into the sort of person she thought *he* wanted her to be, in the hope of getting his approval.

She closed her eyes to think. All she had to do was get through this last lesson and go back to seeing Art only during lesson pick-ups and drop-offs at the hotel. Even she could manage that, surely.

'Jen, let's go! We're getting off here,' Art called. She realised the cable car had arrived and the doors had opened. Art and Newton were waiting for her as the tide of people poured past. She joined them, taking the board that Art was holding out to her, but feeling a bit wobbly. She gave him a weak approximation of a smile.

'Don't worry, the runs we're going to go down are just as manageable as the ones we've been doing,' Art said, mistaking the distressed look on her face for new-piste nerves.

Jen nodded in return, before she and Newton followed Art to the top of a slope. They seemed very high up here, and there were dozens of people swarming down.

'We're heading for that lift there,' Art said, pointing to a spot a hundred metres or so below. 'I'll be with you the whole way, but if for any reason we get separated, we'll meet at the barriers.' He nodded at Jen. It was clear he meant if she and *him* got separated; he would obviously be sticking close to Newton.

'OK,' Jen replied uncertainly. She didn't think that she was capable of aiming towards one specific spot on the slope, even if it was an enormous chairlift station.

'You don't seem so sure,' Art said. 'Give me your phone.'

She unzipped her jacket and pulled it out from an inside pocket.

'Retro,' Art said, amused at her flip phone. He pulled off his glove and tapped at the buttons before handing it back. 'My number is in there, so if we get separated, or you feel like you're struggling and have to stop, you can let me know. OK?' She nodded and he gave her a thumbs up back, as though to settle the matter. His awkwardness towards her had evaporated as soon as the lesson started. He was back to his familiar patter. He quickly demonstrated how to traverse the untried run, moving slowly, and set off with Newton behind him.

Jen scrambled to follow, no longer nervous about being too close to Art, but instead nervous that he was going to be too far away. She kept stopping, anxious about the people flying past her.

'Concentrate on yourself, not what everyone else is doing,' Art called.

He was watching her while not watching her again.

Jen absorbed his words, concentrating on her own path down the slope and slowly finding her rhythm. By the time she took stock of where she was, she was halfway down the piste and flowing from side to side, feeling as though she was soaring.

She stopped to catch her breath and realised Art and Newton were right there at the edge of the slope, waiting for her. Registering Art's eyes on her as she panted was enough to make her immediately fall over.

'Sorry,' she said automatically.

'It's going to be a long day if you apologise every time you fall over,' he replied.

'OK, sorry.'

They all pushed up and off again, and Jen realised Art was giving her enough space to traverse the slope independently, while staying close enough to guide her towards the lift he'd pointed out. Twenty minutes later, they'd puttered to their meeting point.

'Now for the chairlift,' Art said.

To Jen, the chairs on the chairlift looked like they were coming in very fast. She and Newton exchanged a nervous look but Art took no notice and instead scooted over to the queue-jumping ski school lane, gesturing for them to follow. When he reached the front, he told the lift operator, 'Private lesson,' and the liftie slowed the machinery right down.

'Newton, stand next to me in the middle, and Jen, you stand on the other side of her. I'll pull the safety bar down, so don't worry about that. The main thing is to sit right back in the seat.'

'Got it.' Newton smiled, looking perfectly confident. Art and Newton both rode with their left feet forward, in a regular stance and facing the right. With Jen being goofy, she found herself facing the other way, staring over Newton's head and directly at Art's face.

You only have a crush on him because in the context of the lessons, he makes you feel safe, she told herself. *It's proximity, not passion.*

As the lift approached, Art stretched his right arm back to buffer the seat and stop it from bashing their legs. There was a whoomphing sound as the three of them sat down in unison, and a little gasp of wisping snowflakes rose up from the seat. The chairlift flew up with a dramatic swing and started climbing the steep mountain, the cable making cranking noises as they passed through the intermittent pulley terminals. Art was sitting with his left arm dangling over the safety rail and alternating between looking down at the mountain floor and making sure Newton was OK. There was a dusting of snow on his hat and his nose was red at the tip.

The lift stopped abruptly. They were suspended in mid-air, still only halfway to the top.

'Someone must have fallen as they got off,' Art said mildly, as Newton looked at him in alarm. 'The lifties will be helping them out of the way.'

Their chairlift was rocking gently backwards and forwards on its cables. Now they'd stopped moving it seemed to be getting degrees colder by the second. Even the normally chatty Newton was silent, peering at people skiing below them, the occasional muffled yelp or whoop the only noise they could hear. Jen felt too awkward to speak. All she could think about was Art's arm resting on the back of the seat and how close it was to her.

The lift swung into life again, swaying once, twice, and then slowly setting back off, its pulleys making a hypnotic whirring sound as it moved. The landing station came slowly into view and Jen stiffened. 'Don't worry,' came Art's voice, 'I'll get them to slow the lift down again, but get your boards ready, nose pointed forward and flush – that means flat,' he added for Newton's benefit, 'to the ground. I'll lead you both down.'

He tugged the safety bar up from what Jen realised was her iron grip and raised it above their heads. With one hand resting lightly on each of them, he guided them off and to a stop a short distance away. He let go but the memory of the momentary pressure on Jen's side remained. It tingled a little and she felt lightheaded. She inhaled a breath of frigid mountain air to steady herself.

It's the altitude, she told herself. *It's the altitude*. Then she remembered how high up they were and realised she actually *was* a bit scared of that.

Art pointed down to where the terrain spread out below them, and she followed his hand with her eyes. 'Now for the fun bit,' he said with one of those smiles he deployed occasionally.

Wide, gently sloping runs opened out as far as she could see. To each side were cliffs and peaks backed by grey-blue sky and wispy clouds.

'We could do this run and then a couple more greens before getting the cable car back down,' Art explained.

'Or, we have time before the end of the lesson to do one big run all the way to the bottom. There's a route down that takes in only greens. It'll be tiring, but it will also be so worth it. What do you think?'

'All the way down!' shouted a buzzing Newton, and Art laughed. Jen wasn't sure she could do it, but at least concentrating on travelling down an entire mountain meant she couldn't think about the line of Art's jaw that was just visible below his goggles, and how when he laughed you could see a tiny dimple just to the left-hand side of his mouth.

'Let's go,' she said before she could change her mind. Art started moving, managing to bend over and secure his back foot in his snowboard binding while he was already gliding along. The ease with which he did it, using natural talent, but without any hint of showing off, was undeniably sexy.

Jen forced herself to stop watching so she could concentrate on the job in hand, of nailing her first turn and not falling on her face.

Methodically she worked her way down, for the most part keeping up with Newton and Art, and even managing to take in her surroundings: white below her feet and white above, where fat, low-hanging clouds were pelting past. It was unlike anything she'd ever done before and she was actually *doing it.* The knowledge made her furrowed, focused expression crack into a smile. She was completely in the moment, her view full of the Canadian mountains. Her legs ached and the wind whipped at her face, but as they reached the downhill slope that took them to the village, she was practically vibrating with exhilaration. She reached the flat just after Newton and Art.

'Oh my God, I *loved* that,' she said, her chin so numb from the cold that the speaking felt alien. Newton's cheeks were flushed with windburn, but she had a giant grin on her face.

'That was amazing. Both of you,' Art said, pulling up his goggles and smiling at them both. 'Talk about a great way to end the week.'

'Is that my Newt?'

Jen heard a voice over their excited chatter and recognised Mr Oates, Newton's father, standing beyond the boundary netting at the end of the piste. He was surrounded by other middle-aged men in skiwear – all in possession of the sort of Silicon Valley wealth that saw them dress like impoverished eighteen-year-olds. Mr Oates ran over to give Newton a hug, looking delighted. 'We were about to catch a few runs, and look who's here, looking like some sort of snowboarding pro.'

Newton giggled. 'Daddy, did you see me?' she cried. 'I came all the way down without falling over. I can snowboard and these are my friends.' She gestured to Jen and Art, who waved back.

'Jen, hey!' Mr Oates said. 'I didn't recognise you out of the hotel uniform, but my wife tells me you've been keeping Newt company.'

Jen smothered a grin at being described in such a way, as though they were just hanging out, rather than her being a hired companion.

'We've been having a great time,' Jen confirmed. 'Newton's been doing brilliantly with her lessons. She puts me to shame. Even though,' she added quickly, lest Mr Oates think Art was a less than capable teacher, 'Art has been brilliant. You probably just need to learn before you're twenty-nine to be any good.'

'You've been doing really well and trying your best,' Newton said loyally, and mimicking one of Art's jollying-along phrases. Jen suppressed another grin.

'She's been making fantastic progress,' Art chipped in.

'Well done, Newt,' Mr Oates said, pulling her in for another cuddle. 'Hey, if your lesson is over, how about you come up the mountain with Daddy?' Mr Oates looked to Art for reassurance. 'If your teacher thinks you can handle it?'

Art nodded an affirmative. 'As long as you stick to the greens and blues, I think she'll do fine. She's been a pleasure to teach.' Jen was well used to flowing between her normal voice and the faux-posh, ultra-polite one she adopted on the Platinum floor, but it was weird hearing Art sound so stiff and deferential.

Mr Oates whooped and held his ski pole aloft. 'Let's go and catch us some powder, Newt! I'll text Mom to say you're with me. Maybe she can even come and meet us.' He held out his hand to shake Jen's. 'Thanks for everything during our trip. Newton's really enjoyed herself and she's loved having a lesson buddy.' As she pulled her hand away, she realised he'd transferred a hundred-dollar bill into it, proof that the tips Cara told her about really existed.

'Thank you so much!'

He turned his attention to Art. 'And thanks for the lessons, man.' He whistled. 'I couldn't believe it when Tina told me who Newton's teacher was going to be. It's rad, Newt being taught by an Olympian.'

Art's smile froze into a tight, fixed grin, while Jen screwed up her face in confusion.

'You were an Olympian?' she said conversationally. '*How* do I not know that?'

'In the squad, but not an Olympian in the end,' Art said, cutting her off. The polite formality was gone, but Mr Oates didn't seem to notice.

'He hasn't told you? Art Jenkins was a big deal on the British team a few years back. Heading for, what was it, South Korea?'

'That's right,' Art said blankly. All the enthusiasm and joy from a few minutes ago had vanished. He looked like he wanted to be anywhere other than where he was.

'Hell of an accident to come out of,' Mr Oates ploughed on. 'You read stories like that and wonder what happens to someone afterwards. I'm glad you made it through.' Jen stared at Art. She had never seen him look like this before. Arrogant, know-all, drunk, even angry, but never utterly vulnerable like he did now.

'An incredible survival story, wasn't it?' Mr Oates said to Jen.

She had no idea what Mr Oates was talking about. He was one of her clients so she couldn't be rude, but whatever was happening was distressing Art to such a degree that he seemed to be disappearing before her eyes. Her instinct was to shut it down. 'I don't know much about it to be honest,' she said non-committally. 'But we probably should be getting back to the hotel now—'

Mr Oates wasn't letting it go that easily. 'You haven't heard about the avalanche?' he interrupted. She shook her head quickly and shot Art an apologetic look. His face was blank, like he was disassociating from the moment completely. Mr Oates was oblivious, talking as though the whole thing was a great adventure. 'Art here survived the freaking mountain landing on him.'

Chapter Seventeen

ART

Art was aware that he was nodding but the rest of his body was numb. Mr Oates was telling Jen and Newton about his against-the-odds survival, as though the person it had happened to wasn't standing right there, next to him. Worse than that, he was mangling it, talking about how Art got up and walked away from being crushed by the mountain, as though the weeks where his life had hung in the balance had never happened. Mr Oates also seemed totally unaware that there was someone else there that day who didn't get to hobble away from the wreckage.

'Shauna didn't walk away,' he burst out, interrupting Mr Oates's flow about how the story had been all over the news at the time, and how it was such a shame that it had ended his Olympic dream because everyone thought he would have medalled for sure. It was rare for Art to say Shauna's name out loud, but right now it was important for him – for everyone – to know she existed.

After those four words he stopped, incapable of saying anything else. He couldn't – wouldn't – look at Jen. Going to see her yesterday was supposed to make him feel better and reinforce a professional friendliness, but when talk had turned to accidents and emergencies it had done the opposite. She'd continued chatting about her – commendable – workplace first aid skills, oblivious, and he'd had to leave abruptly, churned up and knowing there was no way to avoid someone unexpectedly mentioning life-or-death situations around him.

And that was when she didn't know about the accident or about Shauna, had never looked at him with the cow-eyed sympathetic gaze that everyone else had, or 'made allowances' for him because he must be 'changed by the trauma'.

But now she would, of course. He'd been right before. It was just better to avoid people altogether.

'Sorry?' Mr Oates said with a touch of impatience. Art knew that rich people didn't like being interrupted or contradicted.

He felt suddenly on the verge of tears. He'd said enough and didn't want to explain. But he'd started it.

'It wasn't just me on the mountain that day,' he said quietly. 'Shauna, my . . .' How could he sum up Shauna to someone who didn't know her? Beautiful, smart, difficult, goofy Shauna. She'd briefly been his person, but he never got to see how it would have played out. He cleared his throat. '. . . Shauna, died up there.'

Somewhere deep inside, he knew he should follow up the remark with something for Newton's benefit, something neat like 'that's why it's important to take mountain safety very seriously', to make the situation a learning experience and take the pressure off the faux pas that

Mr Oates was probably mortified about. But he couldn't. He couldn't bring himself to say anything else. He felt hollowed out, as though the mountain wind was howling through him.

'I'm so sorry. I didn't know.' Mr Oates's practised CEO demeanour had deserted him. He was stuttering. 'I'm so sorry for your loss.'

'What's he talking about?' Newton chipped in, with a child's inability to read a room. 'Who died?'

'Someone Art was close to,' he could hear Jen saying. It sounded like she was very far away. He couldn't look at her.

'It was a terrible accident,' Mr Oates added.

'I have to go,' Art said shortly. At this point he'd usually try to confirm some repeat lessons for the following year, but right now he never wanted to see them again. Any of them.

'Mr Oates, did you say you were going to take Newton up the mountain with you?' Jen chipped in.

'That was the plan.' Mr Oates's voice was conciliatory. He clearly wanted this awkward conversation over as much as Art did.

'I have to get back to work now, but I'll call Mrs Oates and make sure she knows she's with you,' Jen added. Somewhere Art could register that she was trying to help him by hurrying it all along.

'I want Art to come with us,' whined Newton, in the same voice she'd used to wheedle her mother into booking Jen as her snowboard companion for the week.

'Art needs to go now, hon,' said Jen. 'But listen, when I get back to work this afternoon, do you know what's happening?' She didn't wait for a response. 'A *dog* wedding! I bet I can get you an invitation if you want to come.'

'Oooh Daddy, can I go to the dog wedding?'

'That sounds so fun, Newt. Let's do a few runs and then we'll get back in plenty of time for it.' Everyone's voices were artificially high.

Art couldn't listen to any more. It was only when he heard them all calling farewells that he realised he'd already walked away, such was the disconnect between his mind and his body. He registered vaguely that he wouldn't see Newton again before her family checked out, and that he should say a proper goodbye. But he couldn't.

He fled.

Chapter Eighteen

JEN

All through Mrs Higham's pug's wedding later that day, with Newton at her side, Jen had fretted about Art and his hasty exit from the slopes, wondering whether she should have gone after him. Then, once she finally got back to staff housing, with a slice of the bespoke, pug-shaped cake to take with her, she'd considered texting him. She had his number now after all. But something in his face at the foot of the mountain had stopped her. The first day she'd met him she'd seen his judgemental face, and since then she'd seen plenty of his pissed-off face. She'd also seen his proud face when Newton's snow-boarding technique came together, and the sweet, smiling look on his face when she and Newton had referred to the dazzle-covered Chocolate Box concoction he always ordered as his 'favourite drink'. In the short time she'd known him she'd come to recognise a lot of his different expressions, and that day, his face had shut down. It was as though he had 'STAY AWAY' tattooed on there, and she had to respect that.

But she hadn't been able to stop herself from Googling him. There were dozens of hits, going all the way back to his days as a junior champion right up to newspaper articles that catalogued his ascension to Team GB. Teenage Art beamed out from photos, flanked by his teammates and an enormous hairy man, identified in the captions as the squad's coach Russ 'Yeti' Sullivan. There was a lightness to him in all the photos that Jen had never seen in the man she knew. Around six years ago the local coverage opened out into the national press: a Q&A on a snowboard brand website that implored readers to get to know the people they were sponsoring, and a profile in the sports section of the *Telegraph* a few months before the last Winter Games.

After that there was a gap, until a slew of stories in both the broadsheets and the tabloids catalogued the avalanche that had ended his career and killed a 23-year-old woman identified alternately as his 'companion on the mountain' or 'his girlfriend', while Art was still unconscious and unable to confirm which was correct. The final references Jen found were small mentions of Art being awake, and then, after the Winter Olympics started in the February, teammates paid tribute to him and his ongoing recovery. After that there was nothing. A handful of Team GB medallists enjoyed their moment on the winners' podium and the news cycle moved on.

After that, she *couldn't* text him, knowing that this was why he could be so distant and so prickly. Plus, if she was honest, she didn't know what to say. And if he didn't want her – or anyone – to talk to him about it, that was his choice, even if the memory of the devastated look on his face as he had walked away from Mr Oates ate her up inside.

She didn't see Art for a week. None of his clients were staying at The Redwood, and as the days passed, and she neither saw nor heard from him, she told herself it was better to let him handle it the way he wanted.

But this morning he was booked in to pick up eight-year-old Etta and her six-year-old sister Janis, and she'd changed her mind. It was wrong to ignore it. Isn't that what they told you in articles about how to support someone who was grieving?

Her mouth formed a smile as he walked in, but he didn't give her the chance to say anything.

'Hi,' he said briskly. 'Just here for Etta and Janis, are they on their way out?'

Jen frowned slightly, but dutifully picked up the phone and made the call to their suite. According to their notes, their parents stayed at The Redwood during the third week of December every year and Art had been teaching the children for three years, so they already knew him.

'Ten minutes,' she said, putting down the receiver. Usually, he just sat down patiently to wait. Today he tutted. Something was off.

Don't ignore it, she told herself.

'Art.' Jen's voice was hesitant and solemn. 'I wanted to say how sorry I am about Shauna, and about your accident.'

'What are you sorry for?' he replied instantly, in a combative tone that put the day she met him in mind. 'Unless you're secretly the God of Snow and it's you who causes avalanches.'

Jen paused, her expression somewhere between shock and hurt. Two weeks ago she would have fired back something equally as cutting. But it felt wrong now. She knew he was in pain.

'I just meant it must have been really hard for you,' she said carefully. 'I can't imagine having to come to terms with losing someone, and only hearing about it long after the rest of the world. I'm sorry it happened to you. And I'm sorry the avalanche also took away your career.'

His eyes narrowed. As though he knew she'd Googled him and found out all the gory details.

'I have a career.' His voice was clipped, forced.

'I know you do. I meant your Olympic dream.' She was blushing and stammering. He was making her squirm. She took a breath and looked him in the eye, trying to force an iota of last week's friendliness. 'Well, you know what I mean.'

'Not really. But then, we don't really know each other, do we?' His tone was dead and distant. His jaw was set, his brown eyes flat.

Jen gave a small, nervous laugh. 'I think we know each other a little by now—'

'It was clear from the off that we didn't really like each other,' Art interrupted. 'So now Newton's gone home there's no reason for us to pretend to be friendly.' The temperature in the hotel now felt lower and frostier than outside on the mountain.

'Right,' she said, removing all the emotion from her own voice. 'If that's what you want. I mean, I wasn't expecting us to have a heart-to-heart but—'

He cut her off. 'It's best not to expect anything from me.'

A door opened along the corridor and the sound of stampeding children hurtled towards the lobby. Etta and Janis's mum was calling out questions about gloves and hats and goggles and whether anyone needed the toilet.

'Janis, how have you grown this much since last year?' Art said, stretching out his arms as high as they would go, his voice filling with a warmth that Jen knew she was now very much excluded from. 'And Etta, who took your front teeth? Let me at 'em!'

'They've gone to the tooth fairy,' she shouted, smiling gappily at him.

'Oh, that's OK, then.' He continued to fire quips at the two girls as he waved farewell to their mum and corralled them into the lift, not looking at Jen as they left.

Chapter Nineteen

ART

Etta and Janis's excited chatter washed over Art as they rode the lift to the lobby and got kitted out with boards at the rental shop. He wouldn't think of Jen's face as he left, or the confusion and hurt written all over it.

He'd succeeded in reinstating the distance between them. Mission accomplished.

So why did he feel so hollow?

Chapter Twenty

JEN

With Jen's clumsy condolences she'd clearly got it wrong and Art had turned on her. She tried to be charitable. He had lost someone. It wasn't up to her to decide how he should grieve.

But still.

He'd looked through her, as though their closeness during the days of lessons had been nothing. It hadn't been nothing. Not on her end, anyway. And by the way the light had extinguished in Art's eyes the second Mr Oates had brought up his accident, she didn't believe he was a good enough actor to spend all that time *pretending* that they were friends either.

After the lift doors closed, she questioned every interaction they'd had, and every small joke they'd shared. If they hadn't been friends, at least they were on their way to being.

Or had she imagined that?

That was what Art had just told her. And it wouldn't be the first time she'd assumed there was more to it than there was.

Stupid stupid stupid.

'Jen, we've got a situation,' Cara called as she burst out of the staff door, not bothering to be quiet. 'We need all hands on deck.' Cara looked genuinely anxious, which was unusual. Even when she was stressed out, she took great pains to camouflage it because she didn't want to give Eduardo the satisfaction of thinking she cared about her job.

'What's happening?' Jen started towards her and then stopped. 'Wait, I can't leave the desk unattended.'

'It's an emergency. Eduardo said to come.'

She followed Cara through the staff door and up the stairs in the concealed labyrinth of corridors to Suite One, AKA the Platinum penthouse. At ten thousand square feet, and at the top of the hotel, it was a floor in itself, one that required a face recognition scan to reach by lift. It had been occupied for the past three days by an aging Russian oligarch and his impressively haughty wife. Since they'd arrived by helicopter, there had been endless requests, all communicated entirely via a translator, who was based eight thousand kilometres away in Moscow but was seemingly on call at any time of the day or night. As far as Jen knew, they'd checked out at 3 a.m. According to the morning's handover notes, Gregory, the night concierge, had been informed by the translator that the penthouse was not up to their exacting standards and they were moving to a private chalet two miles down the road. The translator settled the bill and informed him they wanted to depart without coming into contact with anyone from the hotel. No one from Platinum or the main lobby should approach or make eye contact with them as they did.

Gregory had complied. As he'd mentioned wryly in the note, it wasn't even the strangest request he'd ever had. But as Cara now opened the door to the penthouse, Jen realised there was more to it than a billionaire's allergy to civilians.

The soundproof walls had masked the carnage, but broken bottles and glasses from the complimentary full-size bar were all over the floor, the oligarch's bespoke suits were slashed and the remnants of what could only be an epic drugs binge were all over the gilt-topped furniture.

'Shit,' exclaimed Jen, taking it in.

'Shit indeed,' said Eduardo from his position on all fours in the centre of the room, where he was analysing what looked like a cigarette burn in the silk rug.

'I'll call the police,' Jen said.

'Don't you dare,' Eduardo retorted. 'Fetch some rubber gloves and start cleaning.'

Jen gestured to one of the many surfaces that were dusted with white powder. 'What do we do with this? Surely it's illegal for us to even touch it.'

'Don't be such a baby, Jennifer,' he said with irritation. 'There are facemasks and PPE in the cleaning carts. Suit up and flush it.' He shot a look at Cara. 'And make sure you *do* flush it.'

She widened her eyes innocently, hands held aloft to indicate she wouldn't dream of doing anything else.

'I need to order a new rug,' Eduardo muttered to himself, 'then call Ken to come and decorate. The Hamiltons aren't due for another two days so we have enough time. It'll be fine.'

'If no one saw the clients leave, how do we know they're OK?' Jen said, looking around. 'What if one of them is hurt? Shouldn't we file a report somewhere?'

'No one needs you interfering. *This* is your job,' Eduardo snapped. 'Just get on with it. And don't let *anyone* see the state it's in.' He stalked out of the room.

Cara approached the cleaning trolley. She pulled out a facemask and what looked like two sets of disposable decorator's overalls. 'Put these on,' she said, grimacing. 'And then I'll show you what they've done to the hot tub.'

The second Jen finished work, she texted Snowy.

I need a very long shower and an even longer drink. Lots of drinks. Are you around tonight?

Jen winced at how needy she sounded, but between Art's gaslighting and the Suite One horror, she had no game-face left. She needed a friend.

Seconds later, Snowy messaged back.

DUUUUUUUDE. Always. Canucks, 8? Ps How have you lasted two weeks on Platinum without needing to get pissed??

Jen responded:

Mickey's been teaching me meditation, but it's just not going to cut it today. See you there :)

At 8.p.m, she walked up the snow-covered path to Canucks as wet sleet drove sideways. The evening's soggy weather matched Jen's mood: cold-rinsed and wrung out. She missed Maxie so much right now it ached.

She swung open the door to Canucks and the difference from her last night out here was immediate. Not the smell of damp – if anything that was worse – but there was a din that hadn't been there before and an undercurrent of people singing along to the jukebox that was still blaring out soft rock. At the bar was the cram of jostling bodies that Rob had warned her about. Not quite three deep, but getting there.

Rob spotted her and shouted over the heads of the people waiting. 'Oi, what can I get you? Beer?' Jen nodded gratefully, fumbling for her card.

'I'll start you a tab,' Rob yelled. 'It's easier. Everyone's over there.' He nodded in the direction of a packed corner beyond the pool tables and then bent over to get a bottle of beer from a fridge. She instinctively checked out his bum. He stood back up more quickly than she was expecting, then turned, catching her glance and giving her a little half-smile as though he didn't mind being checked out one bit. His eyes crinkled at the edges. He seemed happy to see her. Thank God *one* person was today.

Scanning the room, she looked for whoever constituted 'everyone' but couldn't see through the crowd. She took a rapid gulp of her drink and entered the throng.

'J-DOG! You made it!' The crowd parted and Snowy's voice rang out even above the sound of Meat Loaf. The surrounding crowd erupted in a cheer. The names came back to her: Darren, Clyde, Kelly – all the people she'd spent that first crazy evening in Whistler with. They scooched around the table to make space and a chair appeared for her to gratefully sink into.

'How's The Redwood?' Snowy yelled, a table of empties already in front of him.

'My boss hates me, I cleaned up what can only be described as a biohazard today and . . .' She paused, thinking about Art. She couldn't bring herself to reduce the situation to an entertaining quip. She lifted her drink. 'Let me have two more of these and then maybe I'll be able to face talking about it.'

'Fair enough. Daz,' Snowy said to Darren, who was getting up to go to the bar, 'get a couple more pitchers. Jen needs to play catch up.' Darren flashed a thumbs up and disappeared, the crowd closing around him in a swarm.

Rob came over carrying a tower of empty glasses in one hand and stacking them higher and higher as he cleared tables.

'You guys are sticking around until I finish, right? I'll be done in half an hour.'

Jen nodded in the affirmative. 'Consider me here until the bitter end,' she said grimly.

Rob winked. 'That's our girl.' She laughed and he gave her a little shimmy as he sauntered off with the glasses, as though inviting her to look at his bum again. This was what she needed: easy company and no hidden meanings. And drinks. Lots of drinks.

'Hey, have you learned to ski yet?' Snowy asked. 'You said you'd never even done it before, last time you were in this bar. None of us could believe you came all the way here and had never been on skis.'

'I've started to learn how to snowboard,' Jen replied, nodding. 'I've been doing it for two weeks now.' Talking about snowboarding reminded her of Art, and thinking about Art made her stomach twist. She remembered that they knew him before the accident. That must have been what he was referring to the day he came in drunk.

She wanted to ask them about it, but the way Art had reacted earlier gave her pause. She stuck to the safer topic of the mountain. 'I had four days of private lessons with a guest – long story – and last week I went up and practised a little on my own, but I need to sign up for some group lessons. My days off aren't regular though, so it's hard to book.'

'Ask Clyde if he can recommend someone.' Another tray of drinks landed on the table, with Clyde the person lowering it down. 'He knows everyone.'

'Shots,' he declared, passing them out to the rest of the table. 'And I do know everyone. Just let me know what you need.'

Jen picked one up and considered it; it was purple. She gave it a sniff. Grape? Her stomach turned over a bit and she lowered it again.

Snowy dropped his shot into his pint glass and then necked the whole thing.

'Gross,' Jen replied, then tossed her own drink back in response. She'd promised Maxie she was coming here to have fun and figure out who she was, and tonight that meant she was a purple-shot-drinking novice snowboarder who would turn up to work with a raging hangover tomorrow. She briefly wondered what Art was doing tonight and what he'd think about her hanging out with his former friends. But then, Art didn't want anything to do with her, did he? So it was none of his business. She poured herself a glass of beer from the jug in front of her and waved at Rob, who was already watching their table from across the bar, to bring over another round.

He gave her a thumbs up and mouthed, 'I love fun Jen,' before shooting her another wink in approval. Her insides fluttered.

Chapter Twenty-one

ART

Thought this would be useful.

Art stared at the words until his vision blurred, his gaze skipping over the link below. It was four hours until his 8 a.m. lesson pick-up at The Redwood, but sleep was once again a distant memory. He'd managed four hours before he'd given up and started scrolling through his phone, trying to escape his own thoughts. But they'd still kept settling on one thing: Jen. Or more specifically, his treatment of her the previous day.

When his phone buzzed, he'd snatched it up.

His mum. A message sent at noon in the UK, probably during her lunchbreak. It was just a link and those five words in the subject line.

His mum used to send him long emails every couple of days, more akin to letters really. They started with 'Dear Art' and were formatted the way you got official correspondence from a bank or employer. They were full of pleas to come home or if not that, to let her come out and see him again. She'd flown out the second the accident happened, but once he started his recovery and rehab, she'd had to return to the UK for work and he'd only seen her once since – when she'd bought a ticket and turned up in Whistler without consulting him first.

Art had barely spent any time with her, claiming that she should have checked because he had immoveable back-to-back lessons. As a single parent who'd had to carefully budget, she had always worried about money so hadn't asked him to cancel them, as he knew she wouldn't. Instead she had spent most of her time at Yeti and Lori's house, where she had stayed, while he avoided her. He'd felt shitty about it, but then, when didn't Art feel shitty?

After that disastrous trip, her emails had dwindled. When they did arrive, they were less chatty, and the shame of knowing it was because he'd pushed her away pressed down on him.

His finger hovered over the link. The url was something to do with horizons, which made him think it was going to be an inspirational quote, as she was sometimes apt to send him. He could do without another banal affirmation, but as he'd already read what felt like the whole of the internet, why not have a look? He clicked.

It was a therapy practice here in Whistler that specialised in PTSD. There was a 'contact' icon below it, for a woman called Maggie. She looked to be in her fifties, with an earnest look in her eye and a kind face. His fingers itched involuntarily above the button before he stopped himself. What would he even say? His barriers were back up before he could even register that was what he'd done. Because that's what he did. He kept

Mum at arm's length – both emotionally and physically – because it was easier.

No, not easier. It took extraordinary effort to keep those barriers in place.

Simpler, then. If he didn't let anyone in then he couldn't get hurt again.

He couldn't remember that last time he'd edged his way out of his comfort zone, the tiny world he'd retreated into. He thought of Jen, who'd left her secure life behind in London. She'd thrown herself into Whistler life despite being a decade older than the average gap year seasonaire, and taken everything – a hospitality job she was having to learn at lightning speed, a total lack of any snowboarding experience, the absence of any sort of network here – in her stride. She was trying new experiences, meeting new people, letting people in, even if it wasn't all going to plan. He liked that about her.

He was like that once. He had liked that about him too.

Art found himself clicking on the different tabs on the site as though his thumbs belonged to someone else. There was a blog, and he found himself wanting to know more about this Maggie person and what made her qualified to listen to people's worst traumas day in, day out. It was written in the form of a problem page, with the words PUBLISHED WITH THE PERMISSION OF THE SENDER emblazoned across the top of the window, followed by a list of letters below. They had titles like 'I can't let anybody in', 'how do I help my partner with their PTSD?' and 'panic attacks'.

His eyes flitted around his bedroom, as though his phone camera was monitoring him, before clicking on 'I can't let anybody in'. His heart raced as he skimmed the letter. The specifics of the sender's circumstances were different, but he recognised everything else they described: avoiding thinking about trauma or anyone connected with what happened to them, avoiding places and situations where people might ask about their lives, occasional black-out drinking binges, pushing friends and family away.

It's not just me, Art thought briefly. *I have PTSD.* A twisted laugh escaped his throat. A sensation of weird relief. *It's unhealthy the way I'm not dealing with it, but it's not* not *normal.*

He found himself eager to find out what Maggie would prescribe in her reply. Her advice began with advising the writer to look into CBT – Cognitive Behavioural Therapy – and seeing a GP to discuss the possibility of medication for anxiety or depression. Art skipped over that part, a firm *no* in his mind. He didn't want to see any doctors ever again. They only brought with them the practised sympathy that came with delivering bad news hundreds of times a week. The one who'd delivered the news about his competitive career being over had undercut it with the idea that things weren't so bad because at least he was alive. As if still breathing was the same as being alive when everything that comprised his life had disintegrated.

He jumped to the more personal part of Maggie's reply, outlining tools to help the writer open up about their feelings.

If speaking face to face feels impossible or it's too much pressure to vocalise your feelings on the spot, try what you've done here: a letter or an email. Write down how you feel or how you've been struggling to express how you feel, even if you never send it. And don't feel as though you have to express everything at once. A small step could be replying honestly when a loved one asks, 'how are you?' rather than deflecting with a default 'fine'.

That's what he'd tried to do with Jen. Compartmentalise. He'd been more himself around her than he'd been with anyone for years but he'd still been holding back, thinking that if he kept his past separate from his present, then he could forge a surface friendship with her. One where they had a laugh but never delved too deeply into who he really was and why he was broken. But it hadn't worked. There *was* no way to keep your past from bubbling up into the present – Mr Oates had proved that. And now this Dr Maggie was confirming it. You had to open yourself up – with all the risk that invited – to forge any sort of relationship, surface or otherwise.

I understand it's nerve-wracking. You're opening a can of emotional worms, when you've worked so hard to put your trauma out of your mind, but as you have realised, repressing your feelings doesn't make them go away. The consequence is that you feel distant from those you care about and even more alone. But you're not alone.

No single thing will 'cure' you, but the longer you wait, the further you are from dealing with it.

Shaking, Art shut down the window, threw his phone across the bed and tried to forget he'd seen it. This Maggie made it sound so do-able. But what if he just didn't have it in him to be happy? What if this was just how he felt now: ninety per cent numb, tinged with ten per cent resentment and fear.

Forever.

A small voice in his head bubbled up.

That's not true. You felt happy only a few days ago. You admitted as much.

The lessons were a situation he'd been forced into, but they had quickly become much more than an obligation. He may have been the instructor, but Jen had quietly been teaching him too. He had watched her open herself up to learn something new, and keep practising it until it became second nature. She had showed him that you couldn't necessarily do something scary on your own, and that yes, you might fall flat on your face – repeatedly, in the case of Jen's snowboarding. But she got back up again, and was making progress. She'd improved at snowboarding *and* started to make a life here. All in less than a month. He recognised now that he'd absorbed her lesson-by-example – he'd started to, anyway. Until he'd ruined it by rebuilding and reinforcing the same old walls. The same way he'd ruined his relationship with his mum.

Before he could stop himself, he reached for his phone again, hitting reply.

Dear Mum

I'm sorry I haven't replied to your emails before now. I wanted to. I just couldn't. But I do want to say this: I miss you.

Tears started leaking down Art's face. For God's sake, he was hardly saying anything soppy, and here he was, racked with sobs.

And I'm sorry. I'm sorry I haven't told you before now and I'm sorry I haven't let you help me. It has been too hard since

He broke off there, his breath hard and ragged. He closed his eyes for a second, saw Shauna's teasing smile next to him on a ski lift. She used to sing on them. Cheesy pop mainly, with a particular penchant for ABBA.

It has been too hard since Shauna died. To be alive when she isn't.

He gave a bitter smile.

She would be utterly furious to be dead.

She would. She was impatient and indignant and there was so much she wanted to do.

I don't know how to carry on.

He knew he was rambling. His thoughts were jumping around on the screen and he didn't know if any of it made sense or if it was making him feel any better. It was making him feel something though, even if it was all churning around in his guts like the bad shrimp he'd pretended he'd eaten the other week at The Redwood.

> Yeti told me to get help. (I've not been good to him either.) Does writing to your mum count? Or does he mean a professional?

He couldn't send this email to his mum, it was all over the place. But it was helping some thoughts come together in his head. Apologies, mainly.

There were so many people he should say sorry to. Yeti. His former teammates. The Misfits. Where to even start?

Jen.

Her name kept popping into his head. Probably because she was the most recent person he had hurt. He checked the time again. 5 a.m. He threw on his jeans and a hoodie, wrapping himself in his boarding jacket and pulling on some boots. Then he forced his thoughts to settle before he let himself get into his truck.

The last time he'd impulsively shown up at Jen's work he'd lied about why he was there. He'd pretended he needed to talk about health and safety when really he'd been looking for comfort. It had backfired, making him feel worse about everything he was withholding. This time he was going to be honest. He'd start with a full apology, which was the least he could do, and then tell her he'd pushed her away because he couldn't acknowledge that being around her had opened something up inside him, and that opening himself up meant he'd have to deal with everything that had come before.

And commit to a life where there was the potential for an after. He felt the spark of possibility.

As Art steered up the drive, the pitch black of the road morphed into a low-lit row of old-fashioned lamps that lined the way to the hotel. It was icy out, but the drive was freshly cleared each day by the valets. They scattered grit along with smiles as they caught keys and parked cars all day long – vehicles that cost more than they'd earn across several seasons. But it was too early for them to be lined up outside the hotel. One lone valet, bundled up in a Puffa coat and waiting just inside the hotel's front doors to spot anyone who returned late or left early, was on guard.

Art pulled over about three quarters of the way up the drive, cutting the engine before he reached the turning circle in front of the doors.

In a couple of hours, the activity would crank up for another busy pre-Christmas day in a ski resort. Then the lifts would open for the first tracks, while the service staff in the bowels of the hotel would swap from the night to day shift, creating a seamless and continuous five-star service. But right now it was quiet. Few of the arriving staff came by car and so he sat there for ten, then fifteen minutes without a single soul passing by, unable to make himself park in the staff car park and go up to the ninth floor. It had seemed so straightforward when he was at home thinking about it.

Just do it, Art. Apologise.

Bright headlights lit up the inside of his car and passed by. He was surprised to see a battered truck pull up in front of him right at the hotel doors, and even more so to register it was Rob's. Canucks was five kilometres west of here and it was long closed. He had no reason to be at The Redwood at half past five in the morning, unless he'd got lucky with a hotel guest. The combination of his easy Aussie charm and an abundance of rich women looking for a holiday romance meant it wouldn't have been the first time.

Right on cue, a passenger leaped out, looking like they were in a hurry. He could see from behind that she was blonde and wearing a sweater with sleeves dangling so far out of the arms of her warm coat that it could only have been something she borrowed from lanky Rob. She pushed the truck door closed and then walked around to the driver's side window to say something, her hair falling over the side of her face as she reached in for a quick hug. She walked away, making for the staff entrance. So, not a guest, then. He'd been dating a chambermaid a few seasons ago – was it Mandy or Mindy? Although she'd moved back to New Zealand when the season ended, and besides, it was years ago. Art had no idea who had been in Rob's life in the intervening time.

Guilt gripped his insides again. Where did he even start with making it up to his friends? He couldn't get out and risk Rob seeing him, not until he'd figured out his next move, so he waited for him to pull away, executing a three-point turn rather than using the hotel's turning circle. He gave the horn a cheeky beep as he drove off, causing the woman to stop briefly, turn and wave. As she did, Art got a proper view of who Rob had rolled out of bed to take to work this morning.

It was Jen.

Chapter Twenty-two

JEN

The only thing that could make Jen's hangover worse was the poisonous look Eduardo shot her as she rushed past him, late, to the staff room to get changed. Thank God her work uniform was already inside her locker, seeing as her only other option was the outfit she was currently wearing: yesterday's pub clothes, plus Rob's hoodie. Did she have time for a quick shower or was another ten minutes of tardiness worse than smelling like a brewery? Her brain was in no state to make that sort of decision.

She dug around in the bottom of her locker for the deodorant she knew was in there somewhere, getting a hand on it just as she remembered it had run out.

'Whew, you had a big night, I'm guessing,' came from somewhere behind her and she wheeled around. Cara. She sniffed the air around her. 'Let me guess. Tequila shots, no, I'm getting notes of aniseed, so . . .' She clicked her fingers. 'Sambuca.'

That decided it. Shower.

'Something like that.' Jen's hands were shaking slightly from the alcohol she could feel seeping out of every pore. 'Hey, do you have a towel I can borrow?'

Cara delved into her own locker and came back with one of the insanely fluffy guest towels that they were under strict instructions never to use. 'Here.' She threw it over to Jen, whose hand–eye coordination was poor enough that she fumbled the catch.

'I didn't know you were working this morning,' said Jen as Cara palmed her some of the Aveda miniatures they stocked in the guest rooms. She tried to hand them back, wondering what the punishment for embezzling high-end skincare from the hotel was.

'Relax, they're all ones that have been opened and then left behind, so we'd have to trash them anyway. The waste kills me, so I collect them and reuse.' Cara stood aside and gave Jen a glimpse of her locker. There was a bulging carrier bag that contained half-empty containers of every product the hotel supplied, along with combs, shower caps, slippers and sewing kits. 'I give it to the homeless shelter in Vancouver when I head back there at the end of the season.' She pointed to an area at the back, where material spilled out of another bag. 'OK, maybe the odd robe and towel make it into the bag too. But only ones where the material is starting to fray.'

Cara started getting changed, and Jen grasped her clutch of stolen merch and headed over to the shower cubicle in the corner of the room. She almost shrieked when the faucet came on. How did they manage to have such tepid water in the staff shower, when the rest of the hotel had facilities that *Condé Nast Traveller* raved about? She squirted shower gel all over her body and started scrubbing as quickly as possible.

'Anyway, I'm here because Sasha's gone, so her shifts need covering,' Cara was saying from the locker room.

'Is she off sick again?' Jen called through the door.

'No. She quit.'

'Didn't she start at the same time as me?'

'Yep. But it seems that being summoned to Suite Eight three separate times and being propositioned by the douchebag staying there made her decide that hospitality isn't for her.'

'What the fuck?' Jen quickly rinsed and turned off the water, shivering. 'What did Eduardo say?'

She wrapped herself in the amazing-but-illegal towel, vowing to muster the courage to nick one for herself, and pushed open the cubicle door. Cara was waiting outside with a wet flannel. 'Use this. Your eye make-up is everywhere, hon. Eduardo, of course, took her side, followed the correct HR procedure and informed the authorities that she was being harassed.' She rolled her eyes. 'Or maybe he just told her to bat him off "because he's a VIP".'

'Is he still staying here?' Jen felt nauseous, and now not just from her hangover.

Cara shook her head. 'He checked out last night but I'm freaking furious. There's a guy like him every season and every season we're told to ignore it.'

Jen scrubbed at her face. 'So, what's Sasha going to do? Is she going to go to HR?'

'Eduardo agreed to transfer her to the gift shop downstairs if she didn't make a fuss.' Cara held up a hand as

Jen started to protest that 'a fuss' was something of an understatement. 'I know, but she has a sick mom who she looks after and the winter is when she makes her best money.'

Jen sat down on the bench, clasping her towel around her. 'What can we do? He can't get away with it.' Jen sighed. 'They always get away with it, don't they?'

Cara flashed a conspiratorial smile and pulled her phone out of her pocket. 'Usually, they do, but I'm gathering evidence. *Don't* tell anyone, but I know someone at the *Vancouver Sun* – an investigative reporter. They got an anonymous tip about The Redwood a while ago and have been building a case – not just what has happened but who's complicit in covering it up. So far they're struggling to get anyone on the record, but they approached me and asked me to keep a record of *everything* I see and hear. You should too. Date, time, person, response from management. Then bring it to me. I'm going to wait until the end of the season, and I'm going to keep Sasha out of it if that's what she wants, but I'm going to at least try and do something.'

'I won't tell anyone,' agreed Jen grimly. 'But be careful. Aren't you worried about losing your job?'

Cara shrugged. 'I'd already decided that this was going to be my last season here. I've got a job at a charity lined up in Vancouver for April, so I'm going to make as much money as I can before that and then bid goodbye to expensive rent in ski resorts in favour of a proper career. If I can take down one small corner of the patriarchy before I go, all the better.'

A thump on the door made them both jump. 'Is anyone actually coming to work today?' Eduardo shout-hissed from behind it.

'Coming!' Cara called back in a sing-song voice. She shoved her phone in her locker.

'SHHHHHH,' came back through the door.

'Help yourself to a toothbrush,' Cara said as she disappeared out of the door. 'I have plenty.'

Jen threw her uniform on, trying not to think about poor Sasha. She was in her early twenties and had been so happy to have a job on the prestigious Platinum floor after several seasons as a chambermaid in the main hotel. Eduardo's reaction made her boil with fury, that his devotion to the clients extended to perverts who should be reported to the police. It was another cover-up, just like that trashed room – but worse, because there was a woman's life and future involved.

The shower had helped a little but Jen's head still thumped from last night, along with the prickle of hungover self-loathing pulsing through her body. Pitchers of beer had kept arriving at the table, and the group got rowdier and drunker before Rob finished work and joined them. He'd been flirting with her and she'd been enjoying it, basking in the uncomplicated glow of his attention. By beer number five (or was it six?) she'd almost drowned out the tiny Maxie voice in her head telling her she was getting dangerously close to breaking their deal. Who cared? She'd stuck to it for two months now and so far it had *not* paid off. Far from fostering an atmosphere of mutual respect, the only guy she'd shown her true, single and unfiltered personality to had stopped speaking to her and run a mile. Proving *exactly* why she didn't rock the boat or try to 'be herself' around guys. So with Rob last night she didn't. Even when he'd been drunkenly imparting his hard-won 'truths' about life: that possessions hindered your freedom and monogamy was a con. She had nodded along, even though it had made her cringe at the time and made her cringe as she thought about it now. She wanted monogamy! She also liked things! When would she stop trying to appease every feckless but good-looking man she met?!

Because going along with things made people like you. For a while, anyway.

It was during that deeply intense conversation that Rob had leaned in close and said, 'You're so easy to talk to, Jen. I think we're on the same page about pretty much everything.' And then she thought he might kiss her.

More than that, she'd hoped he might. After all, he was handsome and interested and they'd been talking non-stop for over an hour. Even if the conversation was mainly Jen staying silent about opinions she didn't agree with.

She pulled out her phone to text Maxie.

> Max, I almost snogged someone last night. Someone you would have massively disapproved of. He doesn't even believe in monogamy. Why am I like this?

She stared at her phone wondering if Maxie would reply, or if she'd spend her whole shift beating herself up about almost breaking her no-man vow just three weeks into her trip and just two months into the agreement.

> The key word here is 'almost'. That means you DIDN'T snog him, and therefore you should actually be proud of yourself. Progress!

Jen smiled. Maxie always knew what to say. And it was true. As she'd leaned closer to Rob across the packed table, maintaining the sort of eye contact where both parties knew what was going to happen next, she'd pulled back and, instead of smushing her mouth against his, she'd deliberately clinked her glass against his beer, spilling half of her drink over both of them and forcing them to jump back.

It would have been so easy to do it. It wasn't long until Christmas and Rob would have been just her type to have a festive fling with. Instead she'd gone back to the boys' houseshare for a pub after-party, before throwing a hoodie on over her clothes and passing out on their musty old sofa for a couple of hours before work. Maybe Maxie was right, and she had made progress. And more importantly, she hadn't broken the deal.

But she knew, as she helped herself to the perfume in Cara's locker and liberally spritzed herself, why she really hadn't kissed Rob.

It was because he wasn't Art.

Chapter Twenty-three

ART

The last week had been interminable.

He had no right to be annoyed about Jen seeing Rob. Not only was she a free agent, but he'd given her every reason to stay far away from him. He'd reverted to drop-offs and pick-ups with only the briefest of interactions, and Jen's icy acceptance of their now non-existent friendship was worse than her pulling him up on it. His mind had been churned up ever since, pinballing between guilt at his behaviour and guilt about what it meant that seeing Jen with Rob had affected him so much. He tried to keep a lid on it all, and his instinct was to retreat, but he felt somehow different after getting to know Jen. Plus, as his now regular visits to Maggie's website were teaching him, emotions didn't work like that. They had a habit of bubbling out of you.

Today the thoughts were even more relentless, because it was the most endless of days: Christmas Day.

There were three hours until his lesson with the Fairfield family at 9 a.m. He'd planned to wear a Santa outfit over his uniform with a supply of candy canes in his pockets. The mountain company always laid on activities to keep the customers feeling festive, from complimentary mulled wine as people came off the slopes to lifties dressed as elves and ringing 'jingle bells' as people queued for the gondola. Christmas songs blared out from the mountain-side cafés and people started singing carols on the lifts with perfect strangers adding fa-la-la-la-la flourishes to each other's songs. It seemed counterintuitive but Art embraced it because it provided distraction from what the day really commemorated for him. He threw himself into his lessons, hamming up his role as 'snowboarding Santa'. It was an act, a character to hide behind, and the kids loved it.

But this year he was struggling to get into the role. He showered and dressed slowly – underwear, thermals, waterproofs – and then decided to make a start on his to-do list sooner rather than later. The rituals he both dreaded and clung to so that the day had structure. There was the dutiful 'Merry Christmas' text to send to his mum back home – something generic enough to be read out to the assembled family at his auntie's in Wakefield – and presents that needed wrapping and dropping off at Yeti's, as well as the booze hamper he always sent to Rob and Snowy's. Tokens of a normal life, from a person who 'did' Christmas, just not with the people who loved him. He changed up the time he dropped off the gifts each year, so neither household stood a chance of anticipating or intercepting him.

Presents delivered, Art went to the mountain, flashed his employee ID and bypassed the queue of tourists waiting for the day's first cable car. He was ascending Whistler

Mountain as soon as the pulleys started cranking, and then he kept riding the lifts until he couldn't get any higher. It was icy, with only a smattering of fresh snow dusting the ground and a clear view right across the valley. When he got off the uppermost lift, he moved over to the boundary rope that separated the patrolled piste from the backcountry, beginning with a cluster of rocks that overlooked the trails. In the other direction he could see the mountains bleed into the valley floor and ant trails of people streaming to and from the restaurants and cabins at the bottom. But he stayed there, next to the rope they'd ducked under four years ago today, and looked out to where they had headed. The fatal spot was out of sight, a forty-five-minute hike away that was – thankfully – difficult to see even from the lifts. Even so, he conducted most of his lessons from Blackcomb, its sister mountain. Not because he felt like he couldn't avoid Shauna here – more because whenever he came he felt disconnected from her, and that in turn made him feel as though he wasn't remembering her correctly.

Art had read that the loved ones of dead people claimed to see them everywhere, all the time. He'd never had that. If anything, he had started to struggle to remember what she looked like. After he'd woken up from the coma and been informed by Yeti that Shauna's funeral had already happened back in her native New Zealand, he'd wondered if he'd dreamed the whole relationship. Only a card from her parents, wishing him all the best in his recovery, marked that it had happened at all.

And so he came here each year, hoping that it would provide him with the closure he hadn't been able to find so far, but he always ended up feeling restless and wrong. The wind whipped at his cheeks and he could feel a storm in the air. He hoped it held off until after the kids' lesson; selfishly he didn't want the weather to thieve the only hours he had in his day that were occupied.

It was no good. Shauna wasn't here and it was a shabby way to try to commemorate her. She would have wanted a rowdy celebration with all of their friends, no room for silent contemplation because they were all too busy laughing and talking over each other. Maybe at some point he could manage that.

He'd so often wished that it was him instead of her, but rarely thought about what she would have wanted for him as the survivor. It's not as though it was something they'd talked about: what they'd do if one or the other died, and if they'd be happy for them to move on. Maybe if she'd passed away after a long illness rather than being snatched away in a split second. But would it have made any difference, really? Would he feel less guilty about being attracted to—

He blew out a shaky breath, watching as it misted visibly in front of him. He was, he was attracted to Jen. Maybe it was a good thing she was with Rob. It meant he didn't have to think about what that meant.

Before Shauna's death, he used to come up the mountain all the time by himself. The light, the space, the air, the possibility – it made him feel free, and that in turn made him happy. Besides, on the competitive circuit it was down to you alone in the end. You needed a sense of self-reliance, a conviction that you contained everything you needed to win. But for Art, alone now meant lonely, rather than solitary. He'd cut himself off to try to save himself from any more hurt.

But it wasn't working. It had never worked, really.

Art wondered how the Misfits would react if he turned up to the annual meal. Just thinking about it made his mouth feel dry. It had been too long, and besides, Jen would likely be there with Rob. His mind replayed seeing her get out of Rob's car, and again he felt the jealousy he had no right to, but that burned all the same.

He stood there for almost an hour, as more and more people started to spill out of the lifts, their moods light. Plenty of them wished him a merry Christmas as they sailed past to start their festive morning on the slopes. He felt like a stationary fixture in a film scene, a subway entrance or crosswalk sign in the busy metropolis of New York, unchanging as the city and its activity ebbed and flowed around it. For something to change, he had to let *himself* change.

Could he?

'You have yourself a merry Christmas, Art. Get yourself something nice.' Mr Fairfield, flanked by his wife and three picture-perfect children, pressed a wad of hundred-dollar bills into Art's hand. Then the family pushed off in the direction of their beautifully appointed ski-in, ski-out cabin, where a private chef had been flown in to prepare their Christmas meal. It was 3 p.m. and if the mountain hadn't already been about to shut down for the day, the biting, high winds that had the chairlifts swinging on their cables was cause for the station technicians to make a call.

The storm had started to come in just after noon, forcing fair-weather skiers and boarders to call time, and leaving only the stalwarts who preferred challenging conditions on the mountain. Mr and Mrs Fairfield were two such people. They enjoyed icy runs and dim visibility because it forced them to concentrate on their form, and so their children had remained in Art's charge until the last possible moment. He had taught them for two years in a row now, so they were competent snowboarders but with the weather as it was, he'd kept them on the lower slopes.

He watched the family disappear into the gloom as they zipped down the lower part of the slope, racing each other back to their cabin and teasing each other. He felt a pull. It was eleven o'clock at night in the UK, the day almost over, but his mum might still be up. She might even have texted him while he was teaching.

What was it Dr Maggie's website had said? Small steps. The idea had prised a tiny part of him open.

He pulled out his phone, and registered that the screen was chock-full of notifications, only one of which was the preview to a WhatsApp from his mum a couple of hours ago.

The other five missed calls and one voicemail had arrived within the last fifteen minutes, and all of them were from Jen.

Chapter Twenty-four

JEN

Mickey's phone went straight to voicemail. Again. Jen remembered he'd thrown his phone onto the kitchen counter last night and declared he was unplugging from the grid, permanently. He may have expressed a theory about 5G that Jen had blocked out because she wanted to remain friends with him.

A sob worked its way up her throat and she began to tremble. All the warmth had seeped out of her body and the cold was settling deep into her core. The fog felt dense with moisture, trickling and freezing into the small gaps in her neckwarmer and coat cuffs. How long did it take for frostbite to set in?

Fucking Mickey.

Inviting her for a post-work Christmas Day snowboarding expedition and then immediately leading her off the side of a piste that he claimed was an 'easy shortcut with an awesome view', in conditions that she knew in her gut were beyond her experience and expertise.

By the time Jen had realised how bad visibility really was, Mickey had disappeared into the mist, leaving her in an area flanked by fir trees, with no signposts back to the main piste and no people gliding by to ask. None of them were stupid enough to go snowboarding in a storm. Unlike her.

She'd shouted for Mickey, but the fog seemed to swallow the sound. The only things she could make out in her range of sight were the trees, stretching metres into the air and with branches hanging low and fat with snow.

At first, she'd given herself a pep talk. All she had to do was keep going downhill and she'd eventually come out at the bottom. She'd seen tree fields like the one she was in from high up on the lifts, and they were always between two slopes. She just needed to be slow and methodical, the way Art had taught her. But when she'd set off, she'd immediately fallen, knocking the breath out of herself as she landed. On the ground, she realised that she'd tripped on a rock. An actual, sticking-out-of-the ground boulder that scraped her board in such a way that she could imagine the damage it could have done to her face. From her position she'd clocked more exposed rocks ahead – and that they weren't even the most perilous part of her journey. She also had a view underneath the fir trees' lowest branches.

There were gaping cavities where the low-hanging branches had prevented the snow from settling – holes at the base of the tree that were wide enough for someone to fall into, and that presumably extended the remaining length of the trunk. A void. And who knew how deep?

She was surrounded by trees. Which meant she was also surrounded by big fuck-off holes.

She'd frozen in place, assuming Mickey would come back once he noticed she was gone, while acknowledging with a rising panic that Mickey was not one for noticing things.

That was fifteen minutes ago and as she hit redial on Mickey's number, she realised her phone – her crappy, flip-up, non-smartphone, with no GPS – was running out of battery.

Think, Jen. THINK.

Mountain Rescue. That was who you were supposed to call if you got into difficulty. Except . . . She had only skimmed the document details but she was pretty sure her travel insurance didn't cover her for any expenses or injury that occurred off-piste. Why would she have taken out a more expensive policy that did? She hadn't *intended* to go off-piste. But she certainly didn't have the money to pay for a private rescue operation if it came to that.

There had to be a solution that didn't involve her having to call Mountain Rescue.

Think.

Art.

His name bubbled up unbidden. During the lessons with Newton, he'd given her his number and said to call him if she was in trouble on the mountain. Sure, that was before he'd stopped speaking to her, but without Mickey coming back for her it was the only idea she had. Her choices were to be embarrassed to death, freeze to death or call the emergency services and pay off the debt for the rest of her life.

She took a shaky breath, trembling from both cold and nerves, as the phone rang. And rang. And rang. And then she got Art's voicemail too.

Of course. It was Christmas Day.

Still, she hit redial, not knowing what else to do, and then started alternating between him and Mickey, praying that one of them would answer. After five tries of each, neither did and her phone was now on ten per cent battery.

A few plump snowflakes started to trickle down, followed by a few more, and then turned into a deluge. It was the sort of snow that looked romantic when you watched it out of a window, but filled you with a creeping sense of dread when you were lost on a mountain. She shoved her phone miserably into her pocket, feeling as though she was being enveloped by the quiet.

Behind her, she heard a noise and started, freaking out that it was a bear. But it was the sound of a branch being overweighted with snow and falling. She watched the flakes collecting in the creases of her coat. How long would it take for her to be completely covered if she didn't move? What was she supposed to do? The memory of Art's lecture on her first morning on the slopes popped up; his talk of safety courses and compliance. She needed someone who would tell her what to do. She reached for her phone again and left a message.

'Art, it's Jen.' She struggled to keep the wobble from her voice. 'I'm on Blackcomb mountain and I was with Mickey but he took me off the side of the piste and now I can't see where I am and . . . and . . . and . . .' She pressed the cancel button, hanging up before she disintegrated completely into tears, and then sat there sobbing, hot tears burning tracks through the frigid cold of her face.

She should never have agreed to come up here. When would she learn to push back rather than go along with things she knew weren't right? It's not that she had no gut intuition, it was that she was too weak to act on it. Especially with anyone male. With Matt at school, she'd pretended to be into Arctic Monkeys just because he loved them, and half the reason she'd taken the job at Proctors was because it had been convenient to get from there to the houseshare where Jay, her boyfriend-at-the-time, lived. With Ollie she'd ended up joining her university's paranormal society and with Nathan, she'd pretended to be fine with a casual relationship to the point where he didn't even consider their break-up a break-up. And for what? So they would like her? So they'd think she was 'no trouble'? Even though it wasn't *her* they liked at all, because she'd never shown them her actual personality. Now she was going to freeze to death and it was her own stupid fault – one of those stories people saw on the news and commented, 'well, what was she doing up there to start off with?' Forget six months, she should steer clear of *all* men forever. If she ever made it off this mountain.

Her phone rang in her hand.

Art.

'Hello!' she shouted. 'Art, I know this is possibly the stupidest thing I've done so far—'

He cut her off. 'There's no time for that now. Where are you?'

'If I knew that I wouldn't be calling you to say I was lost,' she wailed.

He clicked his tongue, but let the comment go. 'What I mean is, where *were* you – *exactly* – when you left the piste? What run, how far down and any identifying markers? I'm coming up Blackcomb mountain now and I'll come and find you, but you need to tell me everything you can. I need to know whether to call Mountain Rescue.'

Mortified, Jen half-heartedly started to tell him not to do that, but with the snow coming down harder than ever, fear quickly overrode her humiliation.

'We came down Heavenly run and it forked off two ways, one down a black run, I think, and the other way down a blue, so I said I wanted to go down the blue, which we did. But then Mickey said there was an easy shortcut back to the lift and led me under a rope. That's where I am now. In the middle of a load of trees that have massive holes underneath and I'm scared I'm going to get sucked into one and it's really really snowing and I'm cold.'

'You're not going to get sucked into one,' Art said calmly. 'And I know where you mean. It's not far from the lift. The important thing is that you stay where you are. Don't try to snowboard but keep moving on the spot to stay warm. I'll be there as soon as I can. How's your phone battery?'

Jen looked at the screen. 'Eight per cent.'

'Right.' He breathed the word heavily. 'I'm going to go now but I'm going to call again briefly in five minutes. We'll keep doing that until I reach you, so we stay in contact but we don't run your battery down. OK?'

Jen nodded, too miserable to respond.

'Jen? I need you to say OK.'

'OK,' she confirmed in a small voice. She didn't want to hang up, even though she knew it was the sensible thing to do, because the sound of his voice was the only thing reminding her she wasn't completely alone.

'I'm ten minutes away, tops. I promise I'm coming. If you need to, call 911, that'll get you through to Mountain Rescue. Or if I don't get you when I call back, I'll call them myself.'

'Yes. Art, please hurry.'

'I'm coming.'

He cut the line and the silence felt denser than before. She pulled her rucksack off her back, having remembered she'd stuffed a load of Christmas cookies from the break room in her bag before she'd left work. The manager from the artisan bakery downstairs in the hotel had dropped them off as he closed the shop for the day and she'd grabbed them to distribute at Rob and Snowy's, where she had been planning on heading after their 'Christmas cobweb-blower' as Mickey had described it. She wasn't hungry but thought she'd better nibble on one in case her body shut down from the temperature. It was so cold she worried she was going to crack her teeth.

When her phone rang again all she could hear was the crack of wind before Art's voice came through, faintly. 'Jen, it's me. I'm just getting on the chairlift to Heavenly now.'

Jen heard another voice mumbling in the background. 'No, I need to go up,' Art said. 'I know you need to shut the lift, but . . .' The sound of wind prevented Jen from hearing anything else.

'Art!' she shouted. 'Art, what's happening?'

'It's the weather. They're shutting all the lifts.' She heard the clanking of machinery. 'But it's OK, he's letting me on. Thanks, man, I appreciate it. I'll radio up to let you know when I've found my friend, so you know everything's OK.'

Despite her shivers and her fear, it didn't pass Jen by that Art had referred to her as his friend.

'I'll tell her, don't worry,' he heard Art say.

'Tell me what?'

'Jen, I have to go, my phone's running low on battery too. I'll see you soon.' He cut her off abruptly and she was by herself again, feeling both worse and better than before. Art was on his way and he was being kind. But what if he didn't make it, or he couldn't find her? What if he went straight past?

Panic rose again and she could feel her edges start to blur, her breath getting shorter and shallower when she noticed the light had dropped even from five minutes ago. That would make it harder for Art to see her. The sun set at around 4 p.m. in December, they really didn't have much time now, and that combined with the fog and snow—

'JEN!' Art's voice cut through the thought. Deep and loud and *close*.

Relief flooded her system. 'ART! I'M HERE. CAN YOU HEAR ME?' she screamed back. Jen had seen Art snowboard and knew his technique was good, but she'd never seen how he must have been at top speed during his pro boarding days. He'd arrived faster than she'd hoped and must have raced all the way from the lift to get to her so quickly.

'Yes! When I shout, shout back, and I'll follow your voice. Jen?'

'Art!'

'I hear you. Again, Jen.'

'Art!'

'Again.' She could hear his voice getting closer and tears brimmed in her eyes, misting up her goggles from the inside, but this time they were tears of pure relief.

'Art!'

He burst through the line of trees behind her, swooshing to a stop just above where she was sitting, hugging her bag and now openly crying. She'd never been so happy to see someone in her life. He pulled up his goggles and leaned down over her, holding out a hand to help her up. The sight of him was blurred from tears and from the snow that was still falling heavily above them.

'You're not hurt, are you?' he said, his face shining red from exertion and the elements. Snow was clinging to the bits of hair poking out from the bottom of his hat. He was wearing a Santa outfit that was covered in snow.

'No, just cold,' she choked out. 'I didn't know what to do.'

'It's OK, I'm here. Can you get up all right?'

She nodded and he hauled her back upright, a tight grip on her arm, before pulling his goggles back over his eyes.

He looked around them and shook his head, a grim look on his face. 'Don't move until I do,' he muttered. 'There are tree wells everywhere.' He pointed to his left. 'We need to get back to the piste that way, keeping away from them. You can easily get trapped.'

'What?' It escaped Jen as a bark. 'You told me that wouldn't happen.'

He flashed a brief, rueful smile. 'I wasn't going to tell you that *before*. Follow me.'

Jen's teeth were chattering. 'You won't leave me, will you?'

'No. I promise. I'll guide you, it's not far. What the fuck was Mickey thinking?' he added as an afterthought, almost to himself. He shook his head again, as though to clear the thought from his head, and snapped back into efficient mode. 'This way. Try and follow my line exactly.'

He inched forward, glancing back at her every couple of seconds. Jen tried to follow and immediately fell over.

'It's OK, you're OK, you're just cold,' he said. All the sharp edges from the last time they spoke had disappeared from his voice, and he flipped easily back into his soothing teacher tone. 'We need to get those muscles warmed up again. I'm here and I'll be no more than a metre in front of you at any time. We're going back to the cable car and we'll go down it together, inch by inch, OK?'

His encouragement infused her with a little confidence, and she shakily made her way after him. 'Great, Jen, a little further,' he coaxed.

Through the gloom and the snowfall, he stayed at a pace she could follow, and never more than a hand's-grasp away. She managed to keep him in her sights. Her legs felt stiff after settling and cooling, and her coordination wasn't up to much, but Art kept up his patter.

'Keep going. Almost there.'

Quicker than she could have predicted, a boundary rope appeared in front of him. He reached ahead and pulled it up, saying, 'Under there.'

She ducked under his arm as he held it up for her and squinted at her surroundings, trying to register anything familiar and get her bearings. It all still looked white and impenetrable. 'We're back on the piste?'

He nodded. 'Yep.'

'How far away from it was I?'

'About fifteen metres.'

Shame and embarrassment flooded through her. 'Shit, Art, I'm so sorry. I should have been able to make my own way back.'

He brushed off her words as though they were the falling snow. 'How would you know that when you had no idea where you were to begin with? Let's get back to the cable car. It's this way.'

He glided past her, still leading and ensuring she was close behind him but without talking now, other than the occasional 'All right?' to check she was following. Away from the relative cover of the trees, and with each metre they travelled, the wind seemed to get louder and the visibility worse, but a few minutes later they made it to where two pistes converged and she saw a familiar sign for the gondola. A kilometre and a half to go.

'How are you doing?' he shouted behind him. 'Do you need a rest?'

Jen's legs were burning and she was breathing hard but she didn't want to stop now. 'I'm OK,' she wheezed. 'Let's keep going.'

She focused all her concentration on watching Art and on staying upright. They didn't pass anyone on their way. The last of the light was disappearing as they rounded the final bend, before a flare of the lamps signalled they were at the gondola.

Just in time.

The piste lights lit up all around them and the sun had officially set for the day. The slope flattened off and she came to a stop, fifteen or so metres from the cable car – a distance Art easily coasted before stopping himself and unstrapping his board. Jen walked the last few metres, feeling wobbly on her feet, as a liftie came out of the little cabin next to the gondola station, the pom-pom of his flashing Santa hat swaying in the crosswind as he approached them.

'Are you the guys Keaton told me about? I was giving you five more minutes before I called Mountain Rescue.'

'That's us,' Art replied, sounding wearied. 'Can you radio him and say "Art found the stray?" He's waiting for news before he leaves his post.'

'Sure.' His radio crackled as he relayed the message and then he gestured at the gondola. 'Slopes are closed, so you can't board to the bottom. You need to jump in.'

Jen didn't need telling twice to board the cable car. As she reached where Art was standing, he grabbed her board, the same way he had when they'd been with Newton, and hooked it into the gondola door. She felt her legs give way as she got inside and she crumpled onto the nearest bench. Art followed her slowly in, walking to the furthermost point from where she was sitting and leaning against the glass sides. The doors closed and shut out the howl of the wind.

As they cruised down the side of the mountain, Jen looked up at where they had just come from, seeing tiny lights twinkling dimly at various points, but not much through the weather. Now the adrenaline had dissipated, the idea of being back up there, somewhere, but without any real idea of where, threatened to overwhelm her.

She had to take a steadying breath. 'Thank you, Art,' she started. 'Thank you so much.'

On the other side of the car, he was standing rigid and motionless. He didn't register her at all.

Then he slowly pulled off his goggles and looked down, holding his face in his gloved hands silently before running his hands slowly back across his face and over his hair, the skin around his eyes crumpling as he rubbed back and forth, back and forth.

'Say something, Art. Are you OK? I know what I did was completely stupid, and I'm so sorry to put you in this position . . .' Her voice trailed off. She wanted him to say something, anything, rather than return to the silent treatment they'd been giving each other for the past week.

'Art?'

He finally looked up and his expression was furious.

'What the fuck were you thinking, Jen?'

Chapter Twenty-five

ART

Jen looked young and scared inside the cable car. She was soaked and an inch of snow sat on top of her woolly hat. Below the hat, her blond hair was stringy and damp, and her slate-grey eyes loomed large in her face. There were even little crystals of ice on her eyelashes. She also looked hugely repentant, an expression that morphed into fear as Art shouted 'What the fuck were you thinking?' at her.

Jen lowered her face inside the front of her jacket.

She seemed to get smaller as he catalogued each and every one of the mistakes she'd made that afternoon, starting with her ill-fated decision to go snowboarding with Mickey again.

'You don't have anywhere near enough experience to go into the backcountry, not to mention any of the right equipment,' he ranted. 'You don't even have a smartphone, which means not even a basic GPS, and you've had what, a week of lessons?' He started pacing up and down the cabin, ticking off her errors on his hands. 'You don't have any knowledge of the pistes themselves, so how would you know what's between them?'

She didn't reply, keeping her face in her coat where he couldn't see her.

'I don't think you realise just how serious it could have been. Tree wells are very bad, Jen—' Art stopped there, the fury draining out of him. The thought of what might have happened if she'd barrelled half a metre closer to one of those fir trees took the breath out of him. He stopped pacing and dropped onto one of the benches along the cabin's inside perimeter. The only sounds were his own ragged breath, the wind outside battering them and the occasional clunking of the gondola's pulleys.

He leaned his head against the window and closed his eyes, as though that was protection against the onslaught of alternative outcomes to the afternoon. He'd been on autopilot once he picked up her call and then as he searched for her, all of the training he'd had kicked in, and – this time – a bad situation had a positive outcome.

But right now he didn't feel any relief. Instead his heart was hammering and he couldn't quite catch his breath. He was shaking as though he'd been sitting out in the freezing snow himself. His teeth were chattering and he couldn't stop his legs vibrating. There was also the very real possibility that he was going to be sick. He concentrated on breathing, elongating his breaths in an attempt to quell whatever was happening to him, but he could feel sweat prickling under his arms and across his back.

'Art, I'm sorry.' Jen's voice was small and muffled. 'I deserve everything you've just said to me and more.'

It wasn't that he didn't want to answer Jen, more that he physically couldn't. The mass of emotions and physical sensations hitting him right now had put him so far into his body that anything outside of it felt very far away. He felt a warm trickle down the back of his neck. Snow melting from the tips of his hair or sweat beading, he couldn't tell.

'Art?' Jen's voice was clearer now. She must have peeped out from her jacket. 'Oh, I see. You're not talking to me. If it makes you feel any better, all I can think about is how stupid I am.'

'Make *me* feel better?' He would have laughed if he could. He opened his eyes. 'Why did you do it?'

She had the decency to look even more sheepish than before. 'I was trying to be spontaneous and in the moment.'

'Right.' He shook his head. 'Except you told me back at the hotel that you like to be *prepared*, what with all your first aid and fire marshal training. Besides, being spontaneous doesn't have to mean dangerous. You know that going along with what your libertarian stoner flatmate says is not actually the same as being a devil-may-care person?'

Jen looked stung. 'Unless it was my idea.'

'Was it?'

'No.'

Art barked out a mocking laugh. 'Well, then.'

He shut his eyes again. Was his ankle really burning or did it just feel as though it was? He clenched his right hand in and out in time with his breath, concentrating on the rhythm. He had to get off this mountain. Now.

'I know you don't want to talk about—' Jen started and then stopped and he could sense the hesitation in her voice '—what happened to Shauna, but I can only imagine what effect idiots like me putting themselves in danger has. I'm very grateful for you coming to help me, and I'm also very sorry for putting you in that position.'

'Please stop talking.' Art's voice was weak. Insides twitching, lungs struggling. He felt dizzy despite sitting very still.

'But I feel terrible, I really do. Tell me what you want me to say.'

'I don't want you to say anything!' he shouted. There was terror in his voice. 'I just want you to be safe!'

His words reverberated around the cabin, and then disappeared.

There was a long silence. Jen nodded almost imperceptibly as though understanding something.

Art was still too hot. He started tugging at the cheap material of his Santa costume, desperate to get it off, but his fingers wouldn't comply. He couldn't get a hold of the zip at the back. Jen tentatively crossed the gondola cabin and, without saying anything, she pulled off her gloves and reached for the zip. Her cool hands briefly made contact with the sensitive area at the bottom of his neck and the contrast between that and his scorching, panicked skin caused him to hold his breath. The unexpected intimacy of it, something that for her must have been just a small, natural act of care, was both a shock and a balm. Every part of him wanted to turn and take hold of her hands, but instead he clenched his into fists, his arms rigid, until she moved away and he could pull the outfit down and step out of it. He yanked the zip of his snowboarding jacket down for good measure, letting the cold air rush in.

'Thank you,' he husked as he stuffed the Santa suit into his bag.

'Let's get off the mountain,' she said eventually, her voice more assured. In one sentence, it was as though their roles as protector and victim had changed.

Jen stayed quiet after that, but jumped up when the cable car doors opened to hop out before Art and grab her snowboard as well as his.

He let her, following slowly behind, still feeling sick. Leaving the gondola station, they found themselves at the top of Blackcomb village after darkness had fallen, which made the Christmas tree lights and street decorations pop. Groups and families milled around them.

'Are you heading home? I'll give you a lift,' Art told her as they reached the parking lot.

Jen gave him a cynical look. 'Thank you, but I can tell that you can't stand to have me in your sight right now so it's fine. I'll get the bus.'

'It's blowing a blizzard and my truck is right over there.' He gestured to the mountain staff car park, where his truck was one of the few remaining cars in the lot.

Jen shrugged. 'OK, thanks. I wasn't going to head home though.'

Of course. She was heading to the Misfits meal at the Creek, where she'd be seeing Rob. The meal he'd once been an instrumental part of. With a guy who used to be one of his best friends.

'Sure,' he said, experiencing a spear of loneliness so strong it physically hurt. He wanted to be beside her, knowing she was safe, even though he knew he couldn't talk about what had happened or what *could* have happened. It was both about her and not about her, at the same time. 'Wherever you like.'

He threw both their boards into the back of his truck, and turned the heaters up as high as they could go before cranking the radio up loud enough that they didn't have to talk.

He roared out of the lot, taking a left. He could feel Jen's eyes on his face, but ignored her, keeping his eyes away from the windscreen and on the snow blustering into it.

'I haven't told you where I'm going,' she said, raising her voice above the music.

He shrugged. 'I assumed to the Misfits meal.'

'The what?'

'Maybe they don't call it that any more. Rob and Snowy's place.' He wondered if she'd notice the way his voice caught a little as he said Rob's name. If she did, she didn't react.

'You're right, I am.' As the heat kicked in, steam started to condense on the inside of the windows, the effect of their drenched coats in the hot air. Jen unzipped hers and pulled off her hat and gloves. She turned the radio down. 'Why did you call it the Misfits meal?'

'Because we were Misfits. Back when we all arrived, years ago. We'd travelled from all over the world to live and work in Whistler and we didn't have any family here at Christmas, or any permanent friends really. Everyone was always just passing through. But at the Misfits meal, every waif and stray was welcome for Christmas dinner.' Art could feel his heart rate slowing slightly, the act of thinking about good times there over the years for once calming him rather than sending him straight into fight-or-flight mode.

The village flashed past in a blur: snow-covered condos, shops and restaurants, all smudged beneath twinkling Christmas lights.

'How do you know Rob and Snowy?' she asked. He looked at her out of the very side of his eye. Her cheeks were all flushed, matching the pink tip of her nose. Was she prying? Or just interested? Was this all a technique to distract him from the panic he had felt in the ski lift? Jen's mere presence, her face glowing from cold and kindness, was distraction enough. He wanted to reach over and brush the flakes of snow from her hair, or shoulders. Anything that would give him an excuse to touch her. Make sure she was safe. Real.

'Everybody knows Rob and Snowy,' Art replied with the merest ghost of a grin. 'They were both working in Canucks when I got here from England, although they were as new as me to Whistler back in those days. They'd arrived from different parts of Australia, and ended up in a houseshare as well as working together at the bar. They were only going to stay for the season, but it's been' – he calculated how long he'd been here himself – 'about ten years now.' He let that sink in. For six of those years, they'd been his closest friends.

A few more minutes and Art pulled off the main road towards the four-bedroom house that he'd spent hours, if not weeks, of his life at, both before he met Shauna and after. Playing computer games, drinking beer, taste-testing whatever weird food combination Snowy had concocted and being impressed when, nine times out of ten, it worked. There were a couple of other people already waiting on the step outside and the door opened as he pulled over, his headlights whooshing across the building as he did a neat turn in the road. It was Snowy answering the door, dressed in a sweater with elves on it that lit up.

'Here you go,' Art said with as much faux-joviality as he could muster.

'Thank you,' Jen said, not making any move to get out and regarding him cautiously. It was as though he was a wounded animal whose reactions you can't predict. 'Listen,' she started. 'I can sense you don't want to talk about it, but I need you to know two things. One is that I am very grateful for what you did for me today, and the other is that I won't be doing anything like that again.'

Dread stabbed at Art's insides but it wasn't as overwhelming as before. He just found himself glad to hear her say it. 'Tell your friend Mickey,' he said, forcing himself to look at her, 'he needs to learn not to be so reckless.'

Jen nodded. 'I will. But you were right. I should never have followed him off the side of the slope. That's on me. And it's something I'm working on. I really am.' She turned to him. 'I want you to believe that I've learned my lesson. It's important.'

She looked so intense. 'OK,' he said slowly, with a sarcastic hint of the same earnestness in his voice. 'I do.' His mind stretched out again, darkening. 'It was a near miss, Jen,' he muttered. 'It isn't always a near miss.'

'I know,' she replied sombrely. She put her hand on his arm and squeezed it. Their eyes locked, before she quickly pulled her arm away as though she'd been scorched. They glanced away from each other self-consciously.

'Why don't you come in? I bet they'd all love to see you.'

Art thought briefly about saying yes, about the in-jokes that probably hadn't changed – not to mention Rob's Christmas playlist, which likely still contained every soft rock version of a festive song this side of the eighties. And then he thought about seeing Jen with Rob. The idea curdled. 'I don't think so, but thanks.'

He pulled off his hat. The heat in the car was making it itch on his head. He ruffled the hair underneath, suddenly self-conscious about it.

Jen moved to unclip her seatbelt and pulled her soggy rucksack out of the footwell. 'I guess you have another Christmas dinner to go to.'

'I do, yes,' Art replied automatically. It was easy to reach for his usual lie.

She hesitated briefly before opening the door, letting in a blast of cold air. Snowflakes swirled into the car. She gave him a long look. 'If you're sure.'

'I am. Merry Christmas, and have a great time with Rob.'

Confusion passed over her face. 'Sure. And Snowy too. Look he's over there,' she said, waving in his direction. Snowy lifted an arm in greeting. 'Merry Christmas to you too.'

Art pulled the door shut from the inside and drove away slowly, taking care that his heavy tyres didn't wheelspin any slush over her as she picked her way to the house. He watched Snowy greet her, dumping a Santa hat on her head. The door shut, the glow of light evaporating as it did.

Time to go home.

As he thought it, he realised he couldn't go back to his empty house. Not this year. He didn't want to be alone any more.

He pulled over again, this time at the liquor store at the end of the street, which was open despite it being Christmas night. He bought twelve bottles of wine without any real selection process and carried the two boxes to the car.

At the house, he knocked, and, in the moment before the porch light came on, he almost got back in his truck and drove away.

He forced himself to stay.

The door opened and the giant mass of his former coach blocked the light from the inside, casting a looming shadow over where Art was standing.

Art thrust one of the boxes of wine at him and tried, but failed, to keep the wobble from his voice.

'Merry Christmas, Yeti. Can I come in?'

Chapter Twenty-six

JEN

'Did . . . Jedi drop you off?' Snowy asked after enveloping her in a hug and plonking a Santa hat on her head.

'Who's Jedi?' Jen wrinkled her nose, confused. 'I got a lift with Art. I work with him at the hotel, sort of . . .' It wasn't anywhere near enough of an explanation as to who Art was, but at the same time, Jen couldn't define him any other way. 'But you guys know him, right? What did you just call him – Jedi?'

'Everyone used to call him that once.' Snowy reached for Jen's coat. 'Did someone pour a bucket of water on you, mate?' he asked, as it dripped onto the floor. 'I didn't realise it was snowing so hard out there.'

'It's not. I mean it is, but that's not why it's so wet.' She took the coat back off him, realising how heavy it was, and draped it over the radiator in the guys' hallway. Steam started rising from it almost immediately. 'It's a long story. Art – Jedi – whatever – is involved.' She felt herself start to shake again with cold. 'Can I have a drink? I need to warm up.'

'A drink I can do. How do you feel about boozy eggnog?'

'Unless it has clam juice in it, I have no adverse feelings towards it.'

Snowy opened the living room door as Jen levered off her snowboarding boots. She'd go and change out of her snowboarding trousers in a minute. She had some jeans in her rucksack – if they weren't soaked through – and if they were, well, her thermals were basically leggings. At least she was free of needing to be immaculately groomed for a while.

As she followed Snowy through, rock versions of Christmas music drifted out from a speaker at one end and there was a chorus of 'Merry Christmas' from the ten or so people assembled there, including the usual suspects, Darren, Clyde and Kelly. Around them a few other people sat on the floor with beer cans or wine glasses at their sides, picking at bags of crisps and flicking through snowboard magazines. Rob approached her from the kitchen area at the other side, holding an 'I Love Whistler' mug. It contained a sickly-looking, cinnamon-smelling drink, which he handed to her with a cheery 'Merry Christmas' before sitting down next to Clyde and picking up a games console to continue playing some football game. She hadn't seen him since he dropped her off at work after the night of their near kiss, and there was no trace of awkwardness coming from him. She could only conclude that he harboured no strong feelings for her at all. Just as she didn't for him.

A series of rickety fold-out tables had been pushed together in the middle of the room and were surrounded by a variety of mismatched chairs. There were bowls of snacks dotted about, but the distinct smell of roast dinner coming from the kitchen indicated that the main event was yet to happen.

Snowy was overseeing everything that was going on there, lifting the lids off pans and squinting at something under the grill.

'Don't open that, mate!' he shouted at Darren, who was about to reach for the oven door. Snowy checked his phone. 'It'll be ready in fifty-eight minutes.'

'I thought it was a potluck thing,' Jen said, pulling the crumpled bag of cookies from her rucksack and putting it on one side as her contribution. They had mostly shattered from where she'd fallen and then sat on them. 'Are you making the whole dinner?'

'Have you ever eaten anything these guys have cooked?' Snowy replied with a shrug. He threw a tea towel over his shoulder and inspected a pan that was bubbling with something unspecified on the hob. 'The only way to guarantee we won't get food poisoning is if I do it myself. Plus, I enjoy it.' He reached into a grocery bag resting against the side of the counter and pulled out an onion, expertly peeling and dicing it as Jen stood in front of him sipping her sickly drink. 'Better?' he said, glancing up quickly.

Jen almost yelped, seeing the knife brushing so close to his fingers, but then realised he could literally do it with his eyes closed. 'A bit,' she said instead. The sensation of being lost and alone hit her afresh and she juddered. 'I went snowboarding with Mickey and then got lost up there, near some – what are they called? – tree wells,' she confessed. Maybe if she talked about it, it wouldn't seem so bad. 'If Art hadn't come to find me, I don't know what would have happened. That's why I was in his truck. He gave me a lift here afterwards.'

Snowy stopped chopping, his eyes widening as she summarised her afternoon. 'Wait. You were lost on the mountain, in the backcountry?' Snowy seemed to be gripping the handle of the knife more tightly than he had been before. 'Jesus fuck,' he muttered.

'I know it was a stupid thing to do. I feel sick just thinking about it.'

'You're damn right it was stupid, Jen. But *today* of all the days.' He went to start chopping again, but Jen could see his hand quivering and he put the knife down. He reached instead for his own mug, emblazoned with the words 'Bitchin' in the Kitchen', and took a deep swig. His eyes were bright with tears and it was obvious it wasn't from the onions.

'What's today?' Dread rose in Jen's stomach.

'If you know Art, you know about his accident, right? Although from what I can gather he still doesn't talk about it.'

Jen nodded. 'I know about the accident,' she said faintly.

'It happened on Christmas Day. Four years ago today.'

Jen's hand flew up to her mouth. 'So Shauna . . .'

Snowy nodded grimly. He ripped off a sheet of kitchen roll and wiped it across his eyes, blinking as he looked at a point in the middle distance. 'We usually raise a glass to her when we eat. And tell any newbies about her, what a great friend she was, try to keep her memory going. We always invite Art but' – Snowy shrugged – 'he never comes.'

Jen struggled to digest exactly how bad what she'd done was.

'Hey Rob,' Snowy called to his friend. He unfolded himself from where he was hunched over his games console and ambled over to the kitchen. He was tipsily singing along to Chris Rea. 'Jen saw Jedi today.'

The happiness evaporated from his face. 'What, really? Where?'

'He dropped her off. Here.'

Rob glanced uncertainly towards the door as though he expected Art to materialise. 'Today? Why?'

'Jen got lost on the mountain in the storm and he had to rescue her,' Snowy summarised. Jen looked at the floor.

'Yeah, she knows,' Snowy said, so Jen knew he was about to tell her she was a moron.

'How's he doing?' Rob said quietly. The easy-going air that he wore so lightly had slipped and he looked sad. 'We never see him.'

'He dropped off the radar after the accident,' Snowy chipped in. 'Wouldn't let us come and see him in the hospital, and then when he was discharged he gradually seemed to disappear. Kept us at arm's length when we texted, said he'd call back but never did. We just thought we were expecting too much from him, that it was his way of dealing with it and he'd give us a shout when he was ready, you know? But he never did. There was always a reason why he couldn't talk or meet up – he needed to go to physical therapy for his leg or had an appointment with the lawyers for the compensation case. We didn't question it, because he *did* need to do all those things. If I got hold of him and told him how glad I was that he was recovering, he just looked shellshocked. I didn't know the right thing to say.'

'None of us did, Snow,' Rob murmured. 'There was nothing right about it.'

'Then I ordered a load of books about how to support people dealing with grief. That was even worse. Like he knew he was being psychologised and backed off even more. I figured it was unfair of me to expect him to confide in us and that he'd find his way back in his own time.' Snowy sniffed hard, and looked down at the knife again, his index finger worrying the handle of it.

'He told me he was going somewhere else for Christmas,' said Jen. 'And that's why he couldn't come in and see you all.'

Rob gave a grim smile. 'Yeah, he would. He says that every year when he texts to say he can't make it. Whether he does or not I've no idea.'

'Where is he supposed to be?' Jen asked.

'Yeti's,' Rob replied. 'But I run into Yeti now and again and he's never mentioned spending Christmas with him, so he's probably not.'

'We could call him to find out,' Jen suggested. 'Well, not me, because my phone's out of battery, but you could.'

'He won't answer,' said Rob. 'He never does.'

'He seemed like he was thinking about coming in tonight,' Jen said quietly. He had, she could tell. He seemed genuinely apologetic that he couldn't. The idea that Art wasn't spending the day with friends or family and instead was sitting alone killed her.

'Really?' Snowy said to Jen.

'Definitely. He seemed torn to me and was about to do it, but then said he had somewhere else to go so I didn't question it.'

Snowy and Rob exchanged a look.

'Maybe you should go over to Yeti's and see if he's there,' Jen said.

Rob looked dubious. 'And if he's not?'

'Then we find him and do, I don't know, an intervention,' Snowy said, nodding as though he was warming to the idea.

'Didn't we try that, like, two years ago?'

'Exactly,' Snowy said, seeming surer of himself now. 'It was two years ago and we haven't properly tried to reach him since. We should never have stopped trying. You heard Jen. She said he was thinking of coming in tonight. That's the closest he's been to seeing us for years. Something's different.'

'I don't know, he's always seemed pretty set on cutting us off,' said Rob. 'He never replies to my messages, cuts me dead when I see him. I know you're into your self-help stuff Snow, but maybe he just doesn't want us to "reach out" any more.'

'Just because your musical tastes are stuck in the eighties doesn't mean your attitudes to mental health should be,' Snowy huffed. 'We're his friends.'

'Not true, but to put it another way,' Rob said, 'is it a good idea to turn up and force him to face us, on today of all days?' He looked at Jen questioningly, and she started to second-guess herself. She held up her hands to abdicate responsibility. 'I almost had to call out Mountain Rescue today because of my own bad choices, so maybe I'm not the person to decide. But Snowy's right, he *is* your friend.'

And mine, I hope.

'It's decided. We're going,' Snowy confirmed. He picked up the knife and pointed at Jen with it. 'Let's go.'

'Me? Not a good idea. *You* should see if he's OK, but I'm the last person he wants to see right now.' Even so, her stomach fizzed at the thought of seeing him again. Had she played a small part in this year being different?

'Tough. You can drive, right?'

'Technically, yes. But I haven't for ages in London, and never on this side of the road—'

'You're the only person in the room who hasn't already drunk their bodyweight in eggnog,' Snowy interrupted, 'so you're going to have to. Besides, you owe him. He saved you today, so you need to help rescue him, even if it's from himself rather than the mountain.'

Jen absorbed what he was saying. 'You're right.' She *did* owe Art. And she cared about him. Maybe he'd shut the door in their faces, but they had to try.

'Car keys are on that table over there,' said Snowy. 'And we can direct you to Yeti's.'

Jen went to retrieve the keys and picked her bag back up. 'OK,' she muttered. 'But you need to give clear directions. And seriously, someone is going to have to start explaining where all these nicknames have come from

– Jedi, Yeti' – she pointed at Snowy's hair – 'at least yours I understand.'

Snowy paused to put the lid on a pan, glance into the oven, and say, 'Daz, I'm texting you now with instructions about this stuffing. Do *exactly* as I tell you.'

He tossed the tea towel onto the counter, took a final slug of eggnog and followed Jen to the door. 'What are you on about? Snowy's my real name.'

Chapter Twenty-seven

ART

'Dinner will be a half-hour,' Yeti announced as though Art being there was the most natural thing in the world.

He took the box from Art and stood aside to let him into his and Lori's one-storey cabin. The smell of cinnamon and cloves drifted down the hallway, which opened up into a living-cum-dining room, where there were three places set at the table. The room was stuffed with festive decorations: fairy lights were strung along the perimeter of the ceiling with candy canes dangling from them, a Nativity scene took up an entire corner and there was a tree so laden down with baubles that it was difficult to see any green beneath. It was the interiors embodiment of a Michael Bublé song. Yeti and Lori's giant hairy rescue dog, Mabel, lay on the floor. She lifted her head in greeting as Art walked in, too ancient these days to be capable of anything more exuberant.

Art started at seeing the extra place setting. 'Sorry. I didn't realise you had someone coming over. This was just a spur-of-the-moment thing – I'm imposing.'

'Nonsense,' said Lori, bustling into the room carrying a bowl of tortilla chips in one hand and two bottles of Kokanee beer in the other. 'It's just us; no one is imposing.'

'But the . . .' Art gestured to the extra place.

Yeti put the case of wine down on the table and intercepted the beers with a grateful smile. He passed one to Art. 'We set that one in case you changed your mind. We do it every year.'

Art took a hurried swig of his drink to hide the rush of embarrassment. They did that *every* year? And every year, he just didn't show up. He sat at home alone, not thinking about how his absence might be noticed, or his presence missed.

'I brought some wine,' he said, to avoid responding to what Yeti had just said. 'There's some more in my truck.'

'We certainly won't run out,' Lori said with a smile. 'You needn't have, especially after dropping off our presents earlier, but thank you. We'll open some with dinner.' She put the bowl down on a small wooden coffee table that Art remembered from his previous visits. In fact, looking around Yeti's place, not much had changed since the last time he'd been inside, during the visit from his mum that made him want to die of shame. The same mid-century-style furniture was in the same place, and Yeti's 'Hall of Fame' – the framed newspaper cuttings that he'd arranged as a gallery on the far wall – was still there. Art couldn't take his eyes off it, even though the stories were too far away and too small for him to read from his spot only a few feet within the doorway.

Yeti saw him looking. 'Probably a few updates since you last came,' he said conversationally, walking over as if to invite him to have a look.

He'd always had ten frames and he'd made sure all of his team appeared somewhere, but rotated which story he displayed about them, depending on the most recent competitions and results. For a long time, Art's stories changed almost monthly and he hogged four or five slots. His mum had faithfully bought two copies of every British newspaper his victories appeared in and posted one over to Yeti in Canada while keeping the other for herself. Yeti had done the same with the Canadian and American papers.

Looking at the pictures now, they were team members who'd come through the ranks after him; four years behind in age but light-years ahead in rankings and podium places. Yeti had five team members on the books right now, three women and two men. Of them, Decca Thomas and Kai Lowry were the ones to watch for the next Games, having shown themselves as strong competition against the American and Japanese favourites in their respective events.

The most prominent article about Decca covered the fact that she'd had a trick named after her for being the first person to ever perform – and land – a particular backflip in an international tournament. Meanwhile, Kai had been nicknamed 'Animal' by the press, both for his wild hair and his erratic-seeming snowboarding style that belied the poise and control he possessed. They'd be deep into Olympic prep now, Art noted, scanning their achievements.

Art expected to feel jealousy or a sense of loss that the years-old articles about him had been usurped. But he didn't. There was a moment of what he could only recognise as nostalgia, before it slipped away, and even that wasn't for the wins or the accolades. It was for the sense of possibility, of being at the beginning of something. He was happy that Yeti had so many potential winners in his crew. He deserved it.

'She's going all the way,' he said, raising his hand to draw attention to Decca. His eye snagged on the article just underneath, a tiny thing, with a small, faded photo next to it.

It was a cutting about Art. But instead of it being one about his 'journey' to the Olympics or a decisive European win, it was the one from the *Yorkshire Post* after Art had won his first event at the indoor ski slope in Castleford as a sixteen-year-old. In the photo, he was beaming and comedically biting the medal he'd been awarded the way he'd seen winners do on the World Championships podium on the TV, even though it was just some local competition. His hair was flattened from the hat he'd been wearing, and his clothes were so baggy, they looked too big, rather than the cool oversized 'real' snowboarding look he'd been going for. He looked young; he looked *happy*. It hit him like a punch.

'Why the hell did you keep this one?' he asked Yeti.

'I show that to the kids I coach all the time.'

Art cast his eye back over the rest of the articles. He found it hard to believe. 'Why? You weren't even my coach at the time. I didn't *have* a coach at the time.'

'Because it reminds me why anyone wants to do this to start off with. That smile, the buzz, the sheer enjoyment of the sport. The achievements don't mean anything if you don't have that.'

'None of it means anything if you don't win,' Art muttered, taking a deep swig of his drink. They were circling dangerously close to 'difficult conversation' territory, but for once Art didn't deploy his ejector seat.

'Not true,' was all Yeti said in response.

Art waited. Yeti did this. He never revealed his whole hand in one go, instead building up to his point.

'Even after everything that happened' – another classic Yeti euphemism – 'you still spend your days on the mountain, teaching kids to ride. There's got to be a reason why.'

Art snorted. 'Yeah, I need to earn a living and I'm not qualified to do anything else.'

Yeti gave him a silencing look. 'Art, you're smart and you have the brains and the money' – Yeti would never be so crass as to refer to the compensation directly – 'to go back to university and retrain if you wanted to. But I think you teach snowboarding for the same reason I coach. You love not just the feeling of being in the outdoors on the mountains, but from getting others hooked on it too. It's the same feeling whether you're helping a complete beginner nail their first turn or a junior champ land their first Backside 900, admit it.'

Art thought about the joy on his pupils' faces when his tuition finally clicked, and how his heart soared *for* them. It happened in the same way it had when he *knew* a medal was on the cards during his competing days.

'Maybe,' he said half-grudgingly.

'It doesn't have to be about podiums and world records,' Yeti laughed gruffly, 'although we both know I only stay in my job as long as they keep coming. But if you lose the love for why you started doing it to begin with, then there's no point. You might as well tune cars if it's purely about mechanics.'

Art nodded, not trusting himself to say anything else. All this time he'd felt like a failure because he couldn't – and wouldn't – do the nail-biting tricks that had once been second nature. Maybe teaching wasn't the consolation prize. Maybe it was enough. He thought about the lessons he'd given Jen, and how it had reminded him of the days he'd spent goofing around mountains with his friends. Having fun, rather than trying to 'win' anything.

Better still, he got paid to do it. It sure beat the waitressing gigs and cleaning jobs the vast majority of mountain resort employees had to do, and for far less money.

Art turned from the wall, took a breath. He headed over to one of the worn leather recliners that faced the flat-screen TV and almost sat down but then thought better of it.

'Listen, Yeti, I owe you an apology.'

The crinkles around Yeti's eyes straightened out in surprise. 'That's not necessary,' he muttered, the rim of his beer bottle held close to his mouth.

Art's mouth twisted into a wry grin. 'The fact that you didn't ask me what for proves that you know you deserve one for something.'

Rather than say anything in return, Yeti cleared his throat and then looked at the floor.

'Because I do owe you an apology. And it's not just for one thing, it's for many many things over the last few years.' Art could see Yeti begin to speak but he silenced him by continuing to talk. 'It's true. Please don't interrupt because there's some stuff I need to say and if you stop me, I'm not sure I'll have the guts to do it again.' To his horror, tears sprang to his eyes. He couldn't break down *now* when he'd barely even started. He swiped the back of his hand over his eyes and gave what could only be described as a disgusting sniff.

'You've only ever done your best to look out for me, and until now I've thrown it all back in your face. Don't shake your head, Yeti, you know it's true. Every time you've offered me help or work or money or friendship, I've withdrawn. It was to help me cope, but as you and everyone else knew a long time before me, it didn't work because I'm not coping. I've been reading all about it on this lady's website that my mum sent me, which I guess is progress, because six months ago I would have deleted the message without looking.' He gave another long, shaky exhale. 'I need to speak to my mum too, that's a whole other situation I have to deal with, but I'm also sorry that I put you in the position of having to keep her informed about me because I was so unreachable that I couldn't talk to her myself.'

Empty of words, Art dropped into the leather recliner, a thousand emotions swirling around in his head.

Did he feel better? Mostly he just felt exhausted and wrung out. But he also felt lighter somehow. As though he'd been pushing something down so hard for so long that now he'd stopped, his body had released, like the game where you press your arms against the inside of the doorframe and when you stop they float up on their own.

Yeti slowly lowered himself down into the opposite recliner, his eyes on Art the whole time. It was hard to tell with all the hair surrounding them, but they looked distinctly damp.

'You done?' he said at last. He was pulling on the hair of his moustache, the bristles making a shooshing sound as he ran his fingers over them.

Art shook his head slowly. 'There are about a thousand other points I need to make, but for now, yes. What I'm saying is, I know I need to get help. I'm trying to get help. This is me asking for help.'

Yeti nodded back. 'I'm proud of you. But just so you know, you didn't and don't owe me an apology. I – we, all of us – just wanted you to come back to yourself again, but I always understood it's not that simple.' His gaze drifted to the window, where it was pitch black outside, but Art knew that in the daylight you could see the tip of Blackcomb over the roofs of the houses. 'I love these mountains, you know I do, but even I don't know how you get over something like that.'

This time Art couldn't stop himself from choking up. 'Honestly, I feel guilty that I'm even trying.' Yeti was at his chair before he could finish the sentence. The giant bulk of his body made a thump as he knelt down next to it.

'Well, you shouldn't,' he said emphatically. 'Of all the things to feel, that shouldn't be one of them. You're twenty-eight years old and have so much life ahead of you. This advice probably wouldn't be condoned by a therapist but the way I see it, you got a second chance. It's up to you what that means, but the only waste I can think of would be not making the most of it.'

Art looked at the ceiling, willing the thumping of his heart to slow down. 'I miss her,' he said softly. 'I can't believe she just doesn't exist any more. It doesn't seem fair that I'm here and she's not,' he said softly.

'What does the universe know about fair, son?' Yeti grunted. 'Fair would mean only good things happening to good people, like Lori being able to have children—' He raised an eyebrow as Art threw him a quizzical look. 'What, did you think me spending my entire adult life dealing with petulant teenagers put us off having kids? No, it just didn't work out for us. My point is, you get what you get, and some get it harder than others. All you can do is deal with it. I'm not saying it's easy, but you can't just exist, you've got to try and be happy too.'

'That's what I'm realising.' Art noticed his beer bottle was empty. 'I've had a few flashes of it recently, but even that feels like a betrayal.' He tore a strip from the bottle's label, weighing up whether to say what he was thinking.

It was harder to get out than the apology, which was fully deserved and long overdue. The feelings he wanted to talk about were so new and terrifying. Would vocalising them release the pressure or just lead to more questions or judgement and guilt?

'There's a . . .' Another thin strip came away. '. . . person. Jen. At work. Sort of. She's made me feel . . .' Art couldn't think of the right word.

'Happy?'

Art snorted. There were small strips of label scattered all over the floor now. 'If happy is the same as feeling tortured and guilty and like a terrible person.' He considered it. 'I think she's just made me *feel* again, as opposed to being numb.'

'If not happy, how about human? You've been trying not to feel anything for so long that if this woman has succeeded in stirring things up, then that's got to count for something. Starting something new doesn't redefine what you had with Shauna. It's different. Separate.'

'I don't even know why I'm telling you. She's seeing someone anyway.'

'Because it's awakened your sense of possibility. And that's all right. In fact, that's what it's all about.'

Necking his beer so quickly had made Art lightheaded. Had someone *Freaky Friday*-ed Yeti and swapped him for Glennon Doyle?

'Dinner!' Lori trilled, bustling back through from the kitchen. She was staggering slightly under the weight of a giant platter. It held a turkey that was far too big for two, or even three, people and was adorned with holly leaves. 'I'll just leave this here to rest for a few minutes and then go back in for everything else.' Art jumped up to relieve her of the plate and put it down on the table. She beamed. 'Seeing as you're here, you can carve while I have a glass of wine.' She looked over at Yeti, who was still kneeling on the floor, and rushed over, extending a hand.

'What are you doing down there?' she chided. 'Your knees.'

Yeti chuckled. 'Seemed like a good idea at the time, but you might have to help me back up.' He grasped for her hand and she heaved, Yeti pushing off the arm of the chair at the same time to lever himself into a standing position again. Once he was upright, he continued to idly hold on to Lori's hand, but his attention was still fixed on Art.

'You don't think that sports psychologist was the last head doctor I've come into contact with, do you? Professional sport is intertwined with mental and emotional health these days, so everyone in the team sees someone to make sure they're ticking along. I just wish it had been more common when you were coming up. Then you might feel less like there's only two categories, fixed and damaged, and instead that it's OK to be somewhere along a spectrum.'

Art nodded, weighing up the possibility.

'And I think you're starting to think about moving on from Shauna but you're still at the start of it. There's no rush.' Yeti ambled over to the dining table and pulled out a chair for Lori, before moving to sit down on his own. 'Give it time. This Jen has made you feel like there could be someone in your future, but it's not something you need to confront *right now*.' He picked up a corkscrew and reached for one of the bottles of red wine Art had brought, opening it before pouring Lori and then himself and Art a glass. He handed Art a knife, and Art had just started to carve when there was a banging at the front door.

Yeti's eyebrows shot up in surprise. Lori shook her head at him in response, a silent conversation between people who'd been married for thirty-five years. The intimacy of it brought a fresh prickle of tears to Art's eyes.

'I'll get it,' he said, wanting to make himself useful. He dropped the utensils. Whoever it was started banging again before he had made it halfway across the room.

'All right, all right,' he snapped, rushing into the hallway and tearing the door open. On the doorstep stood Rob and Snowy. And just behind them was the exact person Yeti had assured him he didn't need to confront right now. Jen.

Chapter Twenty-eight

JEN

They hadn't worked out a plan beyond this point, because they hadn't expected Art to be at Yeti's, never mind to be answering the door. Once she was standing on a snowy porch looking directly at Art, she had no idea what to do next.

'Merry Christmas,' she tried weakly. 'We've come to . . . er . . .' She turned to look at Rob for help.

'Who is it?' boomed a voice from inside the house. A massive and incredibly shaggy person loomed up behind Art, before breaking into a wide smile that showed off bright white, straight, North American teeth. She recognised him as Yeti from her stalking of Art on the internet.

'Rob! Snowy!' he shouted. 'Long time no see, guys. Merry Christmas. Come on in.' He gestured for Art to stand aside and turned his attention to Jen. 'And this is?'

'Jen,' she replied, holding out her hand. She liked this Yeti immediately. The warmth exuding from the house felt like it was being pumped directly from this enormous hairy man and his megawatt smile.

'Oh,' he said, the smile fixing briefly on his face, before he pulled himself together and pumped her hand. 'I'm

Yeti. Well, come in. Are you hungry? Lori's made enough to feed the Canadian ski team.'

Jen glanced at Rob and Snowy to see what they should do, but they were already following Yeti into the house and so she trotted after them. Yeti took their coats and directed them into a living room where she almost tripped over the dog equivalent of Yeti, a massive shaggy thing that was lying on the carpet. It was like something from the Christmas special of a nineties American sitcom, with decorations all over the room and a sofa and armchairs forming the centrepiece of a living room that Jen was sure would be described as a 'den' in North American speak. The air smelled of roast dinners and Jen clocked the turkey on the table. They'd arrived as dinner was about to be served, which made it feel less like a rescue mission and more like gatecrashing someone's family Christmas.

'Er, Rob,' she tried, but Rob was too busy telling Yeti a story about a group of arrogant skiers in the bar who challenged Kelly to a race, not realising that at one point she'd been on the cusp of being selected for the Aussie national squad.

A petite, dark-haired lady in her sixties handed Jen a glass of red wine. 'I'm Lori. Are you a friend of Art's?' she asked.

It was a simple enough question but Jen had no real idea how to respond.

'Yes,' Art said from where he'd come back into the room with them. He had a glass of wine in his own hand. Jen flushed at being described that way for the second time today. 'This is Jen. And you know Rob and Snowy.'

Rob took two lolloping strides over to where Lori was standing and enveloped her in an enormous hug. 'Lozza!' he shouted. 'It's been forever. How the hell are you?'

Lori looked delighted as she embraced him tightly back. 'I miss you noisy boys coming over to my house all the time.'

'That's my fault, Lori,' Art said quietly. An awkward silence fell, until Lori said, 'Oh, that's not what I meant, and anyway, you're here now. Shall we eat before all this food goes to waste?'

'I need you to tell me how you got that bird so bloody moist,' said Snowy, who was inspecting it on the table.

'If you're trying to have your dinner, we don't want to impose.' Jen shot a look at Rob who had already sat down at the table.

'You guys probably have plans,' Art said. Jen detected a note in his voice that she couldn't quite place. Not the distance that she'd got used to during their days ignoring each other, more a wistfulness. She gave him a quizzical look, but he looked away.

'Nah,' Rob said, peeling a piece of turkey skin back from the bird on the table and putting it into his mouth. 'Well, there's a load of people back at ours, but we can go back whenever we like. Snow's left strict instructions, haven't you?'

Snowy nodded. 'They'll be all right. This turkey's amazing, Lori.'

'Stop picking at it with your fingers,' she chided. 'Russell, can you help me fetch the rest of the food?'

'Russell?' Jen mouthed at Art.

Art shrugged. 'She's the only person who doesn't call him Yeti.'

Jen guessed they were staying. She remembered her dead phone. 'Is it all right if I plug my phone in?' she asked. It was too late to speak to her mum, who was staying at her sister's and no doubt exhausted from a day of helping to entertain her six- and four-year-old kids, but Jen wanted to at least text her. As the other person perennially without a partner at the festivities, she'd always taken on the responsibility of looking after her mum on Christmas Day, so she felt guilty for not being more attentive even as she'd felt relieved about getting to opt out and do her own thing this year. Well, until her 'own thing' had involved blindly following Mickey off the side of that slope. Jen fished her charger out of her bag and set it up in the corner of the room.

Extra places were set, Lori's spread covered the table and they all settled down to the sort of family Christmas dinner Jen had definitely not been expecting three thousand miles from home.

They were all groaning from their main course when Jen's phone trilled from its place on the carpet and she rushed over to it. Maybe Maxie was up. Working shifts meant her sleep patterns were all over the place and it may be that despite an early start to Christmas with Noah, she was now too wired to sleep.

She snatched it up, with the phone still attached to the charger. She didn't recognise the number on the screen but was relieved to note that while it was a local area code, it wasn't Eduardo or Platinum. She had *his* number saved under 'OH NO, NOT HIM'.

'Hello?'

'Is this Jennifer Clark?' a formal-sounding voice asked at the other end of the line.

'Yes, it is. Who's this?'

'This is the Whistler Police Department. We've had a report from a Mickey Austin that you're lost on the mountain. We're about to mount a search and rescue operation to come and find you.'

Chapter Twenty-nine

ART

Canucks from 8 tomorrow. You in?

Art's instinct was to say no.

Correction: his first instinct was to ignore the message completely, but it was five days after Christmas dinner at Yeti's, and an invitation to see his former friends no longer filled him with equal parts dread and fear.

But this wasn't just any invitation. It was an invitation to the annual New Year's Eve party at Canucks, which any member of the public could buy a ticket to – but because Rob and Snowy knew so many people, it always felt like their personal NYE bash. A hundred and fifty of their closest friends, a covers band and a night that set the party tone for the whole town. It was a lot.

Nothing like the intimate meal at Yeti and Lori's. That had been an entry-level way of seeing people again. Their house was – and always had been – a safe space, and Christmas dinner had been warm and low-key. Well, until Jen got called by the Police Department, anyway. After that, the gathering had dispersed. Art had spoken to the police on the phone, reassuring them that he'd accompanied her down the mountain himself, but shortly afterwards, she, Rob – of course – and Snowy had excused themselves. First to find Mickey and reassure him that she was safe, and then back to the Misfits meal. They'd invited him to come, but he didn't think he was ready to see Rob and Jen's ease around each other at Yeti's morph into any sort of PDA when they were back at his place and no longer on best-guest behaviour. Plus he'd found himself exhausted: from the drama of the day, from the heart-to-hearts he'd had and from the comfort he found from doing nothing but watching snowboarding videos at Yeti's house. He'd stayed over and slept for twelve hours straight, something he hadn't done for years.

He'd let himself think about Shauna as he'd drifted off, and instead of his memory leaping immediately to that final day, he'd let his mind wander to the parts of their relationship that he'd packed down tight. How she'd loved hot chocolate with Tia Maria in it; that her two favourite films were on opposite ends of the parental guidance spectrum, *The Terminator* and *Elf*; how she'd embraced YouTube as a place to post her snowboarding videos and how good they were. He wondered what she would have made of TikTok, and spent a bit of time inwardly debating whether she would have loved or loathed it as a platform for her work. He had let himself miss her, and his heart ached, but the memories didn't come laced with the same sharp prick of pain they once did, or a total shutdown of his mind against them.

The following morning, back at his own house, he'd let himself search for her videos on YouTube. He cried as he heard her funny, acerbic voiceover and saw the graphics she'd painstakingly edited. One, featuring the Misfits rather than her usual cast of championship hopefuls, was full of them larking about on the slopes, at one point showing a time-lapse video of them burying Snowy up to his neck on a day when twelve centimetres of fresh powder had dumped overnight.

He'd texted the link to Rob and Snowy. He couldn't think of the right message but hoped it conveyed something of what he wanted to say to them.

Snowy's almost immediate response said **The best day with the best people**. It opened up a fledgling line of communication and there had been a steady stream of messages between the three of them – in a WhatsApp group Snowy had christened 'RadsRadsRads' – ever since.

But he wasn't sure he was ready for a big party. Not with *everyone* he knew in Whistler there. Not to mention Jen – with Rob. Then again, he needed to face them some time. He could go for an hour, see how he felt.

He started to tap out a reply and then paused, deciding that first, he needed to send another message. One he needed to get out of the way. He pulled up his email, where there was a draft to Dr Maggie's office waiting.

Re: appointment

Dear Dr Maggie

I'm sure you are very busy, but I would like to enquire about any openings for appointments if you would be able to get back to me after the Christmas break.

Best wishes

Art Jenkins

His finger trembled only slightly as he hit 'send' and he mentally ticked it off his to-do list. He'd done today's small step and now he didn't have to think about it until her office reopened after New Year. Back to Snowy.

I might come for a couple. I'll see how I feel.

He hit 'send' again, and then, nervous that he'd sounded too much of a bummer, added a thanks.

His phone buzzed in his hand and he expected a confirmatory thumbs up from Snowy, but it was Dr Maggie.

My office only shut for a couple of days over the holidays, and due to clients travelling for the Christmas vacation, I have openings for an introductory session this week – this afternoon if it suits, at either 2 p.m. or 3 p.m. Do let me know.

Warmest,
Maggie

Art fought once again against the impulse to pretend he'd never even seen the message. He wasn't mentally prepared for this *now;* he'd thought he had at least a few days before he got a response and then perhaps even a couple of weeks before he had to go and see anyone.

Do it, Art, he urged himself. And quickly, before he bottled it completely.

This afternoon would be fine. I'll see you at 2 p.m.

He sent it before he could reconsider. Torrential rain had cancelled his lessons for the day, so he just had to fill the time until then. He was too antsy to settle on a book or TV show. Instead, he got out the extensive collection of snowboards he'd accumulated over the years, and decided he was going to wax them all.

The rain kept falling all day, along with a freezing wind that made it feel as though water was permeating every pore. Art's legs felt heavy as he stepped out of his truck at the address he'd been given, a large, wooden detached house on timber supports that was about as far removed from a doctor's office as you could get. There was a balcony on the first floor, crowded with outdoor patio furniture and plants, and it was decked out with Christmas lights. A large, twinkling Santa hoisted his sack onto his shoulder above the front door.

His was the only vehicle on the drive but he still dreaded running into another – Art didn't know what you'd call them. Patients? Counsellees? Fellow fuck-ups? – as he approached the door. He could just go. He didn't have to go through with it. He'd pushed everything deep inside for this long, what was a bit longer?

I don't want my life to be defined by sadness, he thought. It would be if he kept fighting moments like this.

So, what did he want his life to be defined by?

The last few weeks, since he'd met Jen, had been a glimpse into a life he *could* have. One where he had Yeti and the Misfits in his life. Not the life he'd envisaged as a hungry-for-success, snowboard-mad teenager, but one that still contained people he cared about. People who cared about him. People like Jen. The memory of Jen getting stuck on the mountain still made his body prickle with fear, but through it she had inadvertently helped him reconnect with his friends, and he was grateful to her for that. For the first time, he considered that moving on didn't have to mean forgetting, so much as recalibrating.

She might never know that she'd had a part in getting him to this spot. Perhaps one day, when he was closer to fixed on Yeti's spectrum, he might tell her.

Art fiddled with his car keys, jumped over a large puddle that had formed at the steps, then took a deep breath and mounted the first step to Maggie's front door.

Chapter Thirty

JEN

'Happy New Year!' Mr and Mrs Moss, who were staying in Suite Ten, called to Jen as they left the Platinum floor in their black-tie finery. They were off to an exclusive dinner being held at the Michelin-starred restaurant at the top of Whistler Mountain, which their friends had hired out in its entirety. They would be seeing in the New Year from the uppermost point in Whistler, marked by a firework display against the backdrop of the inky horizon.

'Happy New Year,' Jen called back from her spot behind the desk. She surreptitiously pulled her phone out of her pocket to steal a look at her messages. Snowy had texted again, an hour after the last time.

> You ARE coming tonight, right?

She checked the time, resisted the urge to huff impatiently and tapped out a reply.

> YES! Being held captive at work but I finish in 20 mins so have a beer waiting for me in 45.

She got a stream of thumbs ups from Snowy in return. At least that's what she thought it was. Emojis didn't really translate on her flip phone, so it appeared as a series of special characters that she squinted to decipher.

'Far be it from me to interrupt, Jennifer,' Eduardo said, pausing afterwards for effect. If the menacing emphasis on her name hadn't sent a jolt of fear through her, then the foreboding look on his face would have done the job. 'But could you please refrain from using your phone and get on with your job?'

'I'm only using it to tell my friends that I'll be late this evening,' she responded, for once forgetting to bite her tongue. But she was fed up. 'I've stayed two hours over my usual shift finish time today.'

'How many times.' Eduardo rubbed his temple as though she was a small child who was testing his patience by refusing to learn a simple point. 'We don't think of our time here as a shift.'

'Right.' She certainly wasn't getting paid enough to think of it as a calling, but now wasn't the time to point that out if she ever wanted to leave and get to the New Year's party at Canucks that Snowy had assured her was the best night of the season. She settled for something less inflammatory. 'It's only good manners for me to let them know where I am, plus I don't want them to worry about my safety, so I thought under the circumstances you could make an exception about the phone rule.'

Eduardo sniffed. Which she interpreted as him having no plans of his own for tonight. If he were one modicum nicer, she would ask him how his Christmas had been, but he wasn't, and so she didn't. Instead her memory reached for something cosier and settled on Christmas Day at Yeti and Lori's. With Art. He'd been relaxed at dinner, and every time he broke out one of those hard-earned smiles her heart had thudded. She was glad they'd seemed to have made up, even if the catalyst for it had been her stupidly going up the mountain during a blizzard. Following him to Yeti's felt like the right thing to do as soon as they arrived, although maybe there was a part of Art that had been upset they'd gatecrashed his dinner, because he'd been a little stand-offish with her and Rob. Not with Snowy though. No one could be stand-offish with Snowy, his personality simply didn't allow any room for it.

She'd heard Snowy mention the New Year's Eve party as they'd left Yeti's on Christmas Day but Art's reply had been non-commital. Since then, she hadn't wanted to ask Snowy if he was coming and she'd felt too uncomfortable to ask Art herself. Because, well, her giant crush was still in place. More so, since he'd heroically shown up exactly when she'd needed him. A flick book of images – his intense eyes, his slightly sulky mouth, the disarming smile that lit up his face when something surprised or delighted him – sped through her mind. Meanwhile he . . . tolerated her? Thought she was an idiot who couldn't stop getting herself into trouble? The only plus was that it meant there was no risk of breaking her vow to Maxie, which was ten weeks old and still going strong – the longest she'd gone without actively trying to change her relationship status.

Even so, the prospect of him being there set off an internal turbulence.

'You should probably get that phone out again, Jennifer.' Eduardo snipped through her thoughts. 'I'm actually going to need you to work a double shift.'

'What? No! I can't.' The words were out of her mouth before she realised how grumpy she sounded, but she couldn't help it. The tight bun she'd pulled her hair into to abide by Eduardo's strict dress code wasn't helping either. It was making her head ache. 'I've been here for twelve hours already and I have the night off. I have *plans*.'

Eduardo wasn't listening. He was frowning at the screen in front of him and muttering. 'I'll just extend all of your hours so you're doing split shifts until the end of the week, and have someone in place for next weekend.' He looked up, seeming to notice Jen was still there.

'Claudia has just quit,' he said as though that explained everything.

'Claudia does nights,' Jen replied reasonably. Then, her suspicion tingling, she added, 'Why did she quit?'

Eduardo ignored her.

'It's not feasible for me to do both earlies and nights in succession,' she told him, her voice still even.

'I'm not asking you to do that,' Eduardo snapped. He patted his hair to put a non-existent stray hair back in place. It didn't move. 'Just stay until I can get Gregory to come in early. I'm sure I can have him here by ten.'

Ten was in three more hours. Jen was already dead on her feet, having not had a day off since before Christmas and having worked overtime on every shift. She'd been looking forward to tonight all week. Since Christmas. Since the last time she had seen Art. Even if there was only a slim chance he'd be there, it was the only chance she had. But Snowy had told her they stopped letting people into the bar at around eight o'clock because Canucks was at capacity by then.

'You know I'm always willing to help out, but tonight I really cannot stay,' she said firmly, before ruining her moment of empowerment by adding, 'I'm sorry.'

Eduardo's eyes flicked up from the screen. 'Are you telling me you can't?' he asked lightly. He looked down again. 'Or won't?'

Jen's heart drummed nervously. 'Can't. Obviously,' she stuttered, as though she was the one in the wrong, for invoking her right to leave work when her working day had finished. 'I really have to go. It's important.'

'Important,' he mimicked. 'I assume that means you have a party to go to.'

She resisted the incitement to explain any further. She refused to be made to feel responsible for a corporation's staffing issue. She earned minimum wage for God's sake, it was not her problem. Not that she could ever have said that to Eduardo.

'I can't work a double,' she said instead.

'I see.' Eduardo's face was expressionless, dead. Which was worse than one of his bollockings-slash-lectures. Who knew how the punishment would manifest if it was served up cold rather than in the moment? She had visions of being made to clean around the claw feet of the rooms' baths again, like when he'd decided that housekeeping weren't doing a good enough job.

'I can stay for another half an hour though, and help see if anyone else wants to pick up an extra shift.' On New Year's Eve, at short notice, when they didn't even pay double time, Jen thought, but Eduardo had a way of making you feel as though you owed him.

Eduardo still didn't look at her, but his tone implied that what happened next was very much her problem. 'In that case, you'd better start ringing around.'

Chapter Thirty-one

ART

Art felt a fluttering of nerves as he opened the door to Canucks, feeling even more anxious than he had before his appointment with Dr Maggie. It was hard to tell how it had gone. She had explained her type of therapy to him and then he'd talked haltingly about why he'd sought her out to begin with. There hadn't been time for much more, and he'd left feeling itchy beneath his skin from emotions churned up but not resolved. She'd explained that might happen and that he was supposed to 'sit with his feelings', which he'd tried for about half an hour. Then he'd grabbed his keys and driven to Yeti's to help analyse some video footage of one of his team members. Art decided that in itself was progress, even if he now knew the constant need to be in motion was a 'pattern', one he and Dr Maggie would need to address when he came back for his weekly appointments.

In Canucks, voices and laughter mingled with the rock soundtrack. It was 8 p.m. and busy. Nothing and everything had changed since the last time Art had spent New Year here. Most of the customers were still in their ski gear, having arrived when the lifts had closed, and were now in for the New Year's Eve duration. Rob was serving behind the bar, tanned arms sticking out of a white Ramones T-shirt, his hair flopping around as he turned his head to joke with the customers as they ordered. Even the same cover band were playing a Mötley Crüe song, their long hair a little thinner and their faces four years craggier, but still rocking.

If Rob was surprised to see him, he didn't show it. 'What can I get you?' he called while simultaneously mixing a cocktail and grabbing some napkins for a man who'd sent his beer bottle skittering across the bar. He was in his element here, always had been.

'Non-alcoholic beer,' Art replied. He knew something stronger would dull the night's sharp edges, but right now it was more important that he knew he could get in his truck and leave at any time.

Rob handed him a bottle and jutted his chin towards the other end of the bar. 'They're all over there. Nah,' he said, refusing the card that Art proffered. 'It's on me.'

'Thanks.' He fumbled to get the card back into his wallet.

Across the bar, he caught sight of Darren and Kelly, plus Snowy in his chef's trousers. Snowy took a sneaky sip from Darren's drink before passing Art on his way back to the kitchen.

'Good to see you, mate,' he said, his face flushed with sweat and, most likely, from several more cheeky sips from people's drinks between kitchen rushes. Snowy had been working at Canucks for as long as Rob had, and his cooking skills far surpassed the burgers and onion rings the job required. He could do it on autopilot, or, as he was demonstrating tonight, half cut. Art made his way through the crowded pub self-consciously, not wanting to make eye contact with too many people. He reached the corner where three tables had been shoved together, and the assembled Misfits greeted him, betraying no flicker of the emotion he was dreading.

As Clyde contemplated his empty glass, he reached forward across the table for a half-full pitcher of a lurid-looking cocktail that had lumps of fruit floating in it. It revealed Jen sitting beyond him. She couldn't have been there long, as her hair, which had a big kink in it as though she'd just pulled it out of a ponytail, was soggy from the rain that had been lashing down for two days now. Her eyes seemed to shine in her face, with the spray of freckles along the top of her cheeks and nose visible where her Platinum-level make-up had been rained off. Art knew she hated the level of maintenance the Platinum look required; she'd complained about how much time she'd had to start spending on make-up during one of the lessons with Newton. She always looked flawless, but he liked seeing the unfiltered Jen beneath. The Jen sitting there with wet hair and in jeans, a jumper and DMs. The Jen who wasn't making as little noise as possible to stop uptight Eduardo being annoyed, and instead was loudly ribbing Darren about something.

As she saw him, she smiled, and the atoms of the room seemed to shift. He was painfully aware of her *right there* and that this was exactly the sort of feeling he didn't want to sit with. He'd assumed she'd be here and thought he'd prepared himself for it; for seeing her and for the inevitable midnight kiss that she and Rob would share. That was half the reason he'd driven here, so he could bail well before people started getting sentimental and tactile.

'Hi,' she called above the band playing.

'Can't drink this shit,' Clyde said, grimacing as he took a swallow of the cocktail. 'I'll get Rob to bring over some more beers. Is that Cally? CALLY!' he bellowed, getting up and gesturing for Art to take his seat in one fluid movement. The faint smell of weed trailed after him as he passed by.

'Sit down,' said Jen, patting the seat beside her. 'How are you?' He sat next to her, getting a whiff of the smell he'd come to associate with her: the room spray they used on Platinum filtered through her own Jen-aroma. He couldn't identify what that was, but it always made him think of rosy cheeks. His heart thumped. The stuffy room started to feel too hot and he pulled his hoodie over his head.

'Yeah. I mean, fine, yeah.' The power of conversation had deserted him and he racked his brain for something to say. 'When Rob gets off shift, I'll obviously, you know, budge up.'

Jen was halfway through taking a sip of her drink and she stopped. Her grey eyes crinkled, puzzled. 'Why?'

'So you can sit together.'

He couldn't work out if the look on her face was surprise or horror, but as it dawned on her what he meant, it was obvious he'd got it wrong.

'Me? And Rob?' She laughed before repeating it with a WTF shriek. 'As in, me *and* Rob?'

Art nodded. A little electrical current pulsed through him, his nerves on high alert. It was a feeling he didn't have the word for, until at once he did: hope. 'I thought you guys were—'

Jen was shaking her head vigorously. 'Don't get me wrong I like him, but not like *that*. We're not together. *SO* not together. And have never, you know . . .' She gave a self-conscious laugh. 'I'm not with anyone right now. Wait, is that why you—' She stopped and looked down at her lap as though deciding whether to continue. 'I'm single right now, very much on purpose. I made a pact with myself before I came here. And also to my best friend Maxie. Not because she's the boss of me,' she added quickly, 'but because I had a habit of drifting into relationships with people I didn't know I wanted to be in relationships with, and then sticking with them despite a whole slalom-load of red flags. Guys like Rob. No offence to him,' she added quickly.

'A pact?' Art was confused. And intrigued. And yes, disappointed. His role as Jen's friend had been confirmed when he'd barely even acknowledged that anything more was possible or desirable. 'What sort of pact?'

Jen winced and took a sip of her drink while she weighed up whether to continue. 'I promised to stay single for six months, or in Whistler terms, for the entire snowboarding season, as a sort of finding myself, palate-cleansing exercise.' She scrunched up her face. 'I'm explaining this badly, aren't I? Like I'm some loser who'll go out with anyone. Which is not entirely wrong. I kept going for guys who weren't right for me, so I decided not to go for anyone for a while so I could figure out who *was* right for me. Does that make sense?'

Art was still trying to process all the information. She wasn't with Rob, and Rob wasn't her type anyway. Or he was, but she wanted to change that. 'Why did you keep going for the wrong sort of guys?' he asked in the end.

Jen gave a self-deprecating smile. 'Well, that's the big question, isn't it? Maxie's theory is that it's because my dad left, and somewhere deep down I've always been trying to prove I can stop other men from leaving. And because somewhere along the way, that particular neurosis got conflated with the idea that I needed a relationship to complete me.'

'And what do *you* think?' It felt good to be having an honest conversation. It had been too long since he'd been open or curious about anything.

'That no relationship will complete me, and a good relationship will simply complement who I am already.' The way she was talking made her sound like she'd got it all figured out, but the angst-ridden look on her face suggested otherwise. She threw up her hands. 'Which I *do* know. Always did, kind of. I just couldn't seem to stop myself being subsumed by whoever I was seeing at the time, through fear they'd dump me. It was hard to stop thinking that I needed the validation of having a boyfriend. So I flew thousands of miles to work out how to stop doing it and to be happy on my own. Oh, and to learn how to snowboard, of course.'

'And how's it going? The pact, I mean.'

'I'm hanging in there. Mostly.' Jen laughed again and reddened in embarrassment. 'I think it's doing me good. It's been weird but good to do things on my own terms and without constantly taking someone else's needs into account. It's so annoying that Maxie was right. God, if you didn't think I was a loser before, you definitely do now.'

'I don't actually.' Art smiled back. It was true. 'I think I understand completely, because I'm trying to learn how to be on my own too.'

Jen's hand flew to her mouth. 'I'm sorry. I didn't mean to compare my sad little love life to what happened to you.'

'Jen,' he stopped her. 'It's fine.' It really was. It actually gave him weird comfort to know that someone else was wrangling with being alone, albeit in a different way. 'It's not sad to work out what makes you happy.' He took a deep breath. Her nearness was so distracting that a little spear of guilt jolted through him, but he pushed through, remembered Yeti's words. 'I should also tell you that you coming here on your own – whatever the reason or pact – helped me see that changing things can be positive.'

Jen's voice dropped, making it hard to hear her above the music, but Art wanted to know what she was going to say next. He leaned a little closer towards her, so that his ear was so close to her mouth he could feel little puffs of breath as she spoke. The sensation of it was like a little vibration starting at his cheek and drifting softly across his face. It felt as though it was just her and him in the room. 'I know you don't like to talk about . . . what happened.

But for what it's worth, I don't think it's sad to miss someone who made you happy, or to struggle to get over it.'

'No, not sad,' Art agreed, pulling up his face to meet hers. 'But it's not healthy to fixate on it for so long that you can't move on, either.' He caught the puzzled look on Jen's face. 'I started therapy yesterday.' He cleared his throat and looked away. 'I didn't anticipate telling anyone that.'

'One therapy session and you can't stop sharing,' she teased. 'What have you done with that grumpy guy I almost took out on the slopes a few weeks ago?'

'He's still in here, don't worry,' Art replied, joking right back. His tone turned solemn. 'But about that. I should have apologised to you a while ago for being a prize dickhead.'

Jen's eyes grew wide in mock disbelief. 'Are you apologising to me? *You*, who are right about *everything*?'

He nudged his chair into hers in response. 'I guess I am,' he said with a smile. 'Apologising, that is. Not right about everything.'

'You had your reasons to be like that,' she said, smiling right back. It was affectionate, instead of the pitying look he expected when anyone referred to what had happened. 'Besides, you were right about the safety stuff. I *should* have known better.'

'That's not what I'm apologising for. I *was* right about that.' He grinned cheekily to show he was kidding. 'It's for those days we spent together doing lessons. Afterwards I cut you off dead. It was nothing to do with you and completely to do with me, but I knew I was making you feel bad. That was out of order in itself, but now I know why you came here, it's even worse. I should have been applauding you for finding your independence, rather than making you doubt your decision. It takes guts to try something new. I mean, look at me, stuck in the same patterns for four years because I was too scared to do anything about it.'

Jen blushed. Damp tendrils of hair were drying fluffily around her face. 'I did think you were a prick when I first met you,' she admitted, leaning in again to be heard above a drum solo. 'I thought you were an arrogant know-it-all, but I had no idea why you kept your distance from people. Plus, you *were* right to think I was an idiot for going snowboarding with no experience.' She hid her face in her hands. 'And then, like, a week ago I did it *again.* So, to be fair, the first impression you got of me was the right one.'

'I don't think you're an idiot now though,' he said. He chanced another joke. 'Or maybe I don't think you're *just* an idiot.'

So where does that leave us?' Jen said lightly, looking up at him through her eyelashes.

The moment was loaded. Their eye contact lingered and there was a crackle in the air between them. They were so close to each other. His gaze trailed down to her mouth. He was all too aware that her lips were centimetres from his face. He wondered what it would be like to run his hands through her damp hair and then kiss her. But Art forced himself to look away, and he stuck out a hand as though to shake on it.

'I guess it makes us friends.'

Chapter Thirty-two

JEN

She reached for Art's outstretched hand and shook it. She wondered if he felt the same electric charge that she did when their hands touched. His skin was warm and soft and she noticed the muscles in his arms tighten, a heat rising across her body. She'd never seen his bare arms before tonight. He always had his snow-boarding layers on when he came to the hotel or was out on the slopes. Bulky coats, baggy trousers and oversized sweatshirts. And he'd had a jumper on at Yeti's. While she knew from his job that he was solid and athletic, she'd never actually seen any *skin*. Or muscle. The thickness of his upper arms led her naturally to meditate on the probability of broad shoulders and solid legs.

Friends.

That was . . . fine. She'd just told him she was truly and happily single, so as far as he was concerned, she wasn't available for anything more anyway. And neither was he. She was staying single, he was staying single, and the only relationships they were committed to were ones with themselves. For once, she recognised a dead end when she saw one. Maxie would be proud. Even if something inside her withered.

Jen's phone buzzed in her pocket and she pulled it out.

'Not the police again, is it?' Art joked. The lazy, handsome curve of a smile. The sight of it made her physically thrum. Maybe it was easier when they weren't speaking. Less to be hopeful about.

She looked at the screen and put the phone face down.

'Your ex?' he asked. His jaw was set. If they hadn't just agreed to be friends – *just* friends – she'd think he was a little bit jealous.

'Neither,' she replied. 'It's even worse than my dating back catalogue. It's Eduardo.'

'Oh. He's not calling to wish you a happy new year, I'm guessing.'

She groaned and took a defiant swig of her drink. 'He was trying to make me work a double shift tonight, because Platinum's short-staffed. But I just don't want to. I'm always working and tonight I wanted to come out, have some fun, and see everyone.' See *you*, she didn't say. She punctuated the thought with a yawn. 'I'm exhausted. I've been doing fourteen-hour days during the busiest time of the year and haven't got a day off for another week. I'm supposed to be back there at 5 a.m. tomorrow.'

'I'm not even sure it's legal for him to make you work that many hours with no days off.'

Jen pulled a face. 'I'm not sure Eduardo "does" staff wellbeing.' Her phone started vibrating again and she flipped it over. 'It's him again.'

Art gave her a sympathetic smile that turned into a chuckle. 'Oh no, not him,' he said, pointing at the screen and the name she had Eduardo saved under.

Jen shrugged. '"Do not answer" unfortunately isn't an option most of the time, so this is the alternative. Go *away*,' she said to the phone. 'I'm off the clock. *For once*. If I pick up, he'll talk at me until I agree to do what he wants. I've seen him do it to other staff members relentlessly. The other week, Eva was visiting her grandmother in hospital and she had thirty-five missed calls from him when she came out. All because he wanted her to change her day off to accommodate some late check-outs.'

'You could switch it off,' Art suggested.

'Yeah,' she agreed. 'But I want to text Maxie and my mum at midnight, and honestly the thought of the voice-mails he'll leave just makes me anxious for when I turn it back on.' She sighed. 'Maybe I should answer.'

'No!' Art picked up the phone. It was ringing for the third time in as many minutes.

'Jen's phone, Art speaking,' he called above the sound of the music. He glanced at Jen as he spoke, his eyelashes flicking up and down in the barest of winks.

'What are you do—?' she started to ask before his voice cut her off.

'Oh, hi Eduardo. The music? It's in my truck. I *love* rock music, didn't you know that about me? I'm just driving Jen back to her apartment from the doctor's and she can't come to the phone. Yes, the doctor's, can you believe it?' Art pressed his lips together as he listened to Eduardo's response, ignoring the alarm on Jen's face as she mouthed, 'What is happening?'

'No, nothing serious – thankfully,' he continued, 'a touch of nervous exhaustion apparently.' Another pause. 'I know, so weird, right? But that's what the doctor said. She needs to rest, which is why I'm answering.' Art's solemn voice was completely at odds with the look of suppressed mirth on his face, and the shared look that told her they were in cahoots fizzed between them. Jen was half anxious, half elated, about what would happen next. She peered around the bar, where the noise and activity were at such a level that there was no way Eduardo could believe him. But he also couldn't force her to come into work when she wasn't rota-d on if she was sick.

'I just hope she's well enough to come to work tomorrow morning. She was so upset thinking she might have to call in sick. The doctor was ready to write her a sick note there and then, but she was determined to rest tonight and make every effort to be back in tomorrow.'

'Overkill,' Jen mouthed. What was he *doing*? He shook his head at her mischievously.

'I *will* tell *Jennifer* –' his eyes flicked up – 'that. Thanks Eduardo.' He went to pull the phone from his ear and stopped. 'Oh, and Happy New Year. I'll be there to pick up for lessons in a couple of days.'

He hung up and burst into laughter.

'What happened? What did he say?' she said quickly. She knew there wasn't anything Eduardo could technically do to her, and if she was ill when she wasn't at work that was her business. But she still felt the icy pinch of his fingers around her freedom.

'He said he was sorry to hear you weren't feeling well, and then passed on the world's least sincere "get well soon".'

'He'll give me hell tomorrow for this,' Jen groaned.

'Jen, you *are* exhausted, and he has no right to try and force you to work so much overtime. You just told me you're here to start living for yourself. So put it into practice!'

'You're right, but it doesn't feel that way.' She checked the time. 'He has a way of getting you to see everything from his perspective.'

'He is awful,' Art agreed. 'I was there when Cara first started. She called him Ed once. You can imagine how that went down.'

Jen laughed. 'Exactly.' She groaned. 'Urgh, I'll be back there in less than nine hours, and I actually could do with some sleep. I'll stay until midnight and then head home to bed,' she resolved.

At the mention of bed, she instinctively looked at Art and found herself locking eyes with him again. They both looked quickly away, which was even worse. Around the table, Clyde had pulled Kelly onto his lap and they were now giving the bar a full-on PDA. Jen pretended she couldn't even see them. She and Art looked back to each other.

'I don't want to leave too late either,' he said eventually. 'I'll give you a lift. But before that, don't let Eduardo ruin the night. Promise me you'll forget about him and Platinum until next year.'

'Promise,' she agreed.

With Art looking at her, she didn't think forgetting about Eduardo would be a problem, although it raised a whole new set of feelings that were more complicated. She couldn't just sit here with him, glancing at those quiver-inducing arms and torturing herself about what couldn't be.

The band finished their first set and a rock song she didn't recognise blared out from the speakers in their place. 'If we're here for the duration, the first thing we need to do is request some different music,' she said.

'Jukebox?' Art suggested, pointing to the other side of the bar.

Jen didn't need asking twice and jumped up. She needed the distraction. Taking one last look at her phone, now mercifully silent, she shoved it in her pocket, along with the worry about how Eduardo would treat her in the morning, and led Art to the jukebox.

Chapter Thirty-three

ART

'Is there anything on this jukebox that was released after 2005?' Jen asked, flipping through the CD books within. Music mingled with laughter and boomeranged around the bar.

'Not if Rob has been in charge of maintaining it,' Art replied. 'He might make an exception if the Black Crowes release some new material, but otherwise his priority is keeping Aerosmith in royalties.' As if the machine could hear him, 'Walk This Way' burst out of the speakers.

'Bruce Springsteen, Bon Jovi and the Rolling Stones it is,' Jen muttered, scrunching her face up slightly as she pressed the buttons to make her selections. It would be so easy to put his hand on hers and see where the night went. Art was hit with a wave of regret, ricocheting off the moment earlier when he'd – reluctantly – suggested they consider each other as friends. But it was the right thing to do, he knew it. He was at the very beginning of his sessions with Dr Maggie, a tentative emergence from an emotional deep freeze, but he was still – in his mind – completely messed up. And from what Jen had told him this evening, the last thing she needed was another relationship that was destined to go nowhere or an unavailable man messing her around, expecting her to fold herself into his life while he 'figured himself out'.

He had to resist the pull he had towards her. But the proximity wasn't helping. She kept brushing against him as she punched in the song codes and shimmied along to the track playing. Metallica had never seemed so seductive.

'Air hockey?' he suggested. That was safe. It was a non-contact game with a metre and a half of table separating the players. 'There's a table over there.' He craned over people's heads. 'And it's free right now. Quick.' He darted through the crush of people. The bar was getting busier and busier with every minute, and the door staff would soon have to stop letting people in. He reached the table a second before another group tried to claim it, and slapped two twenty-dollar bills on the side of it.

'Is that betting money?' Jen called, emerging from the crowd behind him. 'Are you trying to hustle me at air hockey?' Her face had a tipsy, high-spirited glow.

Stop noticing.

He forced out a hearty laugh. 'No, just holding the table for us.'

'How many games will that buy? It's enough for a whole tournament.'

'Good idea, we should make it best of ten or something.' Socialising was easier and less intimate when done around an activity. Especially an activity that involved concentration to achieve the requisite hand-to-eye coordination. That in turn would stop his mind returning to the thought of pulling Jen onto his lap the way Clyde had done to Kelly. And how the thought of that made him feel.

As Jen inserted the cash into the table, Darren happened to be walking back from the bar, laden down with a new pitcher of beer and some glasses. An even better idea: why not make it a group tournament. 'Air hockey?' said Art, catching his attention. 'Winner stays on and we rotate through whoever wants to play.'

'Yessss,' Darren replied. 'Let me round up the troops.'

Before long, there were eight of them, and between the booze-fuelled competitive spirit, and the overwhelming Australian-ness of most of the players, it soon escalated into heats, with new rules like time-trials and forfeits added in. As the hair-rock band launched into their next set, Art realised he wasn't just distracting himself from the energy between himself and Jen. He was having a good time, and catching up between games with people he hadn't spoken to for years. But he had to admit, the boisterous group atmosphere did also nudge them back from the brink, which was the aim. He and Jen were back to being part of a crowd, rather than feeling like the only people in the room, which was safer all round. Plus, Jen had turned out to be so good at air hockey that she was almost constantly the winner staying on the table.

'Er, who's hustling who now?' he said, grinning as she beat him 5-0 for the second time.

'I worked in the students' union at uni,' she said, 'so I had a lot of practice. I'm better at air hockey than I am at snowboarding, put it that way.'

'Snowboarding's the same as air hockey,' he replied lightly. 'You just need practice. Oh, and you shouldn't do it alone.' He gave her a meaningful look. 'Which I think you've learned, right?'

She saluted at him. She'd been drinking her beers slowly but was still a little wobbly on her feet.

'Are we playing or what?' shouted Clyde, stepping up to the table to face her. He had been drinking steadily all night but was his usual playful self. Art didn't know if it was a good or a bad thing that he could put so much away without it seeming to affect him. 'This time, each time a goal's conceded, the loser does a shot,' Clyde announced. 'Will you go to the bar while we play?' he asked Kelly, who was chatting to someone next to the table.

She nodded and started canvassing for orders.

'Hey stranger,' she said as she reached Art. She leaned in for a hug. Art remembered she managed the village's ice cream parlour as the sweet waft of vanilla enveloped him along with her embrace. It was like greeting someone from long ago, welcome but somehow bittersweet. The tears were in his eyes before he knew was happening. He clenched his jaw to stop them spilling. 'What are you having?' Kelly asked, either not noticing or being too diplomatic to say.

Art held up his empty non-alcoholic beer bottle. 'Another one of these, please.'

Kelly held up hers. 'Snap.'

'You're off the booze too?' Art was surprised. Kelly used to love to party as much as Clyde did.

Kelly screwed up her mouth in a way that showed she was bursting with a secret. 'We weren't going to tell anyone for a couple more weeks, but you're not exactly a blabbermouth.' She patted her stomach over her hoodie. 'Me and Clyde thought we might as well get on with having some kids.'

'God,' he said, before correcting himself. 'Congratulations!' Clyde and Kelly were both in their early thirties so there was no reason why they wouldn't start having children, but even so. A wave of something hit him, either envy or realisation. While he was trying to hold life back, everyone else was getting on with living it. He'd barely had time to recover when Kelly added, 'Did you know that Snowy's moving to Vancouver?'

'What?'

'Yeah, he's got a job in some Michelin-starred restaurant, although it's a trainee-type role for now. He decided he wanted to make a proper go of becoming a chef.'

'Wow,' Art said again. These were all normal things that people were doing – new jobs, having babies – but each bit of news still hit him like a slap. He wasn't reintegrating himself into life as it was four years ago, he was reintegrating into what life was now. Everyone and everything had moved on.

A howl of defeat came from Clyde's side of the air hockey table and Kelly smiled while rolling her eyes. 'I'll get those shots because it sounds like *the loser* will be needing them.' She turned around and blew a kiss at Clyde, who didn't look too sad to be forced into drinking more booze.

Jen gave Art a victorious two thumbs up and he felt a buzz as she singled him out from the crowd. The temperature inside Canucks had risen along with the number of bodies in the room, but it wasn't that that made him feel a warm glow. He was enjoying seeing her confident and competitive side. 'Who's next?' she called out to the group.

'ME!' bellowed Snowy, rushing out from the kitchen and undoing his apron. 'The food's finished and the kitchen's closed, so I can finally give Jen an opponent worth facing.'

'Congrats on the job,' Art called as he went past. 'Really happy for you.'

'Thanks. I'll still be able to come up here on weekends. Well, the weekends I get, which won't be at the actual weekend because I'll be working on Friday and Saturday nights now I've decided to pursue "a career".' Art could tell the grumbling was good-natured because Snowy looked pleased.

'I'll have to come in and sample the food after you start. Jen, you know about five-star establishments, do you fancy going to dinner at Snowy's posh new restaurant in Vancouver?' The question was out before Art realised the implication. By the way Jen reddened, she clearly didn't know how to take it. 'Mates have got to support mates, right?' Art added, only drawing more attention to it.

'That's right,' Jen said, fiddling with her air hockey paddle. She smiled, showing she was taking the whole thing as a joke. 'But before that, let me beat Snowy at air hockey. I've finally found something I'm better at than all of you and I intend to rub your faces in it!'

The contenders ran out before Jen's winning streak did, whereby Clyde presented her with a glass of fizz. 'It's real champagne, ask Rob,' he said.

She held it aloft like a trophy before taking a sip. Just then, the band drew out the ending to their final song with a blizzard of guitar solos that bled into an extended drum riff.

'We've been the Wig Factory and I'm here to tell you the bar is now shut for fifteen minutes because it's time to see in the New Year,' the lead singer bellowed over the sound.

The people lucky enough to get served before the announcement raced back to their tables with their drinks, while others followed empty-handed. Rob and the other bar staff jumped onto the counter and joined in as the band started the countdown.

'. . . THREE, TWO, ONE.'

There was an almighty crash of cymbals and the bar erupted with 'HAPPY NEW YEAR' as a heavy metal approximation of 'Auld Lang Syne' started up. Around the air hockey table, Clyde shouted, 'WE'RE HAVING A BABY THIS YEAR' and picked up Kelly. He had an enormous smile on his face.

'So much for not telling anyone yet!' she screamed as he spun her around. She looked just as happy. Snowy grabbed hold of them with a whoop and soon a drunken mass of them were in a big sweaty group hug. Even Rob, who'd seen the commotion from his perch on the bar, jumped down to join in, dragging Jen with him along the way.

'Come on!' Snowy shouted over his shoulder to Art. He found himself clamped between Darren and Rob and they all swayed there together, his nostrils overwhelmed with the smell of booze. As he looked up, Jen was a couple of people away from him. They caught each other's eyes as they belted out 'Auld Lang Syne' and he felt that jolt again, one that even Darren's tuneless singing could do nothing to dissipate. She smiled and nodded at him, as he wished desperately that it was her he had his arms around.

'Right, I'm going to be sick,' shouted Clyde from the middle, and the group hastily dispersed.

'It's good to have you back,' Rob told Art as they broke away from each other. 'We missed you.' For the second time that night, Art felt his eyes brimming with tears. He fought the urge to pretend he hadn't heard. 'I missed you all too,' he said, realising as he did that he meant it.

People drifted back to the bar or to the table or, in Rob's case, back behind the bar. Soon it was just Art and Jen standing next to each other.

'Happy New Year,' she said to him. She was awkwardly rocking on her heels. 'I was going to give you a hug, but I—' She broke off without finishing the sentence.

What could be more normal – more platonic, even – than a friendly hug on New Year's Eve? It was weirder not to. He wanted to hug her. Very much. Too much. She was about a metre away from him, so he shuffled a little closer, until he was right in front of her.

'I'm quite sweaty from how hot it is in here,' Jen murmured as he slowly, gently reached his arms over her shoulders intending to give her the briefest, most companionable of hugs.

Jen's arms reached tentatively around his waist. She *was* a bit sweaty, but not unpleasantly so. Then again, so was he. His body warmed up where she placed her hands on his back, not just from her body heat but from how it felt at that moment. Art instinctively pulled her closer. She pressed her cheek into where it reached to the top of his shoulder. He'd had more physical contact with people tonight than he had in years, but none of the sociable hugs or compassionate arm squeezes had done this to him. It felt electrifying. It felt terrifying. It felt *right.*

Art wanted both to pull away and to never pull away. He forced himself to sit with the opposing feelings as the band launched into another extended guitar solo and the whole time, he kept his arms around her. The noise in the bar seemed to still around them.

Jen had told him she was staying single until the end of the season so she'd be ready for something real. She was sick of being messed around and strung along.

He'd told her he needed to figure out life on his own.

They would both get hurt if this became more than a hug. At the very least, it would destroy the nascent friendship growing between them. It was the wrong time. He felt Jen shift her weight slightly, peeling her face from his shoulder. He sensed her angle her chin up so that now her mouth was *right* there, grazing his cheek. Repositioning his own face by millimetres would bring his lips to hers.

He burned with the want of it: something so simple, so basic as heat between them.

He felt like he used to in the moment before he began his descent down a half pipe on the mountain. The point where you had to ignore how irrational it was to throw yourself down a tube made of sheet ice and simply trust that not only would you make it to the bottom intact, but that when you got there you would feel more elated than you had in your life.

Every atom of his body screamed *yes*. He was on the brink.

But his head told him a resounding *no*.

He couldn't promise her anything, the things she deserved. If he cared about her at all, he couldn't – wouldn't – let her break her pact. Being single was supposed to help her work out what she wanted, and wanting him wasn't going to lead to the relationship she was looking for. He was exactly what she was trying to avoid – another unattainable man whose needs were greater than her own. What she needed right now – what they *both* needed – was to be friends. They'd agreed as much.

Instead of angling his face down, he straightened up, murmuring, 'Happy New Year' onto the crown of her head. His lips were tickled and taunted by the soft hair there. As if picking up on his signal, she gently released her hands and with a small reluctant look, she pulled away.

It left his body as cold as if he'd stepped outside into the freezing New Year's morning.

Chapter Thirty-four

JEN

'You want to go up the hill after work?' The question was tossed out lightly as Art escorted that week's pupil to the lift, holding his tiny snowboard – custom-made and with an exclusive Banksy design on its surface – under one arm. It was the first week of February and so far he'd asked her that question every time he'd come to The Redwood to pick up a pupil. She'd always said yes, and up the hill they had gone.

Friends, Jen reminded herself for the umpteenth time. *We are friends, who go snowboarding together.*

On New Year's Eve, she'd been certain there was a moment where it could have tipped into something more, an almost-kiss that remained uncompleted. Something – no, not something, *Art* – had stopped it. Since then she'd told herself it was for the best. Hadn't she just told him about her vow to stay single, and how much good it was doing her to have to make all her own decisions without them being clouded by second-guessing someone else's desires? And hadn't *he* told *her* just before that his sole aim for the coming year was to learn how to live life on his own? Another guy – the type of guy she historically went for – would have kissed her anyway and not thought of the consequences, but Art, to his credit, at least didn't want her to get the wrong idea. At least right now they could be friends without any of the awkwardness of a drunken snog hanging between them.

Not that it stopped her thinking about it every time she saw him. Or about his toned arms in that T-shirt. Just knowing they were hidden under his giant coat and over-sized sweatshirt brought her out in tingles. As did sitting beside him on the chairlift each afternoon, their sides pressed together, both of them instinctively choosing to do so even when it was only the two of them on a four-seater. They never acknowledged it, but nor did either of them pull away.

'I'll allow you a crush,' Maxie had told her on the phone when she'd confessed. 'Especially with someone who was too noble to just get off with you when he could have. Besides, you've now spent enough non-romantic time together for him to know the real you, like how hangry you get. You're not even bothering to hide it, which means you've broken out of your usual chameleon Jen pattern.' It was true. After Eduardo had made her work through her lunchbreak the previous week, she'd had a meltdown as she and Art queued up for the long gondola line, which was solved only by Art suggesting they stop for a toastie. He'd joked that he was used to over-tired and hungry kids so recognised the signs.

As Art passed the concierge desk now, he pulled a slightly squashed chocolate muffin from one of his coat pockets and put it down in front of her. 'There were loads left in the staff room from some conference this morning. I thought it would keep you going if you don't have time for lunch.' He shot her a grin and for once she stopped trying to hold the tilting feeling of being around him in. She let how much she fancied him wash over her.

'Thank you,' she said, knowing there was a stupid grin on her face.

'Cool. I'll meet you downstairs when you come off shift,' he said. The lift doors shut, and Jen glanced next to her to see Eduardo looking at her with irritation. He was basically the antidote to any amorous feelings, and the tilting sensation dispersed.

'Once you get *that*' – he gestured at the muffin –'off my desk and you've finished organising your social life, Mr Callaghan in Suite Six has a delivery that needs taking to his room.'

Eduardo gestured to an enormous box stationed behind the concierge desk, one that Jen struggled to get her arms around to lift. It wasn't heavy, just big, but aside from muttering at her to ensure she bent her legs, Eduardo offered her no further help.

'Why didn't the bellhop drop it off?' she huffed as she heaved it up. It was so tall she had to crane her neck to see over it.

'They tried, but no one answered, so they left it with us for this morning.' Jen couldn't see Eduardo but could imagine the exasperated look on his face. 'Anything else, or do you want to stand there holding that all day?' he snarked.

Jen rolled her eyes, grateful the box obscured her face.

'I saw that,' Eduardo snapped. She waddled off as fast as was possible with a square metre of cardboard in her arms.

She had to use her elbow to thump on the door of Suite Six. As she did, the door opened a crack because it hadn't been properly shut to begin with.

'Delivery for you, Mr Callaghan,' Jen called into the room.

'Come in, it's open,' a man's voice called back.

'This would be a lot easier if you opened the door properly for me,' she muttered, nudging the door with her toe before shuffling in. She could barely see anything, but she couldn't work out if it was the room that was dark or that her visibility was hindered because of the massive box. Moving into the room, she banged her thigh on the wing of an armchair that had been moved from its usual place in front of the window to somewhere nearer the door. 'Shi—' she started, before swallowing the curse. 'Where would you like me to put this?' she choked out, trying to hide the pain reverberating through her leg. She stood still so she didn't crash into anything else and swivelled left and then right, to get her bearings. It was 8.15 a.m and starting to get light out, but the blinds and curtains were shut tight. She couldn't make out where there was space to put it down.

'Anywhere over here in the bedroom is fine,' the voice said. A side lamp flipped on, giving Jen something to aim for, and she slowly made her way over. She dodged around the couch in the suite's living room, then turned sideways, like a crab, so she could check for hazards over her left shoulder. Like this, she continued to the bedroom. She still couldn't see over the box, but at least could see where she was going on one side.

Would it kill him to come and take it off me, she thought with irritation.

As she neared the source of the light, she pivoted ninety degrees and took a couple of steps backwards, awaiting further instructions. She peeped over the top to where the light illuminated Mr Callaghan sitting on the bed and forced a smile that belied how annoyed she was that he was letting her struggle. Her smile faded as she registered that he was wearing a robe.

Only a robe.

And he had his knees hitched up to reveal that he was stark naked underneath.

'OH!' she shouted, pivoting back and ducking her head back below the cardboard parapet. She pulled the box tight against her body as though it was a shield. He hasn't realised he's flashing me, she thought, an embarrassed laugh threatening to escape from her. She'd save his dignity by hiding behind the box until he sorted himself out. She listened for any sign that he'd changed position.

'What are you waiting for?' Mr Callaghan said. His voice sounded different to the usual polite indifference during their brief exchanges at the concierge desk. 'Just bring it over and put it here.' The next noise she heard was like a hand patting the bed.

Her skin prickled. There was no polite way to say, 'Can you put your bollocks away first?' so she resumed her crab walk. It meant she could creep to where she thought he wanted the box depositing, while blocking all view of him. She got as close as she could bear and lowered it, bending her legs the way the health and safety manual advised so that she could disappear completely behind it. Once it was safely on the floor, she then swivelled another ninety degrees so that her back was to him. She started walking briskly back towards the door.

'Wait,' said Mr Callaghan. 'Don't you want to give me a hand unpacking it?' She now realised *how* his tone was different, and it stopped her dead. He sounded as though he was making an innuendo. Suggestive. It dawned on her that he *had* known he was exposing himself.

Worse than that, he'd done it on purpose.

'I can send a bellboy if you need help with it,' Jen said as briskly as she could manage. Her heart was pounding, and her own voice sounded unnaturally high. She walked the few steps across the room without turning around, noticing that it wasn't just the armchair that had been moved. A lot of the furniture was in a different, haphazard place. If he turned the lamp off again she wouldn't have a clear route to the door. The thought made her pick up her pace.

'But I want you to help me,' she heard him say as she reached the door. 'Stay a while.' She pulled it decisively shut behind her. Stumbling a little, she ran down the hallway as fast as she could, back to the brightly lit reception area and concierge desk. She arrived out of breath, her mind racing.

'Jennifer, I heard you slam that door all the way from down here,' Eduardo hissed in his best quiet-bollocking voice. 'And *what* have I told you about not stamping along the corridors? I've lost all hope of you learning to glide but you could at least *try* to walk quietly.' He glared at her. 'And *why* are you so sweaty? Honestly, I despair.' He turned back to the screen, apparently too annoyed to continue berating her.

'Eduardo,' Jen said in a low voice. Her brain was jumping around. It hadn't quite caught up with what had just happened.

What *had* just happened?

She'd walked in on a half-naked guest. It was barely anything, *wasn't it?* It was the sort of thing that was almost funny.

But if it had been funny, wouldn't she have laughed? Instead she felt uncomfortable, and a bit revolted.

'Eduardo,' she said again. There was a tremor in her voice.

He stopped looking at the screen and fixed her with a look of mild irritation. 'What?'

Jen glanced back down the corridor in case Mr Callaghan had come out after her.

'Mr Callaghan.'

'What about him?'

'He was . . .' She hesitated, trying to thread the disparate elements together. The whole thing had been over in less than a minute. What if she'd been mistaken? She remembered the way he'd spoken to her, the wheedling tone. No. She hadn't been mistaken.

'Any time you want to finish the sentence, Jennifer,' Eduardo said with a tut. 'I have all day.'

'When I went in there Mr Callaghan was naked – well apart from a bathrobe. But that wasn't covering him properly, if you know what I mean.'

'Who knew you were such a prude?' Eduardo snorted. 'For heaven's sake, it was probably an accident.'

'No, it wasn't,' Jen said. 'He set it up so that I'd come in and find him there, like that.'

'How do you know?' Eduardo's voice was flat, dismissive. He clearly thought she was being dramatic.

'I just do,' she insisted. In her gut, she *knew*. 'It felt weird. Not like a mix-up,' she said. 'Deliberate.'

'He's in his *own* suite when you came barging in, and somehow he's deliberately *flashing* you?' Eduardo's tone had segued from dismissive to mocking.

'I wasn't barging anywhere. He told me to come in,' Jen said. 'He set it up.'

'Or he had no idea, and you could have politely mentioned he should cover himself up.'

Could she? She didn't know. Now Eduardo said so, it seemed simple, but it hadn't felt like that at the time.

'You're not listening to me,' Jen pressed. Her head felt muddled. 'He asked me to stay to unpack the parcel.'

'And?' Eduardo said. There was only contempt in his eyes.

'He meant something else.'

'Like what? Because we clear boxes and packing material from rooms all the time.' He was being wilfully ignorant, she knew he was, but she also couldn't bring herself to spell it out. Not here when Mr Callaghan could come out at any time.

'I'm telling you, this wasn't like disposing of the fifty-five Tiffany gift bags the Lambs received all those wedding presents in. It felt off.' Her voice sounded like a bleat.

'Ohh, it *felt* off. You know, you should be careful about making outlandish and unfounded allegations about our most valued customers. Your *feelings* are irrelevant, Jennifer. Grow up.' Eduardo raised his eyebrows skyward, simultaneously shutting down the conversation and making her feel stupid.

The phone rang and Jen jumped. 'Six' flashed up on the screen. 'I'm not answering that, and I'm not going back,' she said without even thinking about it. Adrenaline coursed through her body. She looked at her hands. They were shaking. 'I refuse to go back to that man's room while he's still staying here and I don't want to talk to him.' She had only one instinct: to get away. 'I'm going to check on Suite Nine's breakfast.' She walked away from the concierge desk before Eduardo could stop her.

'Oh, for God's sake,' she heard him mutter, before he snatched up the phone himself. 'Platinum floor, Eduardo speaking,' he said, his silky voice in place.

Jen paused, one hand on the staff door, and listened. Maybe she *had* got it wrong and Mr Callaghan was calling to say there had been a mortifying misunderstanding.

'Jennifer?' Eduardo said. 'She's just stepped out, I'm afraid, but I can come and get the packaging if you need it cleared right away.'

She turned and lifted her gaze to Eduardo's face. He avoided her eye as he listened to the response.

'In that case,' he said in a soothing tone. 'Just leave it outside the door and I'll send housekeeping to collect it later.'

Jen pushed the door. She'd been right. She knew she had. And her stomach burned that Eduardo either didn't, or was choosing not to, believe her.

Chapter Thirty-five

ART

'He did *what?*'

The chairlift they were sitting on was swaying as it made its journey up to a ski run called Seventh Heaven, but Art could feel his body shaking independently of it.

With rage.

As he and Jen rode up to the uppermost point on Blackcomb mountain, and a view he'd been excited to show to her, he'd been blathering on about his latest therapy session: how he'd exchanged a couple of emails with his mum, and how Maggie had talked about building up his confidence to confront the scar on his leg. Jen had been quiet, but he'd thought she was just hunched inside her coat against the biting wind. It wasn't until about halfway to the top of the mountain that he'd realised she wasn't taking in anything he was saying, and that she actually hadn't felt present since he'd met her outside The Redwood at the end of her shift. As Art had registered her ongoing silence, he'd started to feel stupid and embarrassed. He shouldn't have assumed she wanted to hear about his therapy or issues. His voice had quavered as he mentioned the scar and then trailed off.

But when Jen's voice spoke over him, it turned out it was nothing to do with him at all.

'Something happened at work today,' she said. She had goggles on but the strain showed in the set of her chin. She sounded hollow and doubting, as she explained that a guest had deliberately exposed himself to her at work and that Eduardo thought she was overreacting. She stopped and started several times, and kept laughing – but nervously, as though she thought she was supposed to find it funny, and that there was something wrong with her for not. As quick as she finished, she started to question her own story.

'I didn't realise what was going on at first, or as I left, to be honest. Maybe it was all just a weird misunderstanding and I got it wrong. After all, that woman in Suite Two got caught butt-naked by Cara last week.'

'Because she answered the door thinking it was her husband who'd forgotten his room key,' Art replied. Jen looked agonised and unsure, so Art replied as firmly as he could. 'Cara did an impression of her screaming and diving behind the door in embarrassment. What you've told me is not the same, Jen.'

She was nodding. Quick but uncertain dips of her chin. She chewed her lip. 'So, what is it then?'

'Indecent exposure . . . sexual harassment.' He ticked them off on his gloved hands. 'I don't know the exact legal definition, but whatever it's called it's categorically not your fault, and it's also completely fucking wrong. You have to report it.'

Jen looked away, at the crust of snow beneath them and a great slab of rock that rose out of the mountain beyond.

She muttered something Art couldn't catch, her words caught by the wind and carried away.

'What?'

'I said, "That's exactly what Maxie said,"' she shouted, turning back. Her mouth settled into a straight, grim line. 'I left her a message when I was on my break and she replied with a four-minute voice note that was more like a rallying cry in the fight against misogyny, telling me I had to go above Eduardo's head to HR and if not to them, then to the people who own the hotel chain. I could hear the woman she'd been treating in the back of the ambulance agreeing with her. Although it did turn into a rant about some woman she'd just been fighting outside a pub,' she joked flatly. She ran a gloved thumb along the length of the safety bar in front of them, scratching at a frosty patch where the snow had solidified into spiky crystals.

Art could sense she wasn't finished, so he let the silence stretch out. He wanted to vehemently agree with what her friend Maxie had said, but he sensed that Jen was shaken up and that the last thing she needed was some bloke telling her how she should react to what had happened. How *he* wanted to react was to throw this Mr Callaghan – and Eduardo – off the side of the mountain and then to gather Jen up in his arms away from harm. He could feel his pulse ricocheting around his body, his entire being wound tight. A dark shadow threatened to overwhelm him. *See,* it seemed to say. *You can't keep people safe, no matter what you do.*

He forced himself to concentrate on Jen. *It's not about you, Art. Save it for your next session with Maggie.*

'The thing is, I *know* all this,' Jen continued eventually. 'I worked in HR for years. We never had any problems like this while I was there, but I went on enough training courses outlining what the procedures were and what sort of disciplinary steps should be taken. Not just against' – she grimaced – 'Callaghan, but against Eduardo for dismissing what I told him.' She stopped abruptly and looked away again, scanning the terrain for a few moments.

'But,' Art prompted.

Jen didn't answer. The cable car chugged through one of its pylons, juddering through a layer of mist that popped them out above the cloud line. 'But Human Resources work for the company, not for me. Whoever I tell might be just like Eduardo. Or they'll keep questioning me and when I can't remember the details in exactly the right way it will be proof that I made the whole thing up, or misread a perfectly innocent situation. Even *I'm* doubting that it happened the way I think it happened, so why would anyone else believe me?'

'Because you wouldn't make something like that up, for a start,' Art burst out. 'But that's not even the point. The point is that it *did* happen, and he shouldn't be able to get away with it. Anyone who tries to cover up for him is just as bad as he is. He should be arrested and kicked out of the hotel as a bare minimum.'

Underneath her goggles, Jen's mouth twisted into a bitter smile. 'That would be bad for the hotel's bottom line though, wouldn't it? Banning rich people.'

'Far be it from me to speak for the one per cent,' Art fired back, 'but I'm sure at least some gazillionaires aren't sex pests. How about The Redwood appeals to a non-perv clientele instead? Besides, your bottom line is healthier when you don't have to pay hush money to your employees.'

Jen snorted and he panicked that he'd been too flippant, but when he looked closer, she was laughing, albeit with a jagged edge. She sniffed and wiped the back of her glove across her nose.

'You're right, both you and Maxie. And that drunk fighty woman.' She leaned her head back and rested it on the back of the seat, her face in tumult. 'I don't know about Callaghan's history but this is definitely not the first time Eduardo has brushed a staff complaint under the carpet. Another Platinum employee was propositioned – although I'm not sure that's what you call it when it feels threatening – by someone a couple of weeks ago. Cara's compiling a dossier.'

'Shit.' Art was disgusted. Pretty much every woman he knew had a story about a situation that felt off, or had experienced something that was undeniably assault, but this was a huge hotel that apparently had safeguards in place and processes for dealing with things like this. There was a whole section in their website about promoting a respectful working environment, and boasting of 'pioneering' inclusivity initiatives. He'd had to read it all to take their guests on as clients.

But here was Eduardo gaslighting Jen about her experience and refusing to pull the trigger on the hotel's official policy for dealing with it. That implied that this wasn't simply a manager handling a situation badly, but behaviour that was ingrained and insidious.

'We definitely don't go to Eduardo,' he decided. 'We go around him. Above him.'

'We?' She turned to look at him. Even through the reflection of her goggles he could see her eyes, searching.

'Yes, we. If you want me to come with you, that is. You don't have to do it on your own.'

She chewed her lip again. He could see she was veering from steady confidence to uncertainty with every sentence she spoke. 'Eduardo can't find out I'm going above his head,' she fretted.

'No,' he agreed. 'Is there an employee rep? They're always going on about them at our pre-season training sessions. Their name should be in your employee handbook.'

Jen looked at him like he was mad. 'I never had a handbook. Or any training with the rest of the hotel employees. Eduardo said he keeps it all in-house and on-the-job on Platinum, because it's so different to the rest of the hotel.'

Art snorted cynically. 'To keep you away from the people who are aware of employment law, more like.' Again he thought of exactly how he'd like to handle Callaghan, and stopped himself from saying it out loud. 'Straight to HR, then, and I'll come with you.' He corrected himself. 'When you're ready and if you want me to. Whatever you need.'

Jen blew out a plume of air. Her hair was flying up around her hat where the wind was whipping it up, and her face was pale despite it. She shook her head as though to rid it of an unwanted thought. Art definitely knew that feeling. 'Do you know what I want to do right now?'

'What?' Art wanted to help, but he felt so useless.

She shook her head. 'I want you to help me get off this chairlift without falling over, and then I want to spend an hour thinking about how good and slightly terrifying it feels to point a fibreglass plank down a mountain and let myself speed off.'

'Oh-kay,' Art said, not sure if he was understanding. 'You want me to stop talking about it and take you snowboarding?'

'Exactly.' She nodded. 'You're the one who told me that to stay safe up here you have to concentrate.' She pointed a padded finger at him. '*Your* job is to make sure that's what I'm doing. I don't want to think about Eduardo, or Callaghan or *anything* for at least an hour. I just want them out of my head.' She frowned and then added softly but clearly, 'And then on my day off tomorrow, I'll do what I know I have to do.'

Feelings couldn't be buried forever, Art knew that more than anyone, but he could help her get an hour's relief. 'Then that's what we'll do,' he assured her.

The chairlift approached the landing station, where Art knew a steep descent would greet them as they got off. His instinct was to grab her arm and guide her down it, but before he could, Jen pushed the safety bar up and set her face into an expression of grim determination.

'Tomorrow,' she repeated, standing up. Using the chairlift seat to gain some momentum, she slid forward and pushed off down the descent, without needing any help from him at all.

Chapter Thirty-six

JEN

At exactly 9 a.m. Jen knocked tentatively on the Human Resources Manager's office door and reminded herself about what she was going to say. All those early mornings had finally become worth it when she found herself awake early enough on her day off to spend an hour talking to Maxie at a reasonable time in the UK. Maxie had helped her write down a timeline of exactly what happened – both during her time in Suite Six and with Eduardo afterwards – so she had it clear in her mind. Then they'd rehearsed talking through it, with Jen encouraging Maxie to question her version of events and pick holes in what had happened so she felt as prepared as possible for an interrogation. Despite it all, outside the door, her entire body was shaking with nerves.

Art had offered to come with her to the office, but she'd wanted to do it alone, although she'd accepted a lift to the hotel, both for the moral support and for the fact that it was sheeting down with wet snow and she'd wanted to arrive looking sleek and in control, not drenched and bedraggled. When she arrived, the Redwood's main open-plan office was empty aside from one employee typing furiously at her computer screen while looking harassed. It was easy to slip in and right up to the HR manager's door, who she knew worked 7 a.m., to 4 p.m., because she'd looked him up on The Redwood's website the previous night. She'd discovered the information on The Redwood's blog in a post he'd written about 'making flexible working work for *you*'.

'Come in,' a voice beckoned her in.

She hadn't been here since the day Eduardo hired her, but in a different version of her trip to Canada, she would have been working here every day. She could have been in the outer office, beckoning in a lowly hotel employee who was summoning up all her courage like she was. She stood up straight to invoke confidence and went in.

'Oh!' Sitting on the opposite side of the desk to a middle-aged man who she recognised as Matthew Addison, the hotel's Human Resources Manager, was Eduardo. His face was frozen into an expression of disdain, which he rearranged into his superficial shark smile.

'Jennifer,' he said.

'I can come back,' she stuttered. *What was he doing here?*

Eduardo exchanged a look with Matthew, as though to confirm a hypothesis already discussed.

'That won't be necessary, ah, Jennifer, is it?' Matthew said. He looked far less relaxed than Eduardo did. Shifty. He had a sheaf of papers in his hand and was looking from them to Jen. She narrowed her eyes. It was her file. Why was the HR manager holding her employee file? 'I was going to call you in for a meeting tomorrow but as you're here now, we might as well talk today.'

Jen knew it was a myth that people who worked in HR had an inherent gift for dealing with difficult or awkward situations. You could go on all the training courses you wanted but in her experience most company 'reshuffles', redundancies and disciplinary proceedings were overseen by someone who coped with the potential for unleashed emotions by being a disengaged, procedure-led android who cited employee handbook clauses at you. She'd borne witness to plenty of them.

'I see,' she said from her spot just inside the doorway. She kicked herself for not having something to record the conversation on, but her flip phone was incapable of it. 'What would you like to talk about? Because there's something I'd like to talk about myself.'

Matthew gave a low, nervous chuckle. 'We'll get to that. Take a seat and do shut the door.'

The only available seat was next to Eduardo. Jen pulled it as far away from him as she could without dragging it out of the room. 'What's Eduardo doing here?' she asked.

Matthew cleared his throat and fiddled with his tie. It had ice-skaters on it. He had the jockish frame of a man who'd spent his formative years skiing in these very mountains, but now looked as though the dual tolls of the elements and a desk job had softened his edges.

'Eduardo came to ask about doing your probationary review.' He looked at his desktop monitor.

'My what?' It wasn't that Jen didn't know what a probation period was, more that she knew what Eduardo had told her about the hotel's 'imbecilic bureaucratic processes' as he referred to them. He had the same opinion of their review process as he had of training sessions, or job interviews that required candidates to meet requirements other than 'going to a posh school'. Cara told her she hadn't had a performance review in three years, and if it wasn't for her payslips she'd think she didn't exist on the hotel's books at all.

'Your review,' Matthew repeated briskly. 'I have your start date down as November twenty-ninth.'

'That's right,' Jen said. Where was this going?

'Our probation period is twelve weeks and you've now been working here for ten,' Matthew said, looking anywhere but at Jen. His voice had become an emotionless drone, which she immediately recognised as the precursor to bad news. 'I'll get to the point and say that unfortunately Eduardo has found your performance in the role lacking, and so we're letting you go with immediate effect. As per the terms of your employment contract, you're still within the probationary window, so you're not entitled to any severance pay or a notice period, but as a courtesy we will ensure you're paid up until the end of the week.'

He finally looked at her, the bad news delivered, with a blank face.

Jen shook her head, her own face plastered with contempt that she didn't bother trying to mask.

Eduardo was one step ahead of her. Ditching her before she could cause a problem. The same way he'd shunted Sasha into a lesser role at the gift shop but made her grateful for having a job at all. The turnover for staff on the Platinum floor was high enough that what was one more employee who wasn't quite up to VIP standard?

How had she entertained the idea that she could walk in and burst Eduardo's carefully constructed bubble? She'd been worried that no one would believe her. Now she was certain the deck had been stacked so no one would even listen to her to begin with. The worst part was that this all pointed to the fact that this wasn't the first time a staff member had been fired to stop them making a complaint.

She vibrated with fury, but struggled to hold on to her emotions, knowing that any sort of outburst would be construed as the actions of a hysterical and disgruntled ex-employee. Her HR conditioning kicked in.

'Could you please provide me with a breakdown of the tasks I have been underperforming at, and examples of how?' she said coolly, looking directly at Eduardo.

Matthew looked slightly surprised, but Eduardo didn't miss a beat. He smoothed the block of hair. 'Of course. May I?' He produced an iPad from his bag and swiped open a document.

'Appearance,' he began. 'Dress code for the Platinum floor is immaculately groomed. Despite repeated verbal warnings, employee has been unable to meet the standard.'

Jen wanted to roll her eyes. She had no doubt the outcome of this 'meeting' was inevitable, but really? Were these the petty violations Eduardo intended to use to dispose of her? She realised that both men were looking at her and that she'd snorted out loud. Eduardo resumed studying the iPad. 'May I continue?

'Two. Removing hotel property from the Platinum floor – six towels, six pairs of complimentary slippers, and dozens of toiletries meant for guest suites.' Eduardo gave her a cold look. 'Which is theft. And punishable by more than the termination of your employment should we decide to involve the authorities.'

That was Cara's stash. Not that Jen was going to drop her in it. Although, OK, she *had* taken one towel for herself.

'Three. Performance. Employee has cut corners with customer care, being unable to fulfil client requests.'

He was talking about the time she called every single massage therapist within a twenty-five-mile radius because a client announced at four o'clock – peak time – that they wanted a deep tissue in fifteen minutes. She'd managed to secure someone for 5 p.m. This list was a joke, but Eduardo hadn't finished.

'Four. Using her phone during shift. Five. Insubordination to a senior member of staff – I have thirty counts of that recorded. Six. Lying about her education history in order to secure the role. Seven. Tardiness. Employee has been late on shift six times since employment began – I can provide dates if necessary – and on at least four occasions abandoned her post for a period of three hours to go snowboarding.'

This time Jen gasped. She wasn't surprised he was lying but this accusation still sent a shockwave through her nervous system. 'That was signed off by *you* so I could accompany Newton Oates on her lessons,' she said, her voice coming out shrill.

Eduardo only smiled blankly. 'Signed off where? Why would I sanction a staff member leaving the floor and leaving Platinum grossly under-resourced?'

Jen's mouth was hanging open in disbelief. 'How about all the times I've gone above and beyond, does none of that count?

She thought about the overtime, the constant HR-able comments from Eduardo about her own and others' appearances, and incidents like the one last week where a bouffe-haired millionaire asked her to massage his Bichon Frise's belly to try to 'encourage' it to 'pass' the gold and diamond signet ring it had swallowed while his owner was in the shower. Jen had fruitlessly massaged the dog's belly for an hour before Eduardo called a vet. One X-ray later, the ring had been found under the bathmat.

'Do I have any recourse against these accusations?' Jen asked. 'Or is that it? His word against mine, except no one has even asked for my word yet?' There's no way she'd entertain working with Eduardo after this, knowing her every move was being noted and filed away to use against her at any moment, but it was the principle. He was diminishing her so that whatever she said next was viewed as retaliation.

'We usually conduct exit interviews with our employees to gain feedback on the organisation,' said Matthew. 'But as mentioned we have the right to terminate employment at any point during the probation period without needing to enter into our usual procedures.'

'How many times has Eduardo had you do something like this?' Jen said coldly.

Matthew at least had the grace to look uncomfortable. 'Jobs on the Platinum floor are very demanding. Not everyone is suited to the role—'

'Right. It's because of Eduardo's exacting employee standards. *That's* why the female turnover on that floor is so high.' She leaned forward in her chair. 'Where is your integrity, Matthew?'

The silence stretched out.

Jen sat there, glaring at Eduardo and refusing to plead for her job. If this was how it was going to go down, she'd at least retain her dignity. She wouldn't let them have the last word. And then Matthew said, 'Please return any outstanding items of uniform and vacate your staff housing by the weekend.'

Eduardo flashed her a faint, triumphant smile.

Chapter Thirty-seven

ART

Art had respected Jen's decision when she'd said she wanted to go to HR by herself, but once he'd dropped her off, he was too agitated to go home. Instead, he texted to say he'd wait for her in the vegan coffee shop around the corner from the hotel.

> Here if you need me (or a lift!), but if you want to make your own way home, just let me know.

Art knew all about wanting space. But he was learning that sometimes too much of it was as bad as none. The number of messages he'd ignored from well-meaning friends over the years was too high to count, but that didn't mean he hadn't appreciated them being sent or not noticed when they'd stopped.

But that didn't prevent him from fretting that he was being pushy for the half an hour he sat there before Jen roared into the café. She swung the door open with a bang, bringing with her a blast of frigid air and an anger he could feel radiating from her before she made it to the table he was tucked into at the back.

'They fucking FIRED me,' she shouted before he had a chance to ask how it had gone. She looked as strained as she had yesterday but she now also looked energised. The other patrons in the café turned around to gawp. Jen threw herself into the chair opposite Art, shedding her soaked coat and hat as she did, and spattering him with rapidly melting droplets of snow. Her face was flushed and her grey eyes were flashing with a sense of injustice.

'They *fired* you for registering a complaint?' He sat up in his chair, the options instantly running through his mind. 'That's a lawsuit waiting to happen. I have the details of the lawyers who negotiated my payout after the accident somewhere. I'll get in touch with them about who to approach for legal advice.' A sense of relief mingled with a sense of purpose. He could help her sort this out, at least on a practical level.

Jen was fidgeting in her chair, as antsy as if she'd already had three of the very strong espressos the café was famous for, her eyes darting about.

'It's not that simple,' she said, her knees jiggling as she spoke. 'I didn't even get to tell *Matthew*' – she spat out his name with contempt – 'about the harassment or Eduardo covering it up. Eduardo was *there* when I arrived, and they fired me because they can get rid of anyone they like during their probation period.'

'You're kidding me.' Art's stomach lurched. He forgot to be calm and practical, and instead his anger rose to meet hers.

'Nope.' The outraged energy suddenly seemed to drain

out of Jen and she slumped forward, leaning an elbow on the table top and resting her chin in her hand.

'We should go back there,' Art said. 'Together. Demand to see that HR guy without Eduardo there so you can make a statement and they have a record of it.'

She looked at him witheringly. 'So he can tell me it's the ravings of a disgruntled ex-employee trying to get revenge? That's exactly what Eduardo just pre-empted. And who knows how many times he's done something similar before? I actually feel sick. No, actually, I want to stress-eat until I'm sick. I need some cake and an oat milk latte.'

It wasn't much of a way for Art to make himself useful, but it was something. He stood up and hurried to the counter, glancing over from time to time to check on Jen. She was texting furiously on her tiny flip phone, her face scrunched in concentration.

'I'm texting Cara,' she explained as he sat back down with her order, still typing. 'To tell her I have some information for her reporter contact. She's working but I'll be able to meet her later.' She took a sip of her drink. 'Thank you for this. It'll keep me going while I pack.'

'Pack?' A sense of unease spread through him. 'Pack for what?'

'Right. I haven't told you that bit, have I? As I've lost my job, I also lose my staff housing. I have to be out by the weekend.'

Art's stomach lurched. 'As in, forty-eight hours from now?'

Jen nodded, her mouth still full of coffee.

'Where do they expect you to go?'

'Not their problem, is it? That it's still high season and everywhere available for rent is on Airbnb for about a thousand dollars a night could make you conclude that Eduardo timed it to make it as hard as possible for me to stay in town.' She attacked her cake with a fork. 'Because it's not like I can get a reference for another job either.'

Her phone vibrated on the table. 'Oh, that's Cara.' Jen snatched up the phone. 'Hey, where are you? Make sure he doesn't hear.' She jumped up, pulling her coat back on, and disappeared out of the door. Through the steamed-up windows, Art could see her pacing up and down under the café's faux-rustic wooden awning.

He fell back in his chair, his mind spinning all over the place, from the shock of how Jen hadn't just been demeaned, but been literally dismissed, to the prospect of her disappearing from his life in forty-eight hours. He hadn't expected what happened on Platinum to be easily solved – he knew the world didn't work like that – but this was a disaster. Everything good that had happened in Art's life recently was wrapped up in Jen. She had been right there, coaxing him out of his rut, making everything seem better. And now she had to leave staff housing in forty-eight hours. And from the way she was talking, there was nowhere else for her to go.

Should he—

Jen charged back in, looking invigorated. Her eyes were dancing with a sense of purpose. 'Cara said she's almost ready to go with her dossier. Sasha has said she'll talk to the reporter and it turns out the hotel is dotted with people who *used* to work on Platinum and were "moved" elsewhere. I've told her I'll speak to whoever she wants me to. It won't help me, but maybe it'll help someone in the future if the press blow open whatever systemic bullshit is happening at The Redwood.'

'That's good,' Art said, nodding. 'If you're OK with it,' he added quickly. 'I know it's not that easy to speak out, so you have to do what's right for you.'

Jen gave him a determined smile. There was no trace of the hesitant and doubtful woman from the chairlift yesterday. She was fired up and focused. 'No need to tiptoe around it, Art, it's sexual harassment and a corporate cover-up. How far up it goes, I guess Cara's reporter will find out, but either Eduardo needs to be outed or there are a lot more Eduardos higher up the chain of command.'

She took a swig of her coffee. 'How many other people – including people ten years younger than me in their first ever jobs – have been in this position and either felt pressured into going back to work when they felt unsafe or were sacked so they didn't speak out? What happened to me was nothing compared to some of the stories Cara's been hearing, and guess who's at the heart of covering them all up?'

Art didn't need to guess. 'Eduardo.'

'Exactly. I'm angrier at him than at the guy who flashed me.'

Anger flared through Art again. 'When I next see him during a pick-up I'm—'

'No,' Jen said forcefully. 'You're not. You're not going to do anything. Until Cara has everything in place, he cannot find out what she's up to. We have to let him think he's got away with it. Otherwise who knows what he'll do to discredit her and the others at the hotel?'

The prospect of facing Eduardo day after day, knowing exactly what sort of person he was, made Art bubble with rage, but he knew she was right. Jen and Cara were in control of this. Letting it play out the way they needed was the most important thing. He focused on that.

'So, what's the next step?'

'Cara's going to call me later to talk about it. She's on shift so can't let Eduardo get wind of anything.'

'But you'll be here for a while, to help with the case, I mean?' His voice was worried.

I don't want you to go.

Art had only just started to find himself again, and despite reconnecting with Yeti and Rob, and even his mum, his blossoming friendship with Jen felt important. It didn't feel like a coincidence that all the other reconnections had begun when she came into his life and helped open him up to them. But he knew he couldn't demand that she stayed to help him keep growing. He had no right. And what if she felt the opposite? As though meeting him was when everything started going wrong for her? As she sat there, looking fierce but fragile, he desperately wanted to reach over and hold her hand. To recreate the closeness of New Year's Eve when they'd almost kissed. Since then, he'd replayed the moment in his head every time he saw her. What if he'd given in to it?

What if he allowed himself the luxury of a 'what if'? But now wasn't the time. Jen needed him to help her, not make a move.

Jen shrugged. Her eyes were still darting around, and it seemed like she was having trouble concentrating on one idea at a time. 'I don't know. It's all happened so quickly. What I do know is that I can't stay here indefinitely with no money coming in. I'm sure Rob and Snowy would let me crash at theirs for a bit, but' – she shrugged again – 'what would be the point? I'd just be draining my bank balance while putting off the inevitable.'

Her eyes settled on his for an extended moment. He couldn't make a move, but the urge to keep her near him overrode everything else.

Art blurted it out before he could stop himself. 'Why don't you stay with me?'

Chapter Thirty-eight

JEN

Her heart stopped for a second. Move in with Art?

Every conversation on a chairlift over these past few weeks, every time he'd briefly touched her to correct a small part of her snowboarding stance, and every after-slope drink packed tightly around a table at Canucks had reminded her that being physically near him made her body buzz in a way she'd never experienced before. Living together would provide that sensation on tap. She wanted to say yes. More than anything.

But her common sense got in there first. Move in with a guy she had a crush on, and then hope that one day he might want to be more than friends? That was the direct antithesis of everything she'd pledged to Maxie back in October. Even three months ago, she would have seized on his offer as good enough – a drift rather than a decision – but not now.

'No,' she said, watching Art's face fall and feeling her heart drop too. 'Thank you,' she added.

'Sure, sure,' he replied. 'You have to do what's right for you.'

She felt a tug, but she knew she was right to say no. They had agreed to be friends, and while his support was helping her no end right now, confusing what she wanted him to be to her and what he was actually suggesting wasn't a mistake she was prepared to make. Today had been a shitshow in so many ways but it didn't have to end with a classic old-Jen decision. Unless he explicitly said otherwise, he was offering to be her flatmate.

She didn't want to be his flatmate. And she didn't want him to want *her* to be his flatmate.

'At least I have two days to get my life together,' Jen said, with more confidence than she felt. The money she'd arrived with had grown slightly but the basics hadn't changed: she didn't have enough of it to live in a ski resort until the end of the season without a job. And without a local job that classified her as a resident and got her a hefty discount on ski lift passes, her cash would run out even earlier. What was the point of being in a mountain resort if you couldn't even go up the mountain? All the facts pointed to leaving being the most sensible thing to do. She could use her money to travel, or she could move to a different, cheaper Canadian town and earn some more. Plus, she stood a better chance of getting another job without the inevitable blacklisting she knew Eduardo would be co-ordinating. Either way, there were plenty of reasons to go, and only one reason to stay. And that one reason, the man who made her heart thud faster every time she looked at him, wasn't offering anything more than the chance to be his temporary flatmate. It wasn't enough.

The forty-eight-hour deadline wasn't just the end for her job and her apartment, but for Whistler itself.

Chapter Thirty-nine

ART

He ripped the eviction notice off Jen and Mickey's door before knocking loudly enough to be heard over the murmuring of voices inside. The door swung open and Mickey stood on the other side of the threshold. Art hadn't seen him since before his trip up the mountain with Jen on Christmas Day, where he'd abandoned her in the backcountry. Mickey immediately dropped his gaze upon seeing it was Art, fidgeting shiftily.

'Hey man,' he said to a spot on the floor. 'Come in.'

Art gave Mickey a curt nod in return. He wasn't particularly pleased to see him, but now wasn't the time to hold a grudge. There were now only twenty-four hours until Jen had to leave, and everyone here wanted to help her. Beyond Mickey, he could see Rob and Snowy in the minuscule living room. Rob's lanky frame was wedged into a spot between a rickety coffee table and the wall, with Snowy sitting against the opposite wall. Jen was scrunched up on the tiny sofa wearing baggy jeans and a vest top that skimmed her body. Her hair was piled on her head in a messy bun and there was a look of concentration on her face as she said something to Snowy across the room. She caught sight of Art as he entered, and smiled. Heat spread across his body. It had become a reflex when he was around Jen.

Either that, or the small apartment was far too cramped for the now five people inside it and he was overheating. He shucked off his coat, realising why they were all sitting in T-shirts, despite the snow dumping outside.

'Want one?' Mickey appeared from the kitchenette area behind him, holding out a bottle of beer. He seemed to be several drinks in already.

'No, thanks,' Art replied. After she'd turned down his offer to stay with him, he was hoping the other assembled people were going to come up with some solid reasons for Jen to stay put in Whistler, but judging by the number of beer bottles littered around the room, the gathering had already lost its focus from 'Operation Help Jen' and degenerated into a piss-up.

Art found a spare patch of wall in the kitchenette and leaned against that. He got up to speed with where they were in terms of a plan.

'Just stay with us,' Snowy was saying. 'What's one more person?'

'You're moving to Vancouver,' Jen reminded him gently. 'And with Clyde and Kelly's baby, Rob told me you're giving up the house and going your separate ways. I'd only be in the same position in two weeks' time.'

'It's bullshit!' Mickey shouted. 'You should just stay here.' He weaved his way through the tangle of limbs on the floor and flung the window open. The shock of cold outside air gave a moment of relief in the stuffy room, until Mickey sat on the windowsill and fired up a joint, blocking any ventilation coming in with his body as well as creating a hotbox effect. The air started to get thick with smoke and the smell of weed. 'We can stage a sit-in to protest.'

'You're sweet,' Jen said, shaking her head. 'But it's not just the notice on the door that makes me think that won't work. The building manager has already accosted me to tell me that I'll be escorted out on Friday if I'm not gone by 6 p.m., and anyone suspected of harbouring an unauthorised lodger – that's literally the phrase he used – will be evicted. I can't let you risk losing your staff housing too.' She threw a smile at Mickey.

'There's got to be something we can do to help,' Snowy wailed, his blond hair dancing fuzzily above him. 'You're not just going to go back to Pom Land, are you?'

'No—' Jen started to say. Art's ears pricked up, but before she could finish there was another knock on the door. Art was closest, so he leaned over and pulled it open from his position behind it. Cara walked in, dusted in a fine powder of snow from outside and already talking. She stopped abruptly when she realised she wasn't going to get much closer due to the room already being full.

'Don't thank me yet, Jen, but there's a job going here – one that Eduardo has *no* influence over, I might add – pays more than the peanuts we get at the hotel, and you would be perfect for.'

'What? Where?' Jen stood up from the sofa, knees and elbows knocking into Rob as she darted across the room to hear more. She didn't want to leave, this proved it. Art felt a flash of satisfaction and something else – a tingle of hope – that her departure would be averted.

'So . . .' Cara unzipped her jacket. 'Whew, it's hot in here, right?' She pulled off her coat, hat and scarf in a series of fluid movements. 'This guy who knows the guy I'm going to be working with in Vancouver has bought a "portfolio" of cabins in Whistler. Yeah, he's rich. It's a long story but the reason there's funding for the charity is because one of the backers has developed a social conscience about the fact that he made all his money being a dirty property developer and now wants to give back. Anyway, these cabins are being remodelled, and he's going to rent them out to fellow rich guys who want to come ski or snowboard for the weekend, but the profits will all go to the homeless charity in Vancouver. It's going to be called Boarding For Beds or something. Probably a tax write-off, let's face it.'

Art could see Jen trying to keep up. She was smiling at Cara because Cara was beaming at her, but it was clear she had no idea what was going on.

'That all sounds like a great initiative but I don't understand how that helps me.'

'Oh right, yeah.' She held her hands out as she explained the most important part. 'Because he needs a property-manager-cum-staff-supervisor – and who better than someone who knows how to deal with exactly the kind of rich people he's trying to attract, and also has a background in HR? Plus, as my new boss knows all about my upcoming whistleblowing at The Redwood – and he's backing me completely – he's the one person on the planet who knows that being fired from Platinum is actually the best reference you can get. So *he's* going to put a word in for you with Chuck. Who's the property guy. Jesus, why is it so *hot* in here?' Cara stripped off her hoodie as she reached the end of her explanation and left Jen standing where she was to pick her way over to Mickey. She pinched the joint from the end of his hand, took a deep draw and blew a plume of smoke out of the window.

'Only problem is, it doesn't start until May,' she said, talking back over her shoulder. 'He wants to do a soft launch in the summer, so spring is when he'll start getting everything in place. You'd have to support yourself for the next few months.' She took another toke. 'Other than that, I'd say it's yours for the taking. If it works out, they'd probably sponsor a proper work visa for you after your year-long one runs out.'

Everyone looked at Jen, who was now standing next to Art.

'You said you had enough money to last a few weeks, right?' Art said hopefully. 'So a couple of months is do-able if you had a job waiting for you?'

She looked at him properly for the first time since he came through the door, fixing her eyes on his in the way that had started to make him feel both unsettled and grounded every time she did it. A flickering that felt like something just between them and made everyone else in the room seem to disappear.

'Yes,' she said, looking away. 'But I was just about to tell everyone when Cara arrived that I'm going travelling. It's all booked. I leave tomorrow morning.'

Chapter Forty

JEN

The gathering petered out once Jen announced her plan to go from one coast of Canada to the other, using a series of trains and buses to allow her to see as much of the country as she could along the way.

'Blowing Whistler to have an adventure is the biggest fuck you to Eduardo. Good on you, Jen,' Rob announced, dragging her into a hug. 'I've got to get to the bar, but promise me you'll drop in if you have time before you go.'

'I will, if I have time,' she assured him, knowing the last thing she needed was a night at Canucks before the nine-hour bus ride she'd booked for tomorrow morning.

'You coming, mate?' Rob asked Snowy.

'Nah.' He pointed to Mickey. 'He's invited me to go nocturnal snow-shoeing.'

'I know this *great* woodland spot,' Mickey said, his eyes red-rimmed from the joint. Jen's eyes widened in alarm. She had a bad feeling about this.

'Whatever you do, keep your phone battery fully charged,' she pleaded.

Snowy nodded as though she was being over-protective

and started picking up the rucksacks and snowshoes Mickey was directing him to.

'Please look after him, Mickey.'

Mickey flapped a hand at her and left, with another joint stuck to his bottom lip, and Snowy in tow.

Cara pulled Jen into a prolonged and sloppy embrace on her way out. 'I'm happy that you've made a decision that's right for you. And stay in touch while you're away,' she instructed. 'The reporter is going to contact you about the story. It'll drop in a few weeks, when I'm *far* away from The Redwood and working in Vancouver, and you're wherever this awesome trip takes you. You can be anonymous but he'll need to record and verify what you tell him, if that's OK.'

'I'm in,' Jen confirmed. 'Whatever you need.' She was determined to do everything she could to help the case.

'Hero. And let me know about the job. Shall I put you in touch with Chuck anyway? As it doesn't start for a while, you could go travelling and then come back, right?'

Jen nodded but wasn't as sure about this. 'I'll think about it,' she said. 'Who knows how I'll feel when I start travelling?' She gave a little shrug designed to look carefree. The truth was that, despite the research she'd been doing since she got back to the apartment yesterday lunchtime, she was pretty nervous about a two-month solo trip across almost six thousand miles. And about leaving her new friends. And mostly about leaving Art.

'Good for you,' Cara added as she started to close the door. 'But don't drop off the radar.'

'I won't,' Jen said down the hallway after her. She

reached into her jeans pocket and pulled out her iPhone. 'Look, I've even switched back to this.'

'Text me,' Cara called as she disappeared.

Jen shut the door and leaned on it with her eyes closed, a thousand emotions churning. She didn't want to lose touch with any of them, even Mickey. Her time in Whistler had been short, but it had been worth it.

'Hi.'

She opened her eyes.

Art was still there and sitting on the sofa. Now everyone else was gone, it was strange for him to be here, out of context. He'd never been to her apartment before. She was used to seeing him in the hotel or on the mountain. Large spaces. He looked too big for the room, perched on the little two-seater. They'd been wedged next to each other in a crammed cable car numerous times over the last few weeks, but with layers of thermals, woollens and coats between them. There was always a distance. Now, he was sitting there in a faded Burton T-shirt, his defined arms loosely crossed in front of him, she was in a vest and jeans, and there was no one else in the room. It felt perilously intimate. She was so *aware* of him. Aware of her own body and how she wanted it to be closer to his. The opposite of how you should feel when hanging out with a friend.

'Hi,' she replied.

'Travelling, eh?' His voice sounded odd. As though he'd reached for 'enthusiastic' but trapped it in a door. It came out strangled.

She smiled back, but close-mouthed. 'That's right.' She had been feeling good about her decision, excited as well as nervous. But here, now, looking at Art, she knew she was also letting go of something. Something she didn't want to release but had to.

He looked down at his hands. He was clenching his right fist in and out in the way she now knew he did when he was nervous, upset or in pain. She resisted the urge to squeeze onto the sofa next to him and gently press her fingers along his wrist and forearm to see if it would help. 'Jen, I—' he started. He blew out a ragged breath. 'I think you know what I'm thinking.'

'I don't assume I know what anyone's thinking any more,' she said with an almost-laugh. It was true. Her promise to Maxie had released her from second-guessing other people all the time. She flashed him a small smile, belying the nerves this conversation was unleashing. 'Whatever it is, you're going to have to tell me.'

He kept looking to her and then away, as though he was looking for the answer written somewhere on the walls of the apartment. 'I don't know what to say,' he said eventually.

'You could tell me you don't want me to go,' she said softly.

'I *don't* want you to go,' Art fired back immediately. There was intensity in his brown eyes. Her heart leaped. 'But it's not fair for me to ask you to stay.'

'Isn't it?' she said, even though she knew he was right.

Jen thought about Maxie, and how she'd told her to give herself the space to find out what, or who, made her heart beat faster. Planning her trip had done that. The satisfying hum of a decision made purely for herself, and places *she'd* always wanted to go. It wasn't the path Mum had taught her, but she'd found it more fulfilling than any previous decision she'd made with a partner – or potential partner – in mind. She hadn't told Mum about the trip yet but she hoped that when she did, she'd be proud of her regardless. She was proud of herself. She'd stayed up until 2 a.m. putting together the itinerary and cross-referencing her budget to ensure she got the most experience for her money. Right now, travelling was the right thing – she knew it was. The idea of it energised her.

But the thought of Art returning her feelings did too. She couldn't pretend it didn't. And she wanted to hear him tell her that she hadn't been making it up, he *did* think of her as more than a friend, even if they couldn't be together. 'Why can't you ask me to stay?' she asked him.

'Because . . .' Art looked tortured. 'I've just started therapy, Jen. I can't trust how I feel right now. I've only just let myself start feeling at all.'

'And how *do* you feel?' Jen needed to know, even if the window of their time together was shutting.

'That I like you. I *really* like you. As a friend, yes, but as more than that too.' His dark eyelashes flickered as he spoke, blinking. It was as though he'd finally admitted something as much to himself as to Jen.

Relief surged through her, even if it was undercut with a sense of impending loss. She hadn't got it wrong this time. There *was* something between them.

He set his jaw, raking a hand over his stubble. 'I can't ask you to base your life plans on my flimsy emotions. You told me you've always made your decisions based around other people – men – but you've decided to do this trip for yourself. I can't be the one to stand in the way of that.'

'I know,' Jen replied, struggling to keep the anguish from her voice. Everything he was saying made sense. But everything about it sucked.

'And we've both decided we need some time to get to know ourselves and learn how to be on our own,' he said. His voice belied that this decision was supposed to be empowering.

'Yup,' she agreed, looking at the floor. Tears were pooling in her eyes. For two people who weren't together, this was the most break-up-like non-break-up she'd ever had.

'You've got your vow to be single to stick to.' Was she mistaken or was there a questioning note in his tone? 'When does that end again?'

'Mid-April,' Jen replied. 'I mean, it's not set in stone. It was more of an agreement than a promise . . .' She trailed off, thinking back to her conversation with Maxie in October. She didn't *have* to stick to it. But it felt like she should. No, she wanted to, for herself. She'd come so far already. She couldn't backtrack and hang around, waiting to be picked or discarded by a man who was telling her that he didn't really know what he wanted. What had Maxie said to her? Pick yourself.

'Doesn't that job Cara mentioned start around then?' he asked. 'You could come back? For the job?'

Questions, questions, questions. 'I could,' she said. They were still as far away from each other as it was possible to be in her apartment, but she took a couple of steps towards him now, so she was standing above him at the sofa. 'But if I'm going to come back it needs to be for more than a job. I'm super grateful to Cara for putting me forward for it, but is my life's calling to work for a man called Chuck who may or may not have bought some multi-million-dollar cabins as a hobby?' She was trying not to cry now, her voice getting a bit tighter as she held it in. 'I've been in too many relationships where I've waited around hoping the other person will develop a sense of commitment to me, all the time folding my plans into theirs.'

It would be so easy to just say she'd come back afterwards and see how it went. Let Art decide. But she couldn't this time. For the sake of protecting her future heart.

Art reached for her hand and pulled her down next to him. The shock made her gasp. Her thigh was pressed up against his and she could feel the warmth coming from his body. She wanted to slide her hand up it, but she also didn't want to let go from where he was still holding her hand.

'I have to go travelling. I *want* to go travelling,' she said, convincing herself as much as him. Their closeness was jumbling everything up. 'And it's also why I can't come back *only* for a job and to see how it goes. It has to be for the promise of more.'

'I know.' Art was chewing his lip, looking like he might cry himself.

She realised she had to get it all out. Then at least she could leave knowing that for once she'd said exactly what she thought, without pretending to be cool, or hoping the other person would telepathically know what she wanted without her spelling it out.

Be brave, Jen.

'I understand you need time, and that I should take some time too. But I also can't be passive about what I want.'

She took a deep breath. It was a risk. But wasn't everything a risk, really? And living life without taking any risks hadn't stopped Art from being in pain all these years. 'If in two months you still think I should come back – not for the job, or because you kind of miss me and it's weird not having me around – but because you properly, really *want* me to come back, then you have to tell me. Spell it out. I need to know it's what you want rather than something you're letting happen, and that you're willing to give us a go, properly. By then I'll be somewhere across Canada, with some distance between us. I'll have had time to think about it too, and if I come back, it'll be because I want to. Not just because I'm trying to force the thing right in front of me to work, the way I've always done in the past.'

Art nodded slowly, a grave look on his face. His brown eyes were serious but he didn't look as wrung out as before. 'I already know I'm going to miss you.' He gently moved his hand up to her face, cupping her chin as he fixed his eyes on hers. She glanced down at his mouth and her whole body ached with want. She bridged the gap between them and planted a slow kiss on his lips, as her heart hammered and her nerve endings ran wild. There was no hesitation in Art's response. He kissed her back, hungrily, and with none of the uncertainty she might have expected from someone who hadn't kissed anyone for four years. It was electrifying and sexy. Instant gratification. She leaned into it, intending to ignore the conversation they'd just had, stop speaking entirely and complete what the kiss had started. To give in to every moment she'd wanted to do this and just be here, now. Every atom of her body wanted to.

But she couldn't switch her brain off and a sensible voice inside her head – Maxie's? No, *her own* – wouldn't let her surrender to it. The moment could play out, but the whole time she would know that they were still staring down the barrel of an ending. It was a goodbye that could be prolonged, but it was still going to happen.

She pulled away, breathless and shaky, her lips tingling. Art's breath caught slightly, as though hit by the reality of being back in this poky little room, with everything ostensibly exactly the same as it was ten seconds ago, but also completely different. His face was flushed and his lips were slightly parted. She rested her head on his shoulder. She wanted to stay close to him but didn't trust herself to look into his face without kissing him again. What happened next had to come from him. She had to leave to see if he could find it within himself to truly move on. And that, she knew, was out of her hands.

'Will you miss me enough to take a leap of faith in eight weeks' time?' she asked unsteadily, the sensation of his mouth on hers still coursing through her.

He nodded slowly. 'You're right,' he whispered. He moved his hands away from her gradually, reluctantly. He forced a solemn smile. 'We have to choose it and not just drift into it. I mean, how do I know that after two months of freewheeling across Canada you'll still be interested in some fucked-up guy in Whistler?'

'Well, that's the whole thing, isn't it?' said Jen. 'We don't.'

Six weeks later

Chapter Forty-one

ART

To: Jen Clark
Subject: Don't Come Back

Art's thumb hovered over the 'send' button on his phone.

He regretted it the second it left his outbox.

Chapter Forty-two

JEN

She was in Montreal when it arrived, her phone pinging as she waited in the freezing late-March sleet for what four separate people at her hostel had assured her was the best poutine in the city.

From: Art Jenkins
Subject: Don't Come Back

Jen's heart folded in on itself.

That was that, then.

She stepped to the side, losing her place in the queue that she'd just spent forty-five minutes waiting in, but it didn't matter. The chip-and-cheese aroma that had been steadily building her hunger now made her feel only nauseous.

For the last six weeks, his name in her inbox had given her a ripple of excitement when she saw it. She'd looked forward to his messages each day and fired them back during the bus rides and train journeys that had comprised her backpacking adventure so far. If she was busy exploring, she saved up her experiences – the meals she'd eaten, the characters she'd met, or the whales she watched from a boat – and emailed him unfiltered updates once she was at her hostel for the night. She'd told him about someone shaking her awake in a youth hostel in Toronto because she was apparently 'snoring like a bear'; she told him that Nanaimo bars were the most delicious thing she'd ever eaten; she told him that she'd screamed in excitement when she saw a real-life moose; and she'd told him how she was feeling: that amid all the exciting new experiences she sometimes got lonely as a solo traveller or that she didn't always want to 'be on' and socialise with dozens of other backpackers in a hostel. Yesterday, after much agonising, she'd even told him that even though she was having fun, she wished he was here too.

She'd decided that if it was going to work out, she had to be herself, otherwise there was no point. She'd told herself that if he didn't like it and things never progressed, then that was what was supposed to happen, and it was OK.

But the email subject line hit her like a punch. Maybe she *would* be OK, but right now she wasn't. She could delete the email without reading it, along with her latest Uber Eats code and the 3,584 unread mailshots from Refinery29 that languished in her inbox. But she had to see if there was an explanation, to know what aspect of her personality had tipped them from regular, friendly – OK, flirty – correspondence to 'I don't want to see you again' when she still had two weeks of travelling left. Had her admitting she missed him made him realise that he didn't miss her, not the way she wanted him to?

Get it over and done with.

She clicked on the message. It was pretty long for a *thanks, but no thanks* and as she read she realised why.

Dear Jen

Getting your messages these past weeks has been the highlight of my day, and I've been finding myself saving up my news so I could send replies filled with stuff to entertain – and who knows, even amuse – you. Today I was going to tell you a story about hiking with Yeti along the Ancient Cedars Trail and a five-year-old kid screaming to his dad that he'd just seen Bigfoot.

But I couldn't bring myself to, because I wanted to tell you in person.

I wanted to see the competing expressions on your face, feeling bad for gentle old Yeti being mistaken for a beast, while finding it funny that he has the capacity to freak out children.

So, I'm taking some time off.

I could tell you that the back-to-back lessons have slowed down for this season so I have time to take a holiday (true). I could tell you that I've never been to Montreal (true) and I have always wanted to go (also true). But none of them would be the real reason, which is that I miss you and I want to see you. Plus, my therapist – yeah, that's how I talk now – has told me to work on 'engaging' in life. I realised that our original deal, of me telling you if I wanted you to come back, still forced all the proactivity on you. You're not meant to be making decisions based around men any more, and nor should you. And I need to stop avoiding all whiff of risk because I'm scared of getting hurt.

This is all a very long way of me explaining that instead of asking you to come to me, I'm coming to you!

I arrive tomorrow, on the 10 a.m. flight, should you be interested in meeting me at the airport – OK, maybe I am asking you to do something, but I'm hoping it's not a liberty to ask you to travel that far, if I'm flying 2,278 miles (I looked it up) to get to you.

Let me know

Art x

Jen nudged her way back towards her place in the line, not taking her eyes off the message and absorbing a few tuts without hearing them. Her heart was now soaring, miles above the chasm it had dropped into. She felt lightheaded, not quite trusting what she'd just read, and so she read it again, and again, and then again, just to be sure. Her smile grew broader each time.

Her phone pinged again.

From: Art Jenkins
Subject: WTF was that subject line I just sent you? So sorry!!!!

(I realised when I sent it, it was completely tone deaf. In my defence, I'm still learning about sharing my feelings. As you can see, I need to work on how I do it.)

She spotted him as soon as he came through the arrivals portal at Montréal–Trudeau Airport. He had a rucksack slung over one shoulder, and ran his hand nervously through his hair while he scanned the rows of people waiting for their loved ones in the arrivals hall.

His eyes found hers.

She lifted an arm in greeting and he walked steadily towards her. His brown eyes stayed on her as she took in the familiar sight of his snowboarding coat, his hair springing up scruffily, and the curve of his jaw that led to his mouth, a mouth she no longer perceived as bad-tempered and sanctimonious, but as part of her imperfect Art.

'You came,' Jen said softly as he reached her. They were only a few inches apart, his head slightly above hers. He smelled of the mountains, and a bit of damp. It made her wistful for Whistler. 'You're here.'

'I did,' he replied. 'I am. And just so there is no doubt whatsoever, I *wanted* to come.'

'You're two weeks early,' Jen said, laughing nervously. 'You know, technically I still have two weeks left of travelling, and therefore two weeks left of my singledom vow.'

Art took an exaggerated step back. 'Do you want me to go and come back?' He said it solemnly, but his eyes were dancing.

Jen laughed and took a step towards him, resealing the gap between them. 'No. Definitely do not leave. Even Maxie will forgive me two weeks.' She would. Maxie had screamed when Jen had told her Art was flying cross-country to be with her. 'You chose yourself and he chose you,' she'd crowed. 'I couldn't have planned it better!' But even after Art had told her he was coming, there was a part of Jen that wondered if he'd change his mind and distance himself again.

She hadn't thought any further than this moment. Him being here.

'What happens now?' she asked.

'That's for you to decide,' he said. 'You're in charge.' He put a hand on her waist, on top of her heavy winter coat, and then the other around her other side. The same hands he'd used to steady her on the mountain slopes, but placed with a care and deliberation that hadn't been there when he was correcting the mechanics of her posture. His touch was light at first and then she felt him grip her a little closer, pulling her in. 'So, tell me what *you* want to do next.'

Jen thought for a moment, trying to think clearly through the charge she felt from being close to him. 'You can finish exploring Montreal with me and then there's still Quebec City to go on my itinerary. But after that, back west. Now the story has broken about The Redwood and Eduardo has been suspended, there's going to be a full investigation. I want to see Cara and go back to make my official report in person. Plus, Chuck's PA emailed me and said they're still seeing people for that job, so I can go and meet him. If that works out, Maxie reckons she'll be able to afford an off-season plane ticket for her and Noah if I can put her up.'

'They can stay at my place,' he said firmly. 'I can clear out to Yeti's.' He gave her a look, loaded with hope and optimism. 'The thing I want you to know is that wherever you're going, I'm following.' She felt the sensation of being in the exact right place at the right time, and relaxed into the solid shape of him, her head coming to rest just above his shoulder.

Their bodies moved instinctually together. Jen slid her hands up his sides and leaned into him. He lowered his face to hers in response, both of them moving towards each other. She tipped her chin so her mouth would meet his, registering just before their lips touched just how fast her heart was beating.

They were back on the brink, the precipice. But neither of them was holding back this time. And the view was different. This time it was electrifying and sexy, but also perfect. There was no voice telling her not to – no reason for that voice to be there at all. It wasn't a goodbye and it wasn't an ending.

This time, the heat of the kiss spread between them, like a spring thaw after a long winter.

Like a beginning.

Acknowledgements

This book has been bubbling away in one form or another for a long time. A very different version of it secured me my amazing agent Sarah Hornsley back in 2017, and I would like to thank her for not only taking me on back then, but for encouraging me to dig my Whistler book out of the archives in 2021 and completely overhaul it, and then helping me to turn it into the rom-com it has become. It feels like Art should have always existed!

To Amy Batley at Hodder – thank you for signing this book. I'm so glad it got its moment, and your warm and wise edits made the story (and slow-burn steaminess) much stronger.

A big thank you to my publicist Kim Nyamhondera at Hodder for championing the book and to Natalie Chen and Lucy Davey for the gorgeous cover design, and thank you to my copy editor Helen Parham, for her eagle eye in tightening everything up and saving me from myself.

I have had three books published now, and often still don't believe that I am a 'real' author. Luckily, I married someone who does. Thank you to Ian for always supporting me, for giving me the time and space to write books, as well as knowing what to say when I am dejected and when to raise an eyebrow at the whole bloody thing. Two taps, always.

To Ikey, who will always be the best baby even though I'm not allowed to call you my baby anymore. All the children's cutest and cheekiest moments in this book are inspired by you, even if I struggle to capture your joyful cackle in words.

To my dad who has always been so encouraging of me and my books, and John, Yorkshire's best Helen Whitaker library handseller, for being my most enthusiastic monitors of Amazon rankings.

Approximately a thousand years ago (the early 00s), I did a season in Whistler with my best friend Alex, and met one of my now best friends Suzanne. We never did get any better at tricks and I highly doubt our collective knees have it in them these days, but thank you for the fun times and inspiration! Plus, a shoutout to the international cast of transient seasonaires that we worked and played with during those days.

Finally, to everyone who has bought, borrowed, read and reviewed my books, thank you!